GUILTY KNOWLEDGE

GUILTY KNOWLEDGE

LESLEY GRANT-ADAMSON

PERENNIAL LIBRARY

HARPER & ROW, PUBLISHERS, NEW YORK
GRAND RAPIDS, PHILADELPHIA, ST. LOUIS, SAN FRANCISCO
LONDON, SINGAPORE, SYDNEY, TOKYO, TORONTO

90 91 92 93 94 WB/OPM 10 9 8 7 6 5 4 3 2 1.

For Barbara Grant-Adamson

Blood.

The unpleasant stickiness of blood on her fingers.

Rain Morgan stopped running, jolted to a halt. She looked warily around the garden. Lemon trees. Palms. Rampaging roses and brambles. Eucalyptus. Mastic trees. Writhing vines. All struggling for survival and space, the defiant thrusting up spring colour but the weak dying in smothered tangles.

Cypress hedges cut off the villa from its neighbours. A path sloped through the evidence of neglect. It linked the back gate, in a high wall above her, with steps to a stone veranda behind the house. She pulled her handkerchief from her skirt pocket and wiped her fingers. Her mouth twisted with distaste.

Then she went back to the steps.

She ignored the sun-leached pink villa and the snatch of postcard-blue Mediterranean. Instead she felt along a handrail until she found the exact place where someone's bloodied hand had grasped it.

And then her feet were thudding up the path to the gate and the car in the lane. In her haste she stalled the engine. At her second attempt the car moved. In ten minutes she would be at the flat admitting to Oliver West that things had gone awry, that the Great Idea was not living up to expectations.

He had announced it one evening at the London flat they shared. 'I've got a great idea,' he said.

'What's it going to cost me?' She had not looked up from her typewriter.

'Why do you say that?'

'Because it invariably does. So, what's it going to cost me?'

'Not a thing. We'll get Tavett to pay.' He yawned, stretched his length on her sofa.

She abandoned the typewriter in mid-word. Dick Tavett was the features editor at the *Daily Post* where they both worked. 'Did you say . . . ?'

'A few days on the Riviera won't scupper the *Post* . . .'

'No, but . . .'

'Objections? Well, if you don't fancy it . . .'

Rain joined him on the sofa. 'You did say Riviera as in *French* Riviera?'

'As in spring sunshine and good food and . . .'

'And you did say Tavett to pay?'

'As in Great Idea.' He paused, tantalizing her. She jabbed his ribs with a finger. He said: 'You go to Antibes and interview Sabine Jourdain. You know, the painter.'

Rain nodded, hurrying him on to a full explanation. Sabine Jourdain, old now, was less renowned for her own work than as one of a group of artists who had gathered around the Provençal painter Marius Durance. She had tales to tell and had never told them.

Oliver said: 'Women's Word are planning to publish a book on her next year. Jilly Poynter is writing it.'

'She'll do what she always does: hire someone else to do the legwork and put her name to it.'

'Jourdain is going to be news when the book comes out and I thought the *Post* would be happy to pre-empt that. You could go to France and interview her,' he said.

Oliver had never forgiven Women's Word for turning down a book he offered them on women cartoonists, especially as they had then asked someone else to write it. Rain ignored his motives. 'If she's talking then I want to hear her.'

'She doesn't speak much English and Poynter's French isn't good.' He went on gloating about Women's Word's difficulties but Rain switched off. She was picturing the sun and the food and a proud old woman in a paint-spattered smock opening her heart to her.

'It's bankable,' she said, meaning she could work on the feature right away and it could be published any time in the future. 'Of course, there's the risk Tavett might send someone else and keep my nose to the grindstone editing the gossip column.'

Oliver assured her the risk was negligible. Then another thought struck her. 'How do you come in?' It was unthinkable that Oliver, one of the *Post's* cartoonists, was not including himself in a scheme with so many incidental attractions.

'I just come. I'm owed some holiday and I'm prepared to donate that. I'll tell Tavett I'll take any photographs you want so he needn't pay a French freelance. He'll probably accept that, but if not . . . ' He practised a Gallic shrug. 'If not, we can rake up the cash between us, can't we?'

From the air, three weeks later, the South of France was a sepia print: ochre valleys gouged from brown mountains, snow on peaks providing the picture's high-lights. Oliver looked up from the sex-and-crime thriller, *Bludgeon*, he had bought for the journey and nudged

3

Rain's arm. A stewardess wanted her empty glass. She passed it across. 'Tell me,' she said to Oliver, 'how did you coax Tavett to let us go ahead with this? He was muttering about asking Jilly Poynter to write him a piece.'

'He *was* wavering. Even when he knew he didn't have to pay for me to come.'

'So?'

'So I threatened you'd resign.' He turned back to *Bludgeon*.

The captain's assurance they were about to land at Nice drowned her indignation. Not long after they were on their way to Antibes, Rain at the wheel of a hired car and Oliver, who had forgotten to pack his driving licence, alternately criticizing her speed and rejoicing in the scenery.

Rain said: 'The grand object of travelling is to see the shores of the Mediterranean.'

Oliver looked askance. 'A rather narrow view, surely?'

'Oh that's not me, it's Dr Johnson.'

They agreed they could not think why, when Oliver had packed in so much else, he had not included the Côte d'Azur on the journey which brought him from his home town in Australia to London and, not much later, into Rain's life, her office and her flat.

In Antibes they were in a flat, too. A carrot to lead Tavett on to approval of the jaunt was a colleague's offer to lend his apartment and save the features department budget the cost of a hotel. Rain had been dismayed at Tavett's priorities. 'If I was proposing to dig up something salacious about a pop star he'd write me blank cheques. Because this story might be interesting he wants it done on a shoestring.'

They came to refer to the assignment as Operation Shoestring and Oliver, as the car entered Antibes, remarked that even on a shoestring it was the perfect place

4

to be. It wasn't apparent whether he was admiring the huddle of the old town or the sun and the sea or whether he had glimpsed sunbathers, glistening with oil, leaving the beach.

From the flat—small, basic, adequate—in the rue du Bateau they could look out to sea. Oliver led the way on to the balcony and they stayed there until Rain had to set out to meet Sabine Jourdain.

'Where does she live?' Oliver asked.

'I don't know. I'm to meet her at a friend's house. Sabine Jourdain keeps her address secret.'

'That's extraordinary.'

'Not unique—Cézanne did it. Perhaps it's an old Provençal custom.' She felt in her shoulder bag for a notebook. 'I'm to go to the Villa Fièsole in Antibes because Sabine Jourdain's home is some miles away and difficult to find. I gather she simply doesn't want me there, but once we've met I shall charm her into changing her mind.'

She turned a page in the notebook. 'The friend is an Englishwoman called Barbara Coleman. She's a painter, too.'

'While you track the prey I'll investigate the nearest beach,' said Oliver. And did, while Rain, leaving him the key of the flat, drove to the Villa Fièsole and met a locked gate.

She checked the name on the gatepost. The brown lettering was clear: beyond the ornate iron gates was the Villa Fièsole. Stone arches capped with *fleurs de lys* enhanced its shuttered windows, there were black iron balconies and balustrading. But the stucco was roughly patched and in some places had fallen to reveal brick. Weeds had taken over the path, showing no sign of damage from the movement of the gate or the tramp of feet. Flanking the gates were low walls topped with railings.

5

Unless there was a rear access she could see no way in.

She thrust back a strand of blonde hair and tried the neighbours. The other houses were similar but smarter. At the first she got an incomprehensible Portuguese housekeeper, at the second no reply and at the third an ill-tempered Alsatian dog.

Rain drove to a junction, turned right and a few yards on was rewarded with a narrow track. She walked, counting off houses, then tried the latch of a wooden gate and looked into the back garden of the Villa Fièsole.

She rapped on the back door of the villa and heard the echo in the stillness within. On her way round to the front she looked through the only unshuttered window but there was no hint that anyone was home. The front door bell sounded far off, and then silence.

Hurriedly she completed her circuit of the house and started running back to the car. And it was then she noticed the blood on her fingers.

By the time she parked in the cobbled square outside the flat, she had put the bloody handprint to the back of her mind. There were more pressing things. Oliver would never forgive her if she had to tell him Operation Shoestring was aborted because she could find no one to interview. And she imagined herself explaining her failure to Tavett, a fretful man with premature baldness he blamed on the stress of his job.

Oliver was already at the flat. 'This came for you while I was out.'

Ripping open the envelope she saw that Oliver would not be furious, Tavett need lose no more hair. Briefly she told Oliver how the afternoon's arrangements had broken down. 'I'm to meet Sabine Jourdain on board the *Jonquil* in Antibes harbour tonight instead. This is from Benedict Joseph who's staying on the boat . . .'

6

'The American art dealer? How's he involved?'

'He made his name promoting Marius Durance, and Sabine Jourdain was one of the Durance coterie until it broke up.'

'And now Joseph scents that she might become valuable too and so he's doing her favours?'

'You have a cynical mind. But, yes, I expect you're right. He says Durance will be there this evening.'

'Quite a party.'

She caught his expression. 'Oh, it's all right, you're invited too.'

He brightened, pretending he had not. 'That leaves us time for some sightseeing,' he said, and out they went.

Palms in stone troughs flung spiky shadows, washing was strung from high windows. Rain and Oliver crossed the market place and dropped down into a lane. At the end was the Place Nationale with its arthritic plane trees, striped awnings and dark-skinned men wearing the skull caps of North Africa. Pigeons trailed fanned tails in court-ship display, men removed jackets and waiters brought out more tables.

Rain and Oliver chose a table, ordered drinks. 'If you tie up your work quickly,' said Oliver, his face tilted to the sun, 'we could have several days of nothing but this before we go home.'

She gave him a warning look, but his eyes were closed. 'I'm sorry to be so sluggish,' she said, 'but I've a lot to do and I haven't begun yet.'

Oliver made a sound somewhere between derision and resignation. Rain sipped her wine. When she met Barbara Coleman she need not ask why the English exiles in the coterie had chosen to spend their lives painting, most of them fairly badly, in the South of France. In London spring was late, there were low grey skies, a bitter wind and Fleet Street was a mud-splashed hazard.

What interested Rain was why the group—and in particular Sabine Jourdain—had clung to Durance. She ran over what she knew of him. He was a native of Provence, in his youth as famous for success with women as for his precocious talent as an artist. Later he had taught, and his pupils sometimes stayed on as though their talent depended on his proximity. There had been the inevitable slurs that his interest in the young women was more sexual than artistic. Durance and his friends, living and working together, had created an enclosed and protected world that made outsiders suspicious.

Sabine Jourdain, by all rumours, was the most devoted to Durance. It was no secret she had been his mistress through the stormiest years and been supplanted by ever younger women. When she was young her paintings were well received and one critic, according to cuttings in the *Daily Post* library, believed she had the potential to outstrip Durance. Rain hoped to discover why she had achieved so little.

That evening Rain and Oliver walked to the harbour, entering it through a stone arch decorated with an anchor picked out in fairy lights. Ahead of them gleamed hundreds of luxurious yachts. None of them moved. They were like sunbathers, just lying there, showing off their sleek, pampered forms. Soon Oliver had used up all his superlatives and was reduced to wondering how rich he must become to own one.

'People don't,' said Rain, remembering a yacht broker once trying to get some publicity for his company in her column. 'Mostly they charter.'

'That still means somebody owns them.'

'As a business, not for pottering about at weekends. People pay a fortune to charter them.' She dredged her memory for the details. The biggest and best could be chartered for up to $8,000 a day but it did not stop there:

the price included the crew's salaries but nobody's food and if the boat was to be moved the cost could leap by up to 50 per cent because of fuel and port fees.

Rain quoted the broker as saying: 'Chartering is popular with people who are evading tax.' She started to say that a holiday charter could cost half a million dollars. But Oliver cut in: 'Look at *that!* Do you know what that is? It's a satellite communications system . . .'

She gripped his arm. 'Hush! It's also the *Jonquil.*'

Rain and Oliver were the last to arrive, welcomed by one of the English crew and led to the cocktail bar. There was their host, ready to rush forward and clasp hands: Benedict Joseph, an effusive New Yorker whose dark hair was flecked with grey. His wife, Merlyn, was much younger, around Rain's age, a perfectly groomed brunette with the type of skin that tans easily after a lifetime in California. Beside her was a slender elegant Frenchman introduced by Joseph as Philippe Maurin, owner of a Nice gallery.

Marius Durance greeted Rain next. He was a withered old man, in his eighties, his handshake limp but his appearance striking: leonine head, dark, hooded eyes, jaw jutting into the room. And finally Sabine Jourdain stepped forward to take Rain's hand. She had once been gamine and now stood stockily four square, no taller than Rain. She held Rain's hand firmly. Rain said a few words and smiled but the smile was not returned. After her hand was relinquished Sabine Jourdain's eyes were still on her. Their expression disturbed Rain but she had no time to be troubled. She must be affable and interested in everyone and make sure that she went back to London with a story. To that extent she succeeded.

2

The *Jonquil* was sumptuous
in a way which recalled Brighton Pavilion and the most
elaborate of the 1930s' picture palaces. Any chair leg or
banister rail which might be made to look like gilded
bamboo was forced to do so. Chinoiserie, merely hinted
at in the cocktail bar, was everywhere in the downstairs
dining room. Oriental chairs stood around a circular
table edged with gilded bamboo. On a red silk wall a
painted bird alighted on a painted tree. On other walls
hung some of the pictures Joseph had bought since coming to Europe.

Without waiting for the steward, he pulled out a chair
for Rain, and his wife suggested where the others might
sit. The steward, a slim, brown-haired young man with
the trace of a supercilious smile, gave up and went away.
Rain was flanked by Maurin and Joseph. Merlyn sat
between Maurin and Oliver, and on his other side Oliver
had Durance who was next to Sabine Jourdain.

Oliver turned to Merlyn but she was listening to
Maurin. Rain saw Oliver try to talk to Durance, and
then Joseph was telling her she ought to visit Maurin's

gallery in Nice to see some fine examples of Durance's work.

Joseph said: 'Philippe will be delighted to show you the Durances, he's a great enthusiast. He'd never have forgiven me if I hadn't invited him over to meet you.'

Rain was afraid things were getting out of focus. 'But admiring Durance's work will be an indulgence, I'm here to write about Sabine Jourdain.'

Joseph wagged an admonishing finger at her. 'And you're thinking I'm trying to hijack you to publicize Durance.'

'Let's say I wouldn't blame you if you tried.'

He flung back his head and laughed. 'The others looked up. Joseph ignored all but Maurin. 'Rain is going to call at the gallery but we're to remember her prime interest is Sabine and not Durance.'

'But of course,' Maurin said to Rain. 'You will come tomorrow, perhaps? I shall be free tomorrow.' He made the invitation sound an entirely personal rather than a professional matter. Rain surrendered, preferring to fritter half a day in Nice than turn down an offer to see the paintings and discuss them with an expert. Besides, Maurin was a very handsome man. She noticed Oliver overhearing and disapproving.

She noticed, too, when Oliver succeeded in getting Merlyn's attention and hoped he was not going to ask how on earth the Josephs could afford to charter the *Jonquil*. He was quite tactless enough to do so, but the words which reached her revealed they were talking about painting, and Merlyn's tone suggested that she was in a flirtatious mood.

Joseph, a bulky man, blocked Rain's view of Sabine Jourdain although Rain could watch Durance. Seated, Durance was more impressive. His was a head which should be sculpted and Rain remembered that long ago

Sabine Jourdain had done that.

Durance became aware of Rain's gaze. She shifted her eyes. His hands rested on the table, one toying with a wine glass. Rain remembered the feebleness of the handshake, and wondered how it must be to go on showing the world that powerful face once old age had sapped the body's strength.

The talk ran on. Joseph showing off about chartering the *Jonquil* every couple of years so he could entertain clients from all over Europe. Maurin telling Rain about the rise and fall and rise again in Durance's standing. Merlyn revealing she had been a film actress. Oliver pretending he remembered her performance in a film with Michael Caine. Durance, his voice too soft for anyone but Jourdain to hear. Joseph explaining his ambition had been to own a gallery. Maurin insisting that art was an international affair and so it did not matter whether Durance's work stayed in France or went with Joseph to the United States. Merlyn telling Oliver that in her first marriage (to an actor in a soap opera) she had been manipulated but then she had discovered analysis, assertion, acupuncture and Benedict Joseph. Joseph saying that supper aboard the *Jonquil* often ended with a guest making an offer for a painting on the wall. Oliver attempting a second time to speak to Durance and again failing because the artist's lack of English was neatly matched by Oliver's lack of French. Joseph telling Rain he made his name by taking European painters' work to the United States where he had an interest in galleries in New York and San Francisco. Maurin telling her the artists who had gathered about Durance were unintelligent and she would learn nothing by talking to them.

Durance heard his name and looked enquiringly at Maurin. Maurin called over in French: 'I am giving your secrets away, Marius.'

Durance pretended to be alarmed. 'I thought they were safe with you, Philippe!'

Maurin made a gesture of helplessness. 'But how can I help it? The young lady is so enticing.'

Sabine Jourdain leaned forward so that Rain saw her clearly for the first time at table. The grey eyes were warm now, the face merry. 'Shame on you, Philippe, for being led astray.'

Joseph and Merlyn looked blank. Then the steward came to suggest coffee and asked Merlyn whether she would like it served at the table or in the lounge. Rain hoped for the lounge but Merlyn did not hesitate. 'We'll have it here, thank you, Ross.'

When it was all over and there was no more excuse to stay there, Joseph said to Rain: 'Now I have a real treat for you. The others will forgive me, they know how excited I get about these things.'

He shepherded her from the room and upstairs to a study. Against wood panelling hung more of his recent purchases. The prize he had brought her to see was on a plain wall. It was a picture of a woman stepping from the shade of a tree, her face shadowed but her limbs glowing and her movement vigorous. There was a sense of freedom, the essence of summer.

'Well?' Joseph was growing impatient. He mocked his impatience with a laugh. 'The lady is speechless.'

'No, just wondering what to say first.' She made some admiring remarks about the luminous colour, the voluptuous skin, the draughtsmanship. 'When did Durance paint this?'

'Last summer.' Joseph came and rested his weight on the edge of the desk beside her. 'That's got to be among the best. That combination of force and grace . . . The mark of a great painting.'

Rain stepped forward to look at it in detail, then rejoined him by the desk. 'Very covetable. Dare you keep it or have you a buyer?'

'Is that an offer?'

'Not my league . . .' She drawled an Americanism: 'But it's worth killing for.'

Joseph laughed, rocking to and fro. He was like a child with a fabulous toy that everyone must be made to admire but could not resent because it *was* so wonderful.

He said: 'It isn't sold yet, and I might hold on to it for a time. Let the world find out about it, wait until the price is right. You know the dealer's philosophy? "The important thing is knowing when to let go, there always comes a time when the finest picture has reached its top price." '

'If I owned this I should find it exceedingly hard to let go. But what about Durance himself? Doesn't an artist find it hard to let go when he's produced his very best? Doesn't he want to keep it to hand, if only to encourage himself on the days when he's not up to it?'

He wagged a finger at her again. 'Now don't you go putting silly ideas into artists' heads.'

She went up to the painting a second time. 'It's interesting that he's giving up his characteristic use of green in backgrounds. The shade here is well on the way to blue.'

'Yes, that's a little development that's been noticed in his more recent work. He's famous for green, but I guess he's allowed any colour he wants.' He glanced at his watch, stood up.

Rain was still studying the painting. 'And look at the blueness of these tone patches . . . I saw the Durance exhibition at the Hayward gallery in London a couple of years ago. People were speculating then about his shift of emphasis, but there was nothing so pronounced as this.'

Joseph laughed. 'You're not suggesting this is a fake?'

Rain flashed him a smile. 'My only suggestion is that I go and ask Durance about the change.'

'I can warn you what he'll say. He'll tell you art is growth and development and he's lucky in his eighty-third year to be still advancing.' As he spoke he opened the door, held it for her.

They went to the lounge, a plush room with Chinese screens. Only Merlyn and Oliver were there. Rain saw them from a distance, down a passage. Merlyn was wearing her flirtatious air, Oliver did not appear to mind.

Merlyn teased her husband and Rain about slipping away and missing the departure of the other guests. 'Sabine and Durance were tired. I was going to call the car for them but Philippe said he had to leave then to get back to Nice and so he'd drive them.'

Her husband said: 'Fine,' and suggested more drinks. Oliver and Rain swapped glances which meant neither of them wanted to stay. Rain said, in a tone which hid her annoyance: 'It's a pity I missed everyone. I must arrange to talk to Sabine Jourdain and I'm supposed to be going to Philippe Maurin's gallery tomorrow.'

'That's no problem,' said Merlyn, dropping into a turquoise leather chair with a purple footstool. 'Philippe asks that you meet him at his gallery at noon tomorrow. He'll give you lunch and show you his paintings.' She affected a giggle. 'You're going to have a wonderful day, he's such an attractive man, don't you think?'

Rain did not disagree. She said: 'But Sabine Jourdain?'

'That's even easier,' said Merlyn. 'She'll come here again tomorrow evening.'

Joseph said: 'But Merlyn, you know we have to go see someone tomorrow evening.'

'Yes, I know, Ben. We can have an aperitif with Rain and Sabine and then they can eat and talk here while we go out. It'll be more comfortable for them than a restaurant.'

Joseph needed no persuasion. 'There you are,' he cried to Rain, throwing his arms wide. 'All your problems solved.'

Rain contrived a smile. 'What more could I ask?' She knew. She could wish for less interference and to be allowed to get on with her job in the way she wanted. She said as much to Oliver as they walked back through the harbour. 'Not only was tonight a disaster but I'll have to go through it all over again tomorrow.'

'At least you get lunch with Marvellous Maurin.'

'Jealous?'

But Oliver had remembered the moment the three French guests had talked and laughed together. He asked Rain for a translation.

She told him. Then: 'You didn't need French to notice the interesting thing about that episode.'

'What?' he asked.

'That neither of the Josephs speaks French. Their faces showed they didn't follow the exchanges.'

They were approaching the arch to the town. Oliver asked: 'Did anyone say why they switched the meeting from the Villa Fièsole to the *Jonquil*?'

'Joseph said it was more comfortable on board, he'd already invited Maurin to dinner, he was sorry not to have got a note to me sooner and he hoped I hadn't wasted my time going to the villa.'

'In other words the Josephs were interfering again.'

'Yes. But he didn't say where Barbara Coleman was this afternoon, and my questions were brushed aside.' They threaded through the streets to the flat. Rain said: 'Did you make out where Maurin was taking Durance and Jourdain?'

'It was just as Merlyn told you, but . . . I had the feeling that scene was less than spontaneous. Merlyn and Maurin sounded rehearsed and the other two were bundled off the boat.'

'Didn't they object?'

'Oh, yes. Durance gave in quickly when Maurin spoke to him, but Sabine Jourdain stood her ground and then they were both urging her to go so she had to. She said something to me as she left the room but the only word I understood was "Rain".'

They were near the flat when Rain said: 'Do you feel like a short drive?'

Oliver understood. 'As far as the Villa Fièsole, perhaps?'

The gates of the villa were still padlocked but light came from a ground floor window at the side of the house. Oliver said: 'It's too late to go calling on Barbara Coleman.'

'Or Sabine Jourdain.'

'You think she's in there?'

'She's supposed to be staying there.'

'Even so, it's far too late to call.'

Rain looked as though she might argue. Then she said: 'I should have spent most of today talking with her but events have been stage managed to prevent that.'

Oliver slid an arm around her and gave a comforting squeeze. 'Never mind. Tomorrow you'll have her to yourself all evening.'

'Then why did the Josephs go to so much trouble to stop us talking today?'

'Perhaps there's a concentrated effort to persuade her not to tell naughty tales which they think will harm Durance's reputation.'

'When did a forty-year-old scandal injure an artist's reputation?'

'Well, perhaps you're just imagining things.'

17

But she knew she wasn't. She thought of telling him the detail of her afternoon visit but it was impossible to justify the vague fears which had her racing from the garden, and she would not be able to convince him it really was blood she had found. Yet her doubts were hardening into the wish that Oliver had never had the Great Idea.

3

Philippe Maurin's gallery was in the rue de France in Nice. If he was disappointed to find Oliver had invited himself to come with Rain, then he did not betray it. He showed them his Durances, the three he had hung and the portfolio in his upstairs room. Maurin discussed the details which made Durance's work remarkable and some of these paintings especially fine.

Several of them featured bluish-green tones but as he did not refer to the painting on board the *Jonquil* Rain decided not to. It was Oliver who brought up the question of colour. 'Why has Durance gone into a blue period?' He stabbed a finger at the painting on the easel. 'He used to have a rather idiosyncratic use of green, but now . . .'

'Ah, yes,' Maurin agreed. 'But do you not appreciate how . . .' He made a graceful gesture at the upper part of the painting. 'The tone echoes . . . Durance's scope is extended and the painting enriched now he allows himself this further choice. I will demonstrate.'

He whisked the painting down and stood it against a

wall. Alongside it he arranged several more. 'Voilà. This one, here, was painted four years ago. A traditional Durance, you may say. And this one, furthest from it, is the newest I have. There, in five paintings, you have the progress of Durance and for an artist of this calibre to be adventuring—may I say "*adventuring*"?—at his age is a splendid thing.'

'Yes,' said Oliver, and there was stubbornness in the way he said it. 'But seeing somebody who has been almost fanatic about green moving so far towards blue I thought maybe it was more a matter of eyesight than choice. Is colour vision impaired with old age as general vision is?'

'There is nothing wrong with Durance's vision, I promise. And now,' he addressed his remark to Rain, 'we shall lunch at a small restaurant and then I shall show you some magnificent Durances. There is a collector who lives in Nice and she has graciously permitted that you shall see her paintings. You will not be disappointed.'

The restaurant Maurin chose was in Cours Saleya, once the elegant promenade of the old town. From a gallery diners watched their platters of shellfish prepared. Oliver, who was not a shellfish lover and was being brave, was startled that much of the fish was served raw.

Seeing Maurin sucking the claws of a diminutive crab and Oliver chasing a winkle with a pin, Rain had the amusing idea that this lunch was another brilliant means of preventing her from getting on with her job. 'Tell me,' she said to Maurin, before the idea took a grip and she giggled, 'did you ever sell Sabine Jourdain's work?' The woman had hardly been mentioned at the gallery.

Maurin dealt with the crab before answering. 'It is not important. Do not misunderstand me, the woman is important because of what she has given to the man. Sabine Jourdain has been Durance's support and encouragement, perhaps his inspiration, but her own work . . .' He gave the kind of shrug Oliver wished he commanded.

'Does she still paint?' Rain persisted.

'A little, perhaps. She sculpts more.'

'Wasn't there a phase when she worked on Durance's canvases, under his direction?'

Maurin helped himself to another oyster. 'Marius Durance has never lacked the attentions of young women.'

Oliver abandoned the chase of the winkle and took up a mussel. A waiter brought another bottle of expensive wine.

Maurin was busy showing his skill with a winkle pin. Rain said: 'I need to see some of her work. Do any of the galleries in Nice have anything?'

The winkle emerged on the end of the pin. Maurin said: 'You could look in at a place in the Ponchettes. I believe some of her pieces of sculpture were there a few months ago. I should not think they have all been sold. She is not . . .' he hunted down the word ' . . . in demand.' The winkle disappeared into his mouth.

Oliver was discovering the texture of whelks. 'Which gallery?'

Maurin told him the name, Bellanda. 'We are very close. But first it will be necessary to visit the contessa.'

Rain and Oliver looked up in surprise. He said: 'She is the collector we are to see. The Contessa Mantero.'

The Contessa Mantero was no older than forty, very slim and erect with jet hair twisted into a chignon. She wore a dark blue suit, a white silk ruffled blouse, an imperious air and no smile at all.

On the way to meet her Maurin had explained her title was inherited from a family which was venerable when Nice ceded from Provence in the fourteenth century and joined Savoy. The palace was a more recent

21

acquisition. Her family built it in the seventeenth century and had lived there, in varying degrees of happiness, ever after.

It vied for distinction with the Genoese-style Palais Lascari close by. Both were rich in rococo and antiques, both hid behind austere façades in the lanes of Old Nice. The principal difference was that the Palais Lascari had become a museum and the Palais Mantero was still a home.

The contessa went straight to the point. 'I am delighted that you are interested in my Durance collection.'

Rain heard Oliver echo her thanks. Then the contessa was moving away, Maurin making a gesture to Rain and Oliver to follow.

Shutters had been folded back, so they entered the room to the clarity of Durance's colours. Today Rain's reaction was swifter. She did not keep the contessa waiting as she had kept Joseph waiting. 'These are magnificent.'

The contessa nodded solemnly. 'Which is your favourite? I shall be interested to see whether you choose what I choose?'

Rain felt this a shade unfair. The paintings were individually delightful, the collection a wonderful hoard, the contessa magnanimous to let her see them—but she was discomfited to be challenged to choose the best. A different game occurred to her. 'Do you own the best Durance, or is there a prize which has eluded you?' Rain believed she knew of one.

The contessa said: 'There are other Durances—many, he is an elderly man who has produced much work—but there are no better ones.'

At her shoulder Rain heard Maurin say in a deferential whisper: 'The Contessa Mantero has the finest collection in the world.'

The contessa agreed. 'It could not be improved.' A pause. Then: 'Unless Durance himself should improve.' Rain saw Oliver's face spread into a smile and she warned him off with a look. The contessa had not made a joke.

For twenty minutes the four of them paraded the room, making an observation here, a flattering remark there. The paintings spanned Durance's working life, so the development of his use of green and its much later decline in favour of bluer tones was illustrated. There was a little talk about it and Rain was thankful that Oliver sensed that a suggestion of possible decline in the artist's colour vision would be absolutely out of place in the Palais Mantero.

Then the contessa was standing near the door, hands loosely clasped in front of her, ostensibly gazing at one of her paintings but indicating that the visit was over. Maurin stayed on, Rain and Oliver were escorted downstairs by a servant and let out into the street. The sounds and smells of the alleyways of cafés and shops came as an unkind contrast to the air of quiet splendour inside the palace.

'What a daunting woman,' Oliver said. 'She was so . . .'

'Aristocratic?'

'Exactly.' They were passing a café with tables outside and Oliver suggested an espresso. 'I need to recover from the strains of the last half hour.' He signalled to a waiter.

The sun was pleasant, they were sheltered from the day's cool breeze and for the first time able to relax. Oliver said: 'This is the dullest thing we've done and it's easily the most enjoyable. Is that a sign of an ungrateful nature? Should I prefer swanning about on the *Jonquil*? Or going behind the scenes at fashionable art galleries? Or dropping in on contessas?'

23

'It's just as well you don't. We may not be able to keep that up.'

'Probably the gallery in the Ponchettes will mark the downturn. Maurin was rather patronizing about it.'

Rain said: 'I thought he was sneering at Sabine Jourdain's work. He couldn't find much to say in her favour.'

Oliver said: 'What must it feel like to have the sort of reputation Durance has? To produce work you know will endure long after you're dead?'

'That's the sort of thing cartoonists don't find out about.'

'What I admire about the Durances of the world is that they don't care about the rent, they give everything to pursuing their art.'

Rain gave a scornful laugh. 'Durance's pretty young acolytes found boring details like paying for things were delegated to them.'

Oliver sighed. 'You'll be telling me next that great artists aren't superior beings with their minds on higher things.'

'That's right.'

The waiter brought the bill. Rain paid. 'To the Ponchettes,' she said, getting up. 'To search for some Jourdains.'

Oliver closed his eyes, held his face to the sun. 'Couldn't I wait for you here?'

'That's the worst idea of the day. You'd wander off, I'd have to look for you.'

There were a number of galleries in the low seafront buildings which used to be fishermen's stores. The one Rain and Oliver wanted took its name from the tower which topped the hill rising beside the Ponchettes.

Oliver hung back when they went indoors, leaving Rain to speak French with the woman there. After a few sentences the conversation switched to English.

'From Harpenden, actually,' said the woman. 'I opened this place two summers ago. Closed a gallery in Hertfordshire and opened one here.' She held out her hand. 'My name is May Radley.'

May Radley was aged about sixty but would have been very cross if anyone had thought so. She was vigorous with quick movements, friendly blue eyes, springy grey hair and a figure only marginally plumper than she would have chosen. Before either Rain or Oliver could prevent it, she had popped her head through a rear door and asked someone to bring coffee for them.

The visit to the Galerie Bellanda was a success. May Radley had in stock three sculptures by Sabine Jourdain and moved items in her current show to display them for Rain and Oliver. She also knew Sabine Jourdain and Barbara Coleman.

'I told Sabine she must do more, but she laughed and said it's too late for her now. Have you ever heard such nonsense? These days women may be as young as they wish.'

Rain asked: 'Do you know where her studio is?'

'No, she's very secretive. Barbara knows but she's only given me hints.' She repeated what Barbara Coleman had said, but it was very vague. 'Sabine says a studio is a private world and a visitor an intrusion. I teased her that one day I'd drive up to the valley and find her and load up my van with all the pieces she must keep tucked away up there.'

Oliver said: 'Did she bring these to you herself?' He was very impressed with the sculpture, the heads of children and a woman.

'Yes, one day when she came in with Barbara. I've known Barbara for many years, ever since I started coming to the South of France for holidays. Through a friend in England I heard about Barbara who'd joined that group of artists who revered Durance. I suppose these days we'd say it was a commune. Anyway, my friend suggested I look Barbara up, to see she was all right and not just sending brave letters home. Barbara and I took to each other at once, and she introduced me to Sabine Jourdain. Then, one glorious occasion, I actually met Durance.' She gave a self-mocking laugh. 'I was quite young then and it was all rather heady.'

'Who were the models for these?' Rain asked, bringing May Radley back to the sculpture.

'Local people where she lives. Barbara was extremely helpful when I set up here and she persuaded Sabine to let me have some work. I was able to sell it and then several months ago Barbara brought Sabine here. She'd come to offer me these.'

Oliver picked one up. 'I'm surprised you haven't sold these, too.' He sounded as though he wanted one. Rain hoped it was not true. She had paid for him to come to France and did not want to finance such an expensive souvenir.

May Radley said: 'I haven't offered them yet. They'll go into my next show and I'm using the delay to get Barbara to urge her to let me have more.'

A telephone rang in a back room and May Radley was called away. Oliver, still handling the sculpted head of the woman, said: 'I wonder what she wants for this.'

'You could ask her and start saving your pennies.'

'What became of the head Sabine Jourdain did of Durance years ago?'

When May Radley returned they asked her, but she could not remember which collection it was in. Soon after Rain and Oliver left the gallery to drive back to Antibes, sunlight gilding the windows of hotels and villas along the Baie des Anges. 'We'll have to come here again,' said Oliver. 'Just come and do all the touristy things one day.'

'You can't do all of Nice in a day. We'll come on holiday here some other time if you want to see it properly.'

'Maybe I'll follow Barbara Coleman's example and join a commune of carefree spirits worshipping the sun and Art with a capital A.'

'You'd miss the monthly cheque from the *Daily Post* and the reputation you'd get would be the wrong sort,' Rain said primly.

Then Oliver pleaded that, as he might never see Nice again, they ought to stroll along the bay for a while so he could claim to have promenaded on the Promenade des Anglais. Rain refused because she was afraid of being late at the *Jonquil*. Oliver grumbled that he had expected her work to be finished by now so they could spend a day or two of unadulterated pleasure before heading home to London and winter. A sulky silence settled over them. If it had not been for that squabble the horror that was to come might have been avoided.

4

Rain was sure Oliver was doing it deliberately. He had been in the shower room an unconscionable time and it was reaching the point where she would have to forgo her own shower and hairwash before going out. She sat in her dressing gown on the edge of their bed and tried not to get angry about it.

It was so easy to get angry with Oliver that it often seemed as though it would be better to end their jagged relationship altogether. She had been known to move out of the London flat—and then move back in because it was *her* flat and he ought to be the one to go. At other times he did leave, but briefly. If life was uncomfortable together it was more uncomfortable apart.

The water was still running, she was still waiting. Operation Shoestring was becoming sheer exasperation. People had been treating her badly, in the guise of kindness, and she had been incapable of dealing with them. Only May Radley had been interested in Sabine Jourdain and helpful. For everyone else she was a mere sideshow.

Merlyn and Benedict Joseph, Philippe Maurin and

the Contessa Mantero were all dedicated to telling each other and the rest of the world how wonderful Durance was. And now that Sabine Jourdain was on the *Jonquil* for an evening's *tête à tête*, Oliver was going to make her late. Her annoyance surged and she banged on the shower room door, shouting to him to hurry up.

Her hair was still wet as they walked to the harbour. 'Nobody'll notice in the dark,' Oliver said. He was immaculate, having given unusual attention to his appearance.

'I'll notice. I do notice. I've got water running down my neck.'

'You're exaggerating.' He was right. She did not like that, she wanted him to be wrong.

She said: 'I don't know why you bothered to smarten yourself up so much, you haven't been invited, have you?' She presumed he was looking forward to seeing Merlyn.

'Merlyn didn't say I was to stay away.'

'That's not the same as being invited. Maybe they won't have planned food for three.'

'Rain, that boat has a crew of eight. It's a floating hotel. An extra one for supper won't even be noticed.'

They walked through the arch. Her head felt cold and damp, the breeze coming off the water was making it worse. When Oliver snapped that he would rather have supper in the town if she was going to be tetchy she said nothing. They went a little further and then he said he had made up his mind to go to a restaurant. He asked for the key to the flat.

She was reluctant to hand it over. 'Supposing you're not there when I get back?'

'I will be, you'll be talking for hours.' He held out his hand.

Rain gave him the key, then watched his light clothes moving away into the gathering darkness.

The yachts that were so impressive in daylight were dull patches now and she had to concentrate so she did not miss the *Jonquil* or trip and tumble into the water. In one place boat fitters had scattered their materials over the footway, a sailmaker's van was badly parked, and space was reduced to a narrow track. The walk seemed longer than when she and Oliver had made it the previous evening. There were fewer people about, although many of the craft had lights aboard. From some came the happy sound of laughter, from one the frenetic noise of a party. Someone let off a firework.

Then she saw the *Jonquil*. There were lights on the deck with the cocktail bar and a lamp by the gangway but otherwise the boat was ill-lit.

Rain went aboard, found the doors from the aft deck to the lounge closed, and mounted the open wooden steps to the bar. No one was inside and only one light, near the bar counter, was switched on. She could hear distant voices, somewhere below. She returned to the steps and began to descend.

It was odd that no one had noticed her arrival. The contrast with the Josephs' exuberant welcome and the crew's attention the previous evening was marked. Voices welled up again, closer now. A man's voice menacing, a woman shouting back. Rain froze. She was almost sure the woman was Sabine Jourdain. The man's voice she could not identify.

Rain did not know what to do. The row was far too fierce for her to join them and pretend she had not heard. Although much of what they said was unclear—they were arguing in French and both shouting at once—the essence was reaching her. The man was demanding the woman do something, threatening she would suffer if she did not. And she was resisting vehemently.

Rain crept down the steps. There was still no sound or sign of anyone else, no one to rescue the situation. She looked at her watch. She was late for her meeting, very late. The Josephs must have left to keep their own appointment. Someone else had come.

Voices reached her, in a crescendo of anger, as she went ashore. She walked a little way off, wondering whether to wait a while and then return or else go back to the town and make a fresh plan next day to see Sabine Jourdain.

If she put it off until tomorrow they could meet at a time and place to suit themselves rather than fall in with any more of the Josephs' complicated schemes. And it was now unlikely the woman would be in the mood tonight for the sort of questions Rain meant to put to her.

Back through the arch Rain entered the Place Jacques Audiberti near a crowded café, the Bar de la Marine. She hesitated. She could not go to the flat because Oliver had the key and she did not know where he was. She went into the café and ordered a glass of wine. Sitting on the terrace, where tentative ivy climbed a low screen, she could see and be seen by Oliver, if he came.

Most of the customers were English speakers. At one table a mixed group of young Americans and English people were noisily cheerful. They were joking about the attempts of one of the men to sell his pottery on a market stall. Two of the others, a young man with very long straight hair the sun had bleached, and a big-boned woman in patched jeans, were teasing him without mercy.

Even when they were interrupted by a tall, robed Tunisian pedlar selling leather bags and purses, they did not let up. Rain waved the pedlar aside. Most other people did the same until one tourist showed an interest and a little bargaining went on before the pedlar took from his arm a red and brown leather shoulder bag and gave it in exchange for a fistful of notes.

A woman at an adjoining table clutched at the Tunisian, but although she pressed him to let her see one particular bag, he would only offer those of his own choosing. The woman lost patience and began to discuss with her companions the strange ways of foreign pedlars.

The Tunisian went out of Rain's sight to a table where a couple of young Frenchmen sat, but they apparently wanted nothing because he left the café almost immediately. He walked away under the plane trees.

Rain ordered a snack. By the time she had eaten she was regretting backing away from the *Jonquil*, guilty at leaving Sabine Jourdain waiting for her. She went back to the harbour.

The light was much poorer this time. Ropes brushed her ankles and made her nervous of falling. She leapt in fright at the sudden flash and bang of fireworks on the boat with the party. At last she stepped on to the *Jonquil*'s gangway.

A faint light glowed in the cocktail bar but the lounge was silent. With considerable misgivings Rain peered into the bar. Nothing had changed. She tried calling out, but there was no reply. Oliver's words came back to her: 'That boat has a crew of eight. It's a floating hotel.' She wished she knew where they all were.

Rain went through the bar and into a corridor. Carpets smothered the slight sounds she made. A wall light at the far end of the corridor picked up the mellow glow of banisters that looked like gilded bamboo.

Near the stairs she paused. Below her was darkness, ahead a weak light and closed doors. She knew of a room where someone might wait for her: the study. It was at the end of the corridor.

She opened the study door and felt for a light switch. The room was as she had seen it the previous evening, except that there was an empty expanse of wall where the Durance had hung. She turned off the light and went out. Downstairs she found another switch and looked into the lounge. She gasped.

The purple footstool Merlyn had used was upended and leaning against one of a pair of Chinese screens near doors to the aft deck. A heavy pottery lamp lay smashed on the turquoise carpet. Flowers were trampled into the carpet, their vase tipped over and its water a pool on a lacquer table. Curtains had been wrenched from their pole and beneath a fractured panel of the other screen lay a bird cast in bronze.

Rain felt her colour drain. To save her own embarrassment she had gone away and left Sabine Jourdain, and something dreadful had happened. She wanted to put out the light and flee, but knew that first she must go to the aft deck. Her view when she boarded might not have revealed everything.

She forced herself forward, careful to disturb nothing. When she pulled open the doors the room lit the deck sufficiently for her to take in that nothing else had been upset. Whatever had taken place had happened inside.

Then she heard a creak. Someone was on the gangway. Afraid, she retreated into the lounge. She had left the light on in there. Her instinct was to run and turn it off so darkness would cover her escape once the gangway was clear. But the person coming on board would have seen the glow of light and if it went out would know she was there.

She stood by the doorway to the lounge, fingernails gouging her palms. The Josephs would not be so stealthy if they were returning, neither would the strangely absent crew. The person arriving could only be someone who had no right to be there.

She strained to hear which way the footsteps would go—towards the wooden steps to the upper deck and the cocktail bar or towards the lounge? She heard nothing but the sharp crack of a firework and cheering from the people at the party. Pink imitation stars danced across the sky.

Rain convinced herself she had invented the sound of a footfall on the gangway. But no, a rubber-soled shoe squealed. Someone had come aboard and was walking across the deck above her head.

She waited to be sure, waited with frantic breath until she saw the tip of a shoe appear on the top tread of the open steps. Then she dashed through the lounge and into the corridor. She drew the door after her, praying she had been swift enough not to have been noticed.

Next she had to run upstairs and make sure no one was in the corridor or the cocktail bar. There was no time to spare. Whoever had come aboard could be in the lounge. If the signs of a fight came as a shock he would react in some way—run through the boat looking for someone with an explanation, or perhaps telephone the police. And if he did not react it suggested he had known what to expect, that the man who fought with Sabine Jourdain had returned.

Rain opened the door to the bar a mere chink. The small light by the counter was still on, the room empty. But she could not see the deck and it was possible the man had gone back up the steps and was waiting out there for her. Her scalp tingled with fear, she had no choice but to go on to that deck. It was now the shortest route to safety.

The floor of the bar was shiny vinyl, she had to be

extremely quiet if she was not to give her position away. Choosing the darker side of the room, she glided towards the deck. If someone were on either the upper or lower decks, then she would be caught. She concentrated on listening for sounds of movement but none came. Taking a deep, steadying breath, she slid out on to the deck and started towards the steps. There was no one near the bar but the shadows near the lounge below were deep and threatening. Trembling, she reached the lower deck and turned to the gangway.

The cry shocked her. It took a second for her to realize how far away it was. She spun round but saw no one coming after her. And then she was on the gangway and making for land and safety. Her last sight of the *Jonquil* was the livid light from the lounge port where the curtains had been ripped down.

Rain stumbled, cursed the inattention which had nearly sent her sprawling. She took the centre of the road and ran.

Then she saw people, a knot crouching by the water's edge. Her route took her past them where parked vehicles and the sailmaker's van narrowed the footway and created deep shadow. The people were taking up a lot of room and she could not understand what they were doing. Beyond them fireworks were brilliant against the night sky. As each died, it left the night darker than it had been before.

Then she was up to the group, slowing, waiting for them to let her squeeze by. A man spoke to her, over his shoulder, mistaking her for someone else. She saw that his clothes were drenched, there was the blackness of blood on his knuckles. The people were talking in low urgent voices, making suggestions, giving instructions, but all without hope. They were united in their hopelessness.

Another firework lit their anguish. Rain looked over the man's shoulder and understood. A body lay on the ground, a body that was being pummelled and manipulated as though there were a chance that life could be coerced back into it. The body was wet as the man who had brought it out of the harbour was wet. Rivulets ran from its sodden clothes but life had already seeped away.

Rain was there when the people turned it on to its back and the dead eyes of Sabine Jourdain stared at the Mediterranean sky.

5

Rain Morgan darted up the night-black steps of the passageway beside the flat in the rue de Bateau. There was no light visible on the third floor but until she had run upstairs, twisted the handle and thumped on the door she could not be certain Oliver was not back.

Her breath was coming in anxious rasps. She slumped on the stairs and tried to organize her thoughts. She was ashamed of the panic which had sent her rushing away from the harbour. It was not only the shock of looking down on Sabine Jourdain's face, there was another more personal anguish.

The scene on the boat suggested the woman had been attacked there. Rain had not kept her appointment and Sabine Jourdain met her killer instead. Rain had walked away when she heard Sabine Jourdain and a man having a row, a row which had ended in death.

Rain shuddered and covered her face with her hands. She was convinced the figure who came stealthily aboard the *Jonquil* was the killer and she might herself have been seen by him. He could track her to the flat but she

37

had already decided not to crouch there any longer. A street away her car was parked. She sat in it and waited for Oliver.

The street was quiet. Traffic sounded on the coast road running along the town's seventeenth-century ramparts. People's voices came from the Place Massena, the market place where restaurants and bars were busy in the evenings.

Suddenly she started the engine and pointed the car towards the coast road. In a few minutes she was cutting her lights outside the Villa Fièsole. Through the locked gates yellow light flowed from a downstairs window into the limpid black night.

The Alsatian dog in the neighbouring garden began to bark. Rain went to the track that ran behind the houses. There were no vehicles on it. The Villa Fièsole had no visitors.

Barbara Coleman appeared to be at home, because of the light, but she probably did not know her friend was dead. Rain would not tell her that. She slipped the car into gear and went back into the town. There was still no light from the top floor flat but there was a vacant parking space in the cobbled square.

It was very late when Oliver came. Rain heard him arrive humming to himself, hands in pockets as he rounded the corner with a swaggering stride. She got out of the car, stiff and cold. He looked surprised to see her. 'Hello, had a good evening?'

She said: 'I can tell *you* have. Where's the key?'

'The what?'

'The key to the flat. I'd have been inside hours ago but you've got the key.'

'Are you sure? I thought you had it. In your bag.'

'No, I gave it to you at the harbour.'

He looked as though he could happily stand there all night discussing it. She said: 'It must be in one of your pockets.'

Oliver took his hands out of his pockets to demonstrate there was nothing there. In one he held the key. 'Ah, a key. Is that the one?'

'I'm sure of it.' They went up, Oliver stumbling on the stairs, and she unlocked the door.

Oliver was chattering, telling her what a wonderful evening she had missed. He was describing a bar and the people he had fallen into conversation with. Then he had been to their villa. They were English and American and making a living of sorts from crafts. There were some potters and someone who made enamelled earrings and a couple of weavers . . .

Rain cut him off. 'Oliver, Sabine Jourdain is dead.'

He echoed the word. The meaning hit him. It was sobering. 'What happened?'

She told him. He said: 'Have you been to the police?'

'Not yet. I don't fancy spending the night answering questions. What am I to tell them that can't wait until morning?'

In the morning they were woken by the telephone. Oliver reached it first and held out the receiver to Rain. 'Guess who?' he mouthed.

She guessed. 'Dick Tavett.'

'There is no escape from him.'

She spoke into the phone. Listened. Made faces. Then: 'I'll try, Dick, but something else has happened. No, I haven't finished the Jourdain story yet . . .' She explained why not.

Over breakfast Oliver said he had worked out that, rather than curtail their stay in France, Sabine Jourdain's death could usefully prolong it. Rain could tell Tavett she had been made to spend a day or two at the police

39

station and then she would have to research and write about the ending of the Durance–Jourdain relationship for the weekend arts page.

Rain, already scribbling a short obituary for next morning's paper, rewarded him with a doubtful look. 'And what do you do while I do all that?'

'Didn't I tell you last night about the people I met? I'm going to the beach with them today and I wouldn't mind a few more days sunbathing.' He fetched his copy of *Bludgeon* and his sun glasses and appeared ready to set off for the beach.

'But Oliver, I'm not sure I want to be on my own. Last night I was nearly trapped on the *Jonquil* by the killer.'

'You're exaggerating,' he said, and this time she did not know whether he was right or not.

She began to write again. Oliver was flicking through his book, finding his place. He said: 'I'm spending my holiday, remember. I'm not here on behalf of the *Daily Post* or as your bodyguard.'

She said nothing. He thought of another justification. 'Anyway, you didn't want me to go to Nice with you yesterday and prevent Maurin flirting with you and you didn't want me to go to the *Jonquil* last night.'

Rain put last night's panic out of her mind. Oliver would not take it seriously if she described to him how frightened she had been, or if she tried to share with him the underlying suspicions which had disturbed her since their arrival. She finished writing and put the copy in her shoulder bag to telephone to the *Post* later in the morning. Then she went to the police.

They kept her waiting until she could speak to an officer who knew about what they called 'the incident' at the harbour. She talked to him for a long while, after which he said she must tell her story to his senior officer.

He went out, returned ten minutes later to say his superior was not available. She waited some more.

The senior officer, a man with rabbit features, had a good command of English, so where Rain's French faltered the conversation did not come to a standstill. He was courteously interested in what she had to say although the theory was that Sabine Jourdain had fallen, striking her head, and gone unconscious into the water. He chose to act this out with much hand movement including a ferocious blow of the fist on his forehead.

When she emerged from the police station it was nearly noon although the low axis of the early spring sun gave everyone long shadows. Rain knew she could write nothing more explicit than that Sabine Jourdain's body had been taken from the harbour. There could be no mention of foul play being suspected, so far all that might make the police suspect it was Rain's own story. She was confident their view would change once they had the results of a post mortem examination.

Preoccupied with this, she was startled when a woman sitting outside a bar called to her. Merlyn Joseph. Merlyn looking exquisitely groomed, her gleaming dark hair piled above her fine neck, a strappy dress showing off her shapely figure. 'Hi!' said Merlyn. 'Lovely to see you, Rain. Let me buy you a drink.'

Merlyn was positively the last person Rain wanted to chat to over a drink. She accepted. Oliver was on the beach with his new friends and *Bludgeon*, she would have no company at the flat and it was boring to go into a bar on her own. She asked for a glass of wine and waited for Merlyn to tell her Sabine Jourdain was dead.

A pigeon strutted near the table. A couple of elderly Frenchwomen stopped to gossip, their dogs eyeing each other. Merlyn said: 'I'm so sorry we missed you last evening. I told Ben we should hold on a while but he said we had to go right then. We were dining with a business associate.'

Rain gave an understanding smile. 'It was my fault. I apologize for being late.' She took a sip, decided to give in and mention the dead woman. Obliquely. She was interested to know what Merlyn might say, how she might say it. Rain said: 'In fact, I was so late at the *Jonquil* I did not see anyone else, either.'

A faint frown marred Merlyn's face. She said: 'But Sabine . . . She was there when we had to go. I guess you were very late if she'd gone. When we went she was sitting in the cocktail bar expecting you any moment.'

'Have any of the crew mentioned what time she left?'

Another frown. 'No. I asked a couple of them but they didn't know.' Merlyn drank off her wine. She grew confidential. 'I'm not sure I handle that crew right. They're English and Ben says it's like having an English butler: they're supposed to know more than you do. But I guess I just don't care for them making it obvious.' Her neck grew pink. She called to a waiter, who ignored her. She called louder.

Rain asked: 'What time did you and Benedict get back to the yacht?'

'The *boat*,' Merlyn corrected. 'I had Ben tell me a heap of times before I got it right. If you say "yacht" it gives away that you don't know about yachts—I mean boats.'

'Clearly I don't.' She asked herself whether Merlyn was deliberately digressing, decided not. She tried once more, coming at it another way. 'Were the crew all present and correct when you came back?'

'Sure. But where else would they be at two in the morning? Besides, they have a security job to do. You've seen the amount of stock Ben has on board.'

Rain considered the possibility Merlyn did not know

about the woman's death or the evidence of a fight on the boat. Considered it and rejected it.

The waiter came, but Rain chose not to stay. She had the excuse of telephoning her office and left Merlyn sitting in the sun over her next glassful.

On the way to the flat Rain stopped at a charcuterie and bought vol-au-vents filled with ham and cheese for her lunch. There was another errand to do, too. She was just in time to have a duplicate door key cut before the shop closed for the long lunch break.

After phoning the obituary she took her pastries, some fruit and the last two inches of a bottle of wine from the fridge and ate lunch on the balcony. She put Sabine Jourdain's death, her suspicions of Merlyn and her annoyance with Oliver out of her mind. She thought about Dick Tavett's latest way of tormenting her.

She had been known to remark that Tavett tried to snatch all the glamour from her job as a gossip columnist. People who envied her the glossy life had no idea of his penny-pinching, his chivvying and his habit of wasting her time on fruitless stories.

His latest effort was a classic piece of nonsense: he had telephoned before she was out of bed to ask her to trace an English youth who was 'possibly somewhere in the South of France.'

The youth, who had left school and home, was a member of a minor branch of an aristocratic family, and that connection was enough to convince Tavett there was a story to be written. Rain had tried saying: 'Little birds do leave the nest, Dick. It's called natural instinct.' But he had not been deflected. Because of the tenuous ducal connection, Tavett wanted the *Post* readers to be told. He believed in a high count of dukes in the gossip column.

Rain leaned on the balcony and stared out at the iridescent sea. Some miniature sailing boats, crewed by children, came into sight. One of the youngsters was having trouble with his sail, failing to follow the shouted instructions of the man in charge of the boats and tacking in silly directions. He was encouraged, made headway, repeated his mistakes and got left behind. The man helped him again and eventually the brown sail was at the same angle as all the others.

But all the others had gone. There had been a headlong dash away from shore, the boats strung out behind a young leader with a crimson sail and a stout heart. The man roared and soared after them, heading them off and forcing them round and finally capturing them like any pirate. Rain found herself laughing helplessly.

She fetched her notebook and read with more enthusiasm the information she had jotted down from Tavett. She had meant to make some desultory enquiries and tell him his young aristocrat was not to be found and she was on her way home. Now she was willing to treat it as an excuse to stay away from the office a bit longer.

Her notes said Tarquin Poulteney-Crosse was seventeen and had dropped out of school and drifted away from his family in the West Country. Around the time he disappeared silver was stolen from his parents' home. The unpublishable story, which the police told journalists with a nod and a wink, was that the missing youth had taken it. He was seen in London and then no more was heard of him until the story surfaced that he was in the South of France.

Rain could remember nothing of the Poulteney-Crosses, except that they were related to the Duke of Watchet. She telephoned London. Holly Chase, her deputy on the gossip column, was pleased to hear her. Holly was lively, leggy, beautiful and black. She also had an excellent memory.

'Young Tarquin's father was the youngest brother of the Duke of Watchet. Tarquin is the only son. His sister is a good bit older and married a man who farms in Lincolnshire. Her in-laws . . .'

'Holly, this is all-embracing. Do I really need the in-laws too?'

'You'll be surprised. The in-laws are French and there's a link with Sabine Jourdain. She's a distant cousin of Tarquin's sister's husband. Still with me?'

'Just, but I can't cope with much more.'

'That's all right, I don't have much more. I dug most of that out when the Durance retrospective was on in London and the Duke lent some of his paintings. The rest I found out today because I knew what Tavett was up to and I was expecting your call. The rest is this: Tarquin is an odd personality, the type who never fitted in at school and was in trouble on a number of occasions when his temper got out of hand. The family have found him rather a trial, too. In other words, neither the school nor the family seem heartbroken he's gone.'

But Holly could not point which way Tarquin had headed and they talked about Sabine Jourdain's death and Oliver's sunbathing until Rain rang off.

She walked to the harbour. In sunlight last night's horror was dispelled. The white boats were dazzling, their flags crisp in the breeze. Expensive cars were parked near some of the boats, people were busily to and fro on the footway. Rain averted her eyes from the place where the body had lain but noticed her pace quicken involuntarily. Soon she was at the *Jonquil.*

Joseph met her as she crossed the gangway. He was in casual trousers and shirt, his feet in deck shoes. 'Hi, Rain,' he called, and held out his hand to help her aboard. His smile was fragile.

Rain said: 'You can guess why I've come?'

45

He abandoned the smile. 'Because of Sabine. It's the most terrible thing. Who could believe something like that would happen?'

He started to lead her towards the steps to the cocktail bar but some of the crew were up there and he changed his mind. 'We'll stay down here and sit outside.'

Rain looked across to the lounge. It was shadowed, she could see nothing.

Joseph chose them a table in the sun, asked for drinks. Neither of them spoke until they were brought. Then Rain asked: 'Have the police been here?'

There was a flicker of alarm. Rain understood that the last thing Joseph wanted was the police swarming over the yacht. He said: 'No, I heard about Sabine's death from someone else. She's such a loss, a really fine artist.'

She said: 'You'll probably get a visit from the police as she was here last night.'

'But the accident was on her way back through the harbour. She was just fine when we left her.'

'They'll want to know who she'd been with, how much she'd had to drink, that type of thing.'

A frown creased Joseph's face. 'Yes, I hadn't looked at it like that. Do you think it would be better if I went to see them first? I realize this might sound callous when someone I knew has been killed, but I can't afford to be tinged with scandal. In my business an unstained reputation can be crucial.'

Rain anticipated his next thought. He said: 'Now, Rain, you're not thinking of mentioning this in your paper, are you? You're not going to connect me with this story in any way? I don't mind saying I shouldn't care for that at all.'

With amusement Rain recalled how he had given his life story over dinner while hoping, no doubt, to be mentioned in her feature on Sabine Jourdain. She swept aside the plea. 'I must talk to Durance and Barbara Coleman and anyone else from the days of the coterie. If you'll give me addresses, I'll go and see them.'

Joseph shook his head. 'Oh, no. Not Durance. He's an old man. A very old man. He's had a bad shock. I don't think you ought to go troubling him.'

Rain asked whether Joseph had been to see him that morning. He said not and urged her again to leave Durance alone.

'If he sends me away I'll go, but I must try.'

'It's not fair to disturb him now.'

Rain said: 'People often find it helpful to talk under these circumstances.' She put her notebook on the table, took the cap off her pen. 'He's in Antibes, isn't he?'

Joseph was agitated but eventually recited an address. 'I shouldn't have told you, I can only beg you not to upset him.'

Rain finished her drink. 'Are any of the coterie living locally now?'

'No, they took off in all directions, except for Barbara Coleman. Two or three have a house together up in the hills. Durance says one of them, Madeleine Corley, goes to see him sometimes. The village is Tourettes-sur-Loup—there are a lot of artists living up there. Give me a minute and I'll remember the name of the house.' He remembered and Rain wrote it down.

Then she asked to use the bathroom before she left and he said: 'Sure, right ahead and along the corridor.'

Rain stepped into the lounge, her eyes adjusting from sharp sunlight to dimness. There was nothing amiss in the room. She might have imagined yesterday's scene. The curtains hung correctly, the bronze bird was on a table, fresh flowers were in the vases, the pottery lamp and the purple footstool were in position. A glance showed no damage to either Chinese screen.

47

She had made an excuse to come into the room because she expected to see something that might draw from Joseph an admission that there had been a violent scene on board. Instead, it appeared they were both to go on hiding their knowledge.

When she returned to the deck Joseph was gripping the rail, his knuckles white. She was very close before he knew it. He twisted round, managed an unconvincing smile. He waved her off at the gangway, but the smile and the wave and the cheery remarks did not disguise that he was an extremely nervous man.

6

Marius Durance was in his
studio, a dusty room with a view of the sea and infinity.
He was staring out of the window when the caretaker of
the flats let Rain in.

Rain had persuaded the woman to take her upstairs
because Durance was not in his ground-floor flat. 'I say
these stairs are too much for an old man,' the woman,
elderly herself, said as she puffed up the steep flights.
'But he cannot have a studio on the ground floor, there
is no light, so what is he to do? You will understand that
he is very old, he does not force himself to make this
journey often.'

'How long has he lived here?'

'Not so very long. Three years, maybe? There was
a villa before this, a big place but there were people
there and it was not easy for him. When he was younger
he enjoyed people around him, but now . . . he is very
old.'

They came to the top floor and brown double doors.
The woman said: 'You will be kind, I hope. He is upset.
A friend has died, he tells me. And the man who came

49

this morning was not kind. There was shouting and arguing. From downstairs, in my rooms you understand, I could hear the shouting.' Rain understood she had been listening on the stairs.

The woman tapped on the door but before letting Rain enter she said: 'It is so sad to see him like this. It was a dear friend. He has been up here all day, mourning his loss.'

Durance stayed by the window, as Joseph had stayed by the rail of the *Jonquil*, but there was no tension in him. Durance was slouched, a thin, miserable figure. He turned and Rain saw how the fire had died in the dark eyes.

'I came to see whether you'd like to talk about Sabine Jourdain,' she said gently.

Durance held her gaze as though he could not think who Rain was, did not understand why she was there. Then he stiffened, the jaw jutted a little as he made an effort to cope. 'You knew Sabine?'

'I met her the night before last on board the *Jonquil*. We were all there, guests of Benedict Joseph.'

'Ah yes.' She was not sure he remembered. The white head moved away and he looked across the sea.

Rain said: 'You knew Sabine Jourdain a long time. Perhaps you would like to tell me about her. I have to write an article for an English newspaper about her work and her life.' A pause. 'Tell me, where did she live?'

The old man did not reply. Rain waited. A gull perched on an ochre tiled roof outside the window and wailed. Rain let a few more minutes slip away. Then she said: 'It doesn't matter. I'll leave you now. I'll go and see Barbara Coleman.' No response. She ripped a page from her notebook and wrote. 'This is my address and telephone number in Antibes in case you change your mind and feel like talking.'

She held it out but Durance did not look at her and she cast around for somewhere to put it down. There was a table nearby, a very neat table with tubes of paint, brushes in a jar, artist's things. She put the note there. 'I've left it here, on the table.' No reply, she could not reach him.

She said goodbye and started to the door. Durance spoke. Not looking at her, staring at the empty sea. 'She was more to me than you could know.'

As she ran downstairs Rain saw the caretaker's black skirt whip out of sight. She pretended she had not and knocked on the woman's door to tell her she was leaving. The woman said: 'I wonder who this friend was whose death is so distressing? Monsieur Durance is very old; very old people are not alarmed when their friends die, they expect it. It is natural.'

'This friend was younger, not much more than sixty. She was a painter called Sabine Jourdain. Perhaps you met her? They had known each other many years, I expect she called here.' She knew the caretaker would not have missed her.

'A woman of sixty, you say?'

'Short steely hair, a gamine face, about my height but broad.'

The caretaker was definite. 'No, no one like that. Younger women, painters from the villa where he used to live. But there was only one woman of the age you describe, very thin with fluffy white hair. An English-woman. She came sometimes, but he did not always want to see her. He has reached the time of life when people are a trouble to him.'

Rain went to the cobbled square where she had parked the car, but then delayed driving to the Villa Fièsole again. He would hate it, but she wanted Oliver to go with her. She drove to the beach.

It was sandy, with a view of Cap d'Antibes where black pines curved down to the sea. There was only a glimpse of the harbour: boats, green slopes and distant blue Alps through an archway. She singled out the group of sunbathers which included Oliver and headed towards it. Against rocks at the far end of the beach were a huddle of sleeping figures wrapped in blankets.

Rain felt the scratch of sand in her shoes and bent to slip them off. While she was doing so another figure crossed the beach, the Tunisian pedlar she had seen in the café. He offered sunbathers his leather bags and moved on until he came to the sleepers.

Rain saw him rouse one with his foot and angry voices were bounced off the rocks. The pedlar was asking for something, the blond sleeper denying him. Then the pedlar strode angrily up the beach.

Feeling absurdly overdressed Rain reached the group Oliver was with. He looked up from *Bludgeon*, saw her and looked down at the page. A red-haired girl close— very close—to him narrowed her eyes, watching Rain as though she were a spoilsport come to ruin a good party. Rain smiled a greeting, which the girl ignored, then concentrated on Oliver instead. 'Can we talk?'

'Sure. What's the problem?' He turned over a page. He was not making it easy.

'I mean can we talk privately?'

'What about?'

'Oliver, *please* . . .' She made an impatient gesture.

Oliver sat up, holding the book, keeping his place with his thumb. Rain walked a few yards away. He joined her.

'What's all this about?'

'I've got to go to the Villa Fièsole and I don't want to go alone.'

'You went alone before.'

'I know, but . . .' She thought of her fright in the garden. 'All sorts of things have happened since I saw you at breakfast, and something happened at the villa the other day which I didn't tell you about.'

He did not look impressed. He was still holding the book open at his page. 'What happened?'

'I found blood.'

'Blood?'

'In the garden.'

'Probably an animal injured itself.'

'The blood was on a handrail. An animal couldn't . . .'

'All right, not an animal.'

'Somebody had been injured shortly before I got there. That blood was wet, fresh. In this weather it would have dried quickly.'

His face showed distaste, but he made light of her fear. 'So you want me to come and protect you from an old lady with a cut hand?'

'Oliver, I'm just asking you to come.'

He gave the shrug he had been practising for weeks. It was getting better. He closed the book, said a general farewell to his friends and rejoined Rain. 'What other things have happened today? More blood?'

She told him about the police, Merlyn Joseph, Benedict Joseph being worried, the *Jonquil* being tidy, and Durance being shattered.

He said: 'It wasn't the time to ask him whether his colour vision has gone wonky, then?'

'Nor to discuss Sabine Jourdain's distant connection with Tarquin Poulteney-Crosse.'

'*Who?*'

She told him the detail of Tavett's phone call and

the extra information from Holly. Oliver asked: 'How would it be if the young Tarquin, having melted down and spent the stolen silver, decided to use the family connection to sponge off Sabine Jourdain and when she refused . . . ?' He made a chopping motion with his hand.

'I admire your invention but not your lack of taste.'

'You're wrong there,' he said. 'You *need* my lack of taste, it allows you to feel extremely superior.'

She grinned at him. He might even be right, although she was not going to admit it. As she felt in her bag for the car keys she discovered the spare door key and held it out to Oliver. 'A duplicate seemed a good idea.'

'I'm impressed by a woman who can get a door key cut in French.' He dropped it into his trouser pocket and got into the car.

Low-powered but noisy motor cycles raced past them as they drove towards the Villa Fièsole. Its tiles were vivid in the sun, its faded stucco patchily pink. Rain turned down the track behind the row of villas and cut the engine.

She said: 'We are behind the Villa Fièsole now. The back garden is through this wooden gate.'

'And the car is poised for a swift getaway in case we find more blood?'

They did not. They descended the path and steps without incident, knocked on doors and rang doorbells without effect. The breeze had dropped and shadows of trees fell like iron bars across the stone veranda.

'It's exactly the same—deserted,' Rain said.

Oliver said it had not been deserted all the time because on the first evening they had seen a light and it had been enough to persuade her Sabine Jourdain was there.

But as they passed the unshuttered window he broke

off with an exclamation. An overhead light shone inside, its effect lost in the sunlight lying obliquely across the room. 'Was it like this when you came alone before?'

'I don't think so, surely I'd have noticed?' She was not sure at all. She had been there rather later, the sun would have travelled further and flooded the room. It was possible that without looking up to the ceiling she would not have detected the glow of the bulb.

She said: 'If the light has been on all along, perhaps the house wasn't occupied that night. Barbara Coleman and Sabine Jourdain might not have been here for days.' She shuddered. 'I sensed something was wrong, and then there was the blood . . .'

Next door's Alsatian heard their voices and began to growl beyond the cypress hedge. Rain said: 'He's enormous. I'd hate to think he could get in here.'

'We needn't wait to find out.' Oliver was first across the terrace and up the steps. They both kept clear of the bloodstained handrail. At the top of the garden they looked down. The land dropped away. Brilliant flowers struggled through a mass of greenery, palms reached skyward. There was the right degree of dilapidation to qualify for adjectives like picturesque.

The dog's growls died away. Beyond the villa was the sea, some boats came into sight, and sunshine made everything pleasant. 'I expect,' said Oliver, now the threatening atmosphere had gone, 'there's nothing more sinister about this than that Barbara Coleman is a bit dotty. She could be in there now, peeping at us from a window.'

'Her friend has just been killed.'

'The police are regarding it as an accident.'

'They won't once they've got the post mortem report. I'm sure that will show there was violence before she died.' She took a map from the car and unfolded it on the bonnet.

Oliver said: 'Aren't we going back to the old town now?' He meant the beach. She knew.

She said: 'This is roughly where Sabine Jourdain lived. From the hints Barbara Coleman gave May Radley it must be in this area.'

'But it's miles away.'

'I'm a fast driver.'

'Is it really worth going all the way up there in the hope of discovering the right village, the right house?'

Her finger moved an inch on the map. 'Joseph gave me the address of a woman who used to be a member of the coterie. She lives here. She can probably tell me Sabine Jourdain's address.'

As she spoke she was folding the map, her mind made up. When she asked Oliver whether he was coming he knew she would go alone if he did not. He thought fleetingly of the suck of the sea on yellow sand but said: 'I wouldn't miss it, I want to see what goes wrong next.'

Rain was indignant. He explained: 'I'm puzzled why you're being baulked at every turn.'

She started the ignition. He said: 'You were supposed to be interviewing an old woman. Now she's dead, Joseph is pretending there was no violence on board the *Jonquil*, Maurin is inventing elaborate ways to keep you away from Antibes, and Barbara Coleman has vanished into the Mediterranean blue leaving nothing but a bloody handprint.'

Rain paused at the end of the track to allow traffic to pass. She was relieved Oliver was with her, she felt safer. She chose not to say so. He was puzzled at the way things were going wrong but he would laugh off her nervousness.

Oliver broke the thoughtful silence. 'I think you ought to back off this enquiry as fast as you can.'

'So we can be tourists for a few days?'

He surprised her. 'No, because if Sabine Jourdain was killed there's probably someone who thinks you already know too much. Haven't you thought you might be in danger?'

7

The medieval village hung on a mountain ledge. Oliver said: 'This can't be safe.'

'Then don't look down.'

Rain tugged him away from the alley that ended in a sheer drop to the valley floor. She said that when they found the house they should be careful what they said to Madeleine Corley. 'She might not know Sabine Jourdain is dead.'

They hunted through the streets of grey weathered houses with tip-tilted roofs slanting this way and that and rising to a belfry that was a white rectangle against a blue sky. Rain found the house: tall and skinny with steps across the front to a low first floor doorway. The door was open and cooking smells wafted out. She knocked while Oliver studied the discreet ceramic shop sign.

The woman who answered the knock had draped her large frame in voluminous colourful garments. She had an open face, loose golden-brown hair and exuded the confidence of the well-bred Englishwoman. As she walked towards them between the display of paintings, pottery and hand-blocked fabrics, she switched on a sales lady's smile and Rain prepared to disappoint her.

'We're not customers. I'm a journalist and I'd like to talk to you about Sabine Jourdain.' She introduced Oliver.

The smile barely shifted. 'I'm Madeleine Corley. Come inside and meet the others.' No word of regret about the death, she probably had not heard of it.

The others were two women in the kitchen. One stirred a deep pot on a stove and one stirred sugar into her coffee. The woman with the coffee cup was slender as a knife, her jet hair scraped tight back and looped earrings swinging. The one at the stove was less striking than her companions: mousey brown hair loosely plaited and hanging over one shoulder. But all three dressed in brilliant floating fabrics. Oliver thought of Macbeth's three witches, and Rain thought that they were a hangover of Bloomsbury with espadrilles. They were some of the 'younger ones' from the Durance coterie, and they were in their forties.

'This,' said Madeleine, wagging a hand at the woman with the plait, 'is Jane Stevens and this . . .'

'I'm Linda Mackie.' Although the appearance was Italian the accent was Scots.

Jane offered Rain and Oliver coffee but Madeleine overruled her by fetching a bottle of wine. 'Why don't we carry this upstairs?' she suggested in the tone of one whose suggestions were usually adopted.

'Yes,' said Linda, 'and put the lid on that pot, Jane. The whole house reeks of daube.' Jane meekly did so.

They all trooped up to an airy fifth-floor studio with astonishing views along the valley.

'That's fantastic,' said Oliver.

'Do you like it? It isn't finished yet but I'm awfully pleased with it.' Madeleine thought he was looking at a painting on an easel.

59

Rain tried to cover up the misunderstanding with a remark about the picture but Linda would not allow that. 'Maddy, it's the view he means.'

But Madeleine was not the type to be put out or even put off. She held her glass up to the window. 'It was this effect I was after, the fiery glow the palest colours give you in the brightest light.'

Everyone looked at her glass, bright as a diamond in the sun, the wine a yellow warmth within. Everyone looked away and drank.

She glided down the room, saying: 'Sabine was terribly good with colour. She could do quite effortlessly all the things I struggle for.'

Rain noticed the past tense. Maybe they did know she was dead, but she was not sure.

Jane spoke up. 'Durance could, I'm not sure about Sabine.' Durance in the past tense, too.

'Oh yes,' said Madeleine contradicting with a nodding head. 'She underrated herself, but she didn't fool me. She had a terrific understanding of colour.'

Jane persisted: 'That's because she worked so closely with him.' There was an awkward pause during which Rain considered whether any of the three had been Durance's mistress. Jane said to her: 'By the time we all came he'd lost interest in teaching anyone anything. The older ones used to talk about the days when he was virtually running a school . . .'

'You mean the disciples,' Linda said with a cruel smile.

'You can laugh at them, call them that if you wish, but he gave them a great deal.' A flush warmed her cheeks.

Madeleine said: 'Rain wants to hear about Sabine, not about what a marvellous teacher Durance could be when he chose.' She turned to Rain: 'Sabine is the best person to tell you about Durance's teaching, but we all know she won't say anything about herself.'

Irony apart, Madeleine had unwittingly confirmed that the women did not know of the tragedy. Rain said: 'Whatever you can tell me will be helpful.' And began to put the questions which elicited some straightforward information about Sabine Jourdain during the years the women had known her.

They were in agreement: she and Durance had always had a special relationship, long after they ceased to be lovers. The relationship survived all his others, she was tremendously loyal to him, absolutely devoted. Madeleine grew rather excited talking about it and Linda's eyes gleamed sardonically.

The women differed on Sabine Jourdain's history before they met her. They offered alternative versions of the legends about the coterie in the years before and after the Second World War.

Oliver contributed a question: 'Didn't any of the older ones talk to you about the things they did in the past?'

Madeleine threw up her hands with a theatrical gesture. 'There you have it. They didn't talk. We'd hear snippets and references to the old days but no one was terribly keen to discuss exactly what the truth was.'

Jane said she had been fobbed off. Linda believed it was Durance himself who discouraged such talk. 'He'd decided it was all to be a secret and most people accepted his word without challenge. We're not typical of the coterie, you see. Our loyalty to him didn't extend so far. We've not been dominated by him as the older ones were . . .'

Madeleine jumped in to defend Durance. 'He simply didn't see why people were interested in the past, because all he was concerned with was his work. Whatever he might have been like in his youth, in the end all he cared about was art.'

'You mean when he got old?' asked Oliver.

'Yes, that too. But I really meant the last years of the coterie. We three were just in time to see the last of the Durance magic. There were still about a dozen living and working with him but he was no longer a king holding court. He was withdrawing. I'll confess this is hindsight, it took me an awfully long time to appreciate it.'

Jane fiddled with the end of her plait, which was coming undone. 'It was very sad the way it ended.'

Linda snorted. 'No, it was not. It had to end because it was no longer necessary to live that way. They didn't talk about the scandals of the old days because in modern times they would not have been very shocking at all.'

Madeleine and Jane looked shaken by this. Rain quickly asked: 'Were you the last people to leave him?'

'Yes,' said Madeleine. 'The remnant of the coterie went to a villa in Antibes...'

'The Villa Fièsole,' explained Jane.

'... but Durance decided it was a mistake, the place was a burden and not convenient. He sold it to an American art dealer, Benedict Joseph, who wanted a house here. Over the next year or so everyone drifted away until there were only us and an older woman called Barbara Coleman. She's still there, as a sort of caretaker. After Durance moved out I heard this place was vacant so I asked Jane and Linda to share. We've made the ground floor a shop, to sell our work and other people's, and there's still lots of space. I don't know what's happened to the rest of the group, except that they're terribly scattered.'

'Some even went back to live in England,' said Jane and caused a frisson.

Rain squeezed a little more information about Barbara

Coleman but soon gave up, deciding their reticence was because they did not care for the woman. 'If you met her she'd tell you everything,' Linda said waspishly.

'Except about Durance,' Madeleine corrected. 'I don't think one would ever accuse her of disloyalty to him.'

Their views on Joseph and Maurin were coloured by the suspicion that the dealers had somehow stolen Durance from them. Rain asked whether any of the women ever saw Durance now.

Madeleine said: 'Very rarely. I have a friend in Antibes and when I drive down to see her I call on him. Actually, I went yesterday but he was out. I couldn't wait, it was well into the evening and I had to drive all the way home.'

Linda went to her easel and took up a brush. She was doing a portrait. Oliver commented that it was a good likeness.

'It would be better if Maddy would sit still,' she said.

'I don't think she's quite got my eyes,' said her subject.

Linda touched the canvas with a teasing stroke. '*Ars addit naturae!*' She looked at Oliver as she added: 'That's Corot: "Art must be able to correct nature." '

When they had all considered her canvas they moved, as in natural progression, to Jane's. Jane finished redoing the end of her plait and stood aside for them to see her agitated splashy design. 'It's for fabric,' she said.

Madeleine spoke again. 'I don't envy those who were here in the old days, when the Riviera was full of Americans pretending they'd invented the place. We know quite well the English did.'

'All Britons abroad are "English." Have you noticed?' asked Linda, the Scot. She made another dart at her canvas.

Madeleine went on: 'Perhaps it was just the coast which was intolerable. Durance didn't move to the coast until he bought the Villa Fièsole.'

Jane asked Rain: 'Did you know he calls himself after the river which flows through the region where his family has its roots? The poet who revived the Provençal language named himself after the Mistral wind that blows through Provence and so Marius chose to take the name of the river.'

'Another old Provençal custom,' said Oliver mysteriously.

He did not offer to explain and Madeleine said: 'The river was known as the Torment of Provence because it was so temperamental.'

Jane said: 'Marius is a curious name, too. It's come down from the Roman soldier who defended the region against invading Teutons. There was a terrible battle at Mont Sainte-Victoire—the hill Cézanne loved to paint—and when the Teutons began to flee their women killed them and then strangled their children before committing suicide.'

Madeleine, who obviously enjoyed the tale, gave a dramatic shudder. 'Jane, that's a horrible tale, and it probably isn't true. You know how history exaggerates!'

Jane clung to her story. 'It's fascinating, Marius became a hero but the women played an extraordinary part in his victory.'

Linda said to Rain: 'While we're talking about unusual names, why Rain?'

'A childhood misspelling for the Welsh Rhian. An English schoolteacher who believed me.' And, she might have added, a snappy and memorable byline for the journalist she had become and a usefully classless name for the varied life she led.

Madeleine said in a wistful tone: 'I think it's beautiful.'

'You mean it reminds you of England,' Linda said to provoke her.

Oliver helped himself to the last of the wine. He took his glass to the window and gazed down the valley. He seldom bothered to disguise his impatience or his boredom.

Rain had an important question to ask but held it back. Instead she followed on from Linda's comment. 'Will any of you ever go back to England?'

There was a chorus of 'noes' and 'certainly nots' and she read into the responses three little histories of rejection and disappointment and escape. It was more comfortable to eke a living in the sun with their middling talents than to go home to the hard Northern light and the harder questioning of the people they used to know.

She put her question, gambling that their curiosity would not be aroused if she asked where Sabine Jourdain lived. They ought to wonder why she, having met Jourdain, did not know. Madeleine suspected nothing. 'It was meant to be a secret when she left the Villa Fièsole but Barbara Coleman knew and she dropped so many hints . . .'

Linda laughed, and named a village. 'That's not far from here but I'm not thinking of calling on her. She meant to cut herself off from us when she went there.'

'That was odd.' Jane's voice was quiet. 'She used to be so friendly.'

Madeleine said: 'We only know it's an old farmhouse where the coterie once lived.' She challenged Linda's named village and Jane had no opinion.

Linda insisted: 'Barbara Coleman said it was hard to find but one could ask at the village because people were sure to remember Durance.'

'Nonsense,' said Madeleine, and offered conflicting instructions.

When Rain and Oliver left the house the disagreement

was still not settled. 'What shall we do, then?' asked Oliver.

He hoped she wanted to return to Antibes. She said: 'Find *chez* Jourdain.' She showed him the map, urging that whether Linda's version or Madeleine's was correct, they could not be very far away. Oliver was pushed into agreeing that they begin the search.

8

'**Y**ou're driving as though you expect a man with a chequered flag around the next bend,' Oliver said.

'We have to get there as soon as we can.' They had left the scattered houses of the high slopes and were winding downhill through mixed woodland.

'I was hoping to come back, too.'

The car slowed for a few kilometres and Rain felt Oliver relax. Then she picked up speed again. She expected more criticism but before he spoke they came to the bridge over the river and Pont du Loup, the village Linda Mackie had mentioned. Rain pulled up outside a bar.

Oliver sat, the car window down and the sun on his skin, while she went into the bar. There were three old men inside, two customers and a lean lank-haired proprietor. 'I'm looking for an old farmhouse, the home of a woman painter called Sabine Jourdain. Do you know whether she lives near here?' She made an effort to keep the dead woman in the present tense. If she found anyone who knew her she did not want to explain her death.

Three pairs of eyes stared at her through tobacco smoke. The proprietor spoke. 'We don't know this woman.'

One of the men took his pipe from his lips and she felt a glimmer of hope that he was less ready to dismiss her. She concentrated on him. 'Is the name familiar to you?' He shook his head.

She said: 'But perhaps you've seen her. She's about sixty, her hair is grey and she's short.'

The man replaced the pipe and after an interval shook his head again. Rain gave up and turned towards the door. A voice held her. The other old man, thin and hunched, was saying: 'There were many painters but they went with their *maître*.'

'Ach, that was many years ago,' said the proprietor.

Rain asked: 'Did they live in this village?'

'No, no,' said the proprietor with impatience. 'And it was so long ago, madame, the woman you speak of can be nothing to do with them.'

But Rain's eyes were on the bent figure at the table. He said: 'Durance. Like the river. That was his name. They went everywhere with that man. He was a god to them. They called him *maître*.'

The proprietor took a damp cloth and began to wipe a table, demonstrating the unimportance of Rain and her enquiries. 'You can't come to Provence and ask for a painter, just like that. Everywhere in Provence there are painters, more painters to the kilometre than any-where else in the world perhaps.'

Rain tried the thin man again. 'Did Durance and his friends live near this village?'

The man waved a curled hand. 'Not here, up that way.'

'Don't ask me,' said the proprietor. 'Up the valley somewhere. They were not to be seen here. We heard stories, that is all.' He finished the table, wrung out his cloth and flung it down with a noisy slap as though he were slamming the door on her questions.

Rain thanked them profusely for the help they had given, thanked as much as she would have done if they had really told her all they knew. It sometimes worked. People generally liked to help, always liked to be thanked. The man with the pipe softened. A little warmth came to his eyes.

'They called the place the Villa Souleiado, but it wasn't a villa, it was a farmhouse.'

Rain felt a flush of excitement. 'Do you know where it is?'

He waved in the direction his companion had waved and spoke the name of another village. 'You could go there. It's possible somebody there will remember.'

The village was miles further up the valley. The car flashed along tunnels cut through the limestone, raced beside foaming fast water and came to a bend where another road ran down from higher land. There were two women talking in the sun and Rain stopped to ask directions. The very old woman flung her hands into the air with a shriek of joyful astonishment. 'Villa Souleiado! How many years it is since I've heard that name spoken!'

The younger looked left out. 'What is this villa, Fernande?'

'But it's not a villa, it's only a name.' More gestures. 'That way, the old farmhouse.'

Her companion tipped her head towards the minor road. 'The old house over that way? On the road to Courmes?'

'Yes, that's it.'

'But I thought its name was something like . . .'

'Yes, but the artists named it the Villa Souleiado. Who knows why? They lived in their imaginations. Perhaps they saw the sun where we saw only the wind and the cloud choking the valley. Many of them were English.'

'Ah!' Fernande thought that explained any excesses.

Rain broke into their conversation. 'Does anyone live there now?'

Fernande nodded. 'In the cottage close by there are Madame Alègre and her son.'

The younger woman was now deeply interested. 'And how is Madame Alègre, Fernande? She had a bad back. Is she improving? I know what pain a bad back can be.'

'I've heard nothing of Madame Alègre's bad back lately. I haven't seen her for months.'

Rain intervened once more. 'Have you heard, perhaps, of Sabine Jourdain, a painter? I wonder whether she lives at the Villa Souleiado?'

The old woman was unsure. 'Madame Alègre has said nothing about anyone living in the house.' She looked for confirmation and the younger woman agreed: not a word had been said about it. Fernande said: 'I shouldn't think anyone lives there. It has been empty many years. If someone had moved in, it would have been said.'

Another car stopped and a man came over. Rain got directions to the house and left. She hoped the old woman might talk to her some more, but there was another stranger for Fernande to inspect and she stayed where she was.

Oliver was strolling about, looking deep into the limestone gorge where green and white water ran. 'Isn't this perfect?' he said.

'For what?' Rain knew that country peace would frustrate Oliver in less than a week. He would hanker for wine bars, lively conversation. Maybe he could manage the switch from London to Nice or Antibes but rural life in Provence would defeat him.

'For doing nothing,' said Oliver, still fooling himself.

'Did you get any help from those two?'

The directions were accurate—take the branch road and rise high into the mountain, towards the bare limestone crags and the village of Courmes perched like an ornament on a shelf, but before you reach it watch out for a path dropping sharply away to your right . . . As they were not drivers the women had given a false impression of the time it would take to get there. Rain got lost once by turning off the road too soon, but eventually there was a cottage just where she hoped to find one, and some way from it a building she guessed was the farmhouse. The valley was green and wooded and it was not easy to tell.

'We'll go to the house first and only try the cottage and Madame Alègre if we need to,' Rain said.

The car lurched along a dusty trail towards a house that appeared derelict. Oliver said: 'It's falling down, no one's been living in that.'

'I've got to go into its yard to turn, it's too narrow in the lane. Then we'll ask at the cottage.' But once the car had bumped into the yard and the rest of the house was visible, they realized it was not all near-ruin. At the far end the roof was sound, windows intact and clean.

Rain did not expect anyone to answer her knock on the door and no one did. So she repeated what she had done at the Villa Fièsole and peered through a window. 'There's a kitchen, with crockery and pans. I'd say that's been used recently.'

No reply. She looked around. Oliver was not behind her. She called. Walked out into the yard. Called again. Nothing. From very far below she heard the river Loup crashing over boulders on its way to the sea. The only other sounds were the cicadas. Then there was a sharp tapping noise. Startled, she turned to the house—and saw Oliver waving to her from inside the kitchen. She ran up to the glass. 'How did you get in there?'

'The back door wasn't locked. Come round.'

'Are you sure we ought to go in? It might not be what we're looking for.'

'It is. Come and see.'

He met her at the back door, stooping at the low doorway. 'Look.' He pointed at a couple of pairs of shoes. Women's shoes. Elderly women's shoes.

'There are a lot of elderly women who wear shoes.'

Unabashed, Oliver opened a door and showed her a bedroom with heavy old-fashioned walnut furniture. Then he opened another door and revealed a flight of bare wooden stairs. Before Rain could dissuade him he ran up, and gave an excited cry.

She followed and they were standing in a big room above the inhabited ground floor part of the house. Clear sunlight made it brilliant and the grey wooden floor was broken by the shadows of tables, an easel bearing a partly completed painting and a row of sculpted heads on a shelf.

'Are you convinced now?' asked Oliver. 'This is obviously where she lived.'

'And worked. She *did* have more sculptures, just as May Radley hoped.'

'And she hadn't entirely given up painting.' He was looking at the canvas on the easel. Against the wall leaned several prepared canvases. 'It's sad she kept it up. Even if she was good she'd always be overshadowed by Durance.'

' "Even if"? You'd decided her sculpture was very good.'

Oliver's glance went to the heads on the shelf. Among them was another of the woman who had been the model for the piece he so admired at the Galerie Bellanda. Rain sensed a wicked idea flash through his mind.

'Don't you dare, Oliver! Don't even think about it. If you really want one so badly you can buy the one May Radley has.'

Oliver, disconcerted that his mind was so easily read, muttered that she could not possibly have thought he was considering stealing the head. 'Although I don't see what harm it would do. The artist is dead, she discouraged visitors and it's probable no one else knows about these . . .'

She let his voice trail away as she fixed him with her most superior expression. Oliver sauntered over to the easel. He touched the canvas and said: 'The paint is dry.'

'It's not only dry, it's dusty.' Rain stroked it and held up a dirty fingertip. 'She wasn't interrupted within the last weeks while working on this.'

Oliver went to a table where brushes and rags lay and began to fiddle with them, Rain watching with a half smile until the inevitable happened and he got paint on his hand and needed her to wipe it off. 'Here you are.' She handed him a paper handkerchief.

'Where would I be without you?'

They both thought of the beach and the redhead and Rain said swiftly: 'Even though the painting isn't still wet the rag she wiped her hands on is. She painted something else here recently, and it's gone.'

He screwed up the tissue and tossed it on to the table beside the rags. 'I wonder who took it?'

'She might have taken it with her when she went to stay with Barbara Coleman.'

Oliver sat on the edge of the table and swung a leg, his shadow long on the floorboards. Rain thought he was considering the unlikelihood of Sabine Jourdain transporting a wet oil painting when she went visiting in Antibes, but when he spoke next he said: 'It must have

73

been pretty good living and painting up here, away from it all.'

'You'd hate it, you know you would.'

'Sabine Jourdain didn't, yet she was used to a gregarious life.'

Rain sighed. 'I'll never know whether she was happy or not. I'll never be able to ask her and the only person I've met who was close to her is Durance and he's too distraught to talk . . .'

Oliver stiffened. Somewhere below there were sounds. They changed into heavy footsteps pounding up the stairs. A furiously angry woman burst into the room.

She came at them shrieking that they had no right to be in the house and were to leave immediately or she would set her dogs on them. Rain, who understood, and Oliver, who did not, were equally intimidated. They found themselves being edged into a corner of the room as the woman's arm-waving advance made it impossible for them to do as she asked and get out.

Her skin was an unhealthy high colour, her crinkled greying hair had escaped from its pins and tufts sprang out from her head, her black clothes were worn to greenness and she had heavy laced shoes. The sole of the left shoe was built up several inches but could not correct her rocking gait. She brought with her a smell of stale sweat, unwashed clothes.

'Madame Alègre?' Rain shouted through the verbal onslaught. The name was partly guesswork, partly recognition.

The woman faltered. Rain repeated the name more quietly. The woman fell silent, as though all her words had been used up and she would never utter again. The silence was as frightening in its way as her explosive entrance had been.

Rain said: 'We came to see Sabine Jourdain's home, Madame Alègre.'

Wild black eyes moved from Rain to Oliver. Rain saw her take a deep breath and feared the attack would be renewed. Rain introduced herself, said she was a journalist come to write about Sabine Jourdain. She was scrutinized for deception.

Eventually the woman spoke, her voice high, her face reddened and the eyes darting. 'I mustn't tell you about Madame Jourdain. No, no, I mustn't tell you.' Her right hand plucked at the sleeve of her cardigan.

Rain said: 'I'd like to know how long she lived here, what she painted . . . Just that sort of thing.'

The hand teased the sleeve. The eyes swivelled from Rain to Oliver to the easel. Rain said: 'I was told to come here. I was told Madame Alègre would know.'

The woman softened a shade. Rain felt Oliver behind her, deathly still, not risking spoiling what she was doing. Rain saw the woman's eyes go to the easel again and said: 'That's an old painting, isn't it? It seems funny to find it on the easel. I wonder why Sabine Jourdain put it there.'

The woman's mouth opened but she changed her mind and it snapped shut. She jerked her head round and her eyes seemed to check everything else in the room as though she were making sure Rain and Oliver had not stolen anything. Rain thought what a blessing it was that Oliver had not helped himself to the sculpture. She saw the woman in profile for the first time and then she was certain. She said: 'Tell me, Madame Alègre, did you model for Sabine Jourdain very often?'

The woman's eyes settled on the row of heads on the shelf. 'A few times,' she said. 'Seven, maybe eight.'

'And the children? Who were her models for those heads?'

75

'Two brothers in the village. They came here to be naughty, to play in the old house, and she found them and made them come in and sit still. As a punishment, she said, but she was laughing and they didn't mind. They'd never been in an artist's studio before and they were proud to have their heads made. So they came again.' Madame Alègre discovered she had been tricked into conversation and grew wary, but Rain was smiling at her.

'The heads Sabine Jourdain did of you are very fine. Did you enjoy modelling?'

'Oh, it was nothing. It was sitting still, that was all. "Put your head like this, Madame Alègre, put your head like that." There was nothing to it. It was sitting still and listening to her talking about the days when she was young and the house was full of people and she had no need to take poor models like Madame Alègre and the Laurier brothers.'

Bit by gentle bit Rain eased her along until Madame Alègre was telling how, when Sabine Jourdain was busy with her paintings, no one was allowed to disturb her, but then she would break off for a while and enjoy herself sculpting.

'What were her paintings like?' Rain asked.

Madame Alègre gave the room a puzzled look. She became guarded. 'I don't know.'

Oliver threw in: 'But you must have seen them.'

The woman tensed, her fingers resumed twisting the cardigan sleeve. 'No, no, I never saw them. She wasn't to be disturbed. It was said, she mustn't be disturbed.'

Rain asked softly: 'Who said?'

Madame Alègre's eyes flashed. 'You must go, you shouldn't be here. No one is to come here.'

'Very well. Come on, Oliver.' They went to the staircase, Madame Alègre's uneven walk sounding behind them.

Rain waited for her at the bottom of the stairs, talking up to her as the woman descended. 'Did she live here very long?'

'Three years.'

'And was the house empty before that?'

'Oh yes, it was in a very bad way, but then part of it was put right and Madame Jourdain came.'

'And you looked after her? Cleaning and so on?'

'It was a job for me. I have a bad back, because of the leg. And my son isn't strong enough to work.' She reached the foot of the stairs and gave a harsh laugh. 'Oh, I know what you're thinking. You're thinking that if Madame Alègre was cleaning then Madame Alègre was looking at the paintings.'

Rain gave the embarrassed smile of someone caught out. 'And you were, weren't you?'

'I wasn't to clean in the studio. Artists don't like dust being made. I was only in the studio when I was modelling for her, and then the canvases were facing the walls so I saw nothing. I don't know if they were plain canvases or painted canvases, I saw only the backs.'

'But?'

'But there was the smell of paint and sometimes she was away and it so happened I had some reason to go up to the studio. Oh, she knew about it. I'd tell her: how can an artist work if the windows are dirty, and who is to clean them if Madame Alègre doesn't?'

'She didn't mind that you went in there?'

'Why should she mind? I wasn't disturbing her if I was in there when she wasn't.'

Madame Alègre went outside and looked around at the sun-warmed stone walls, Rain's car in the yard and the clear sky overhead. She said: 'She's away now. It's a pity you've missed her. I'll tell her you came.'

'You've made it sound as though she doesn't have many visitors.'

'Very few, but I know when they come because I hear the cars go by my cottage. Today there have been two cars and she's missed them both.'

'Did you know her other visitor?'

Madame Alègre was staring upwards at the roof above the studio; or perhaps she was gazing at precarious Courmes, the crag curving above it like a protective arm. 'It'll go soon, you see. I told her she must get the man to mend the roof or it'll be like that . . .' She pointed at the collapsed section at the other end of the building. 'And then she'll have no studio. What did you say?'

'I asked who else came today.'

'I've seen him once before but I don't know his name. He comes in a big car, a grey car, and he drives fast. Last week I was in Madame Jourdain's kitchen when he came. That time he was with another man who told me to go home. I was very annoyed, I had my cleaning to do.'

'What does he look like, the man who came today?'

As Rain suspected, she had missed no detail. Madame Alègre gave a precise description. Rain thought she identified Joseph. Then she was sure of it. Madame Alègre said: 'He had the boot of the grey car open and he loaded the paintings into it. He doesn't know I saw him. When I went into the studio after he'd gone there were no paintings left, except that old one he'd put on the easel.'

Madame Alègre became engrossed in the state of the roof. 'You'd think the man would fix the roof for her.'

'The man with the grey car?' Rain asked.

'No, the famous man. He sometimes comes here with the man in the grey car and sometimes with a different

78

man. He's so famous and he won't even fix the roof of his old home.'

'Who do you mean?'

'Another painter. Durance.'

'Were you here years ago when Durance lived here?'

'With all his women? No, but people still talk about it. Do you know, some say they were all mad? Most of them were English.'

'I heard they gave this place a funny name.'

'Villa Souleiado?' Madame Alègre's laugh echoed off the walls. Oliver wished he understood the joke, but saw from Rain's face that she did not, either.

'It's not French, it's Provençal,' said Madame Alègre. 'It means sunstruck.'

There was not much more to be had from Madame Alègre. She became nervous and restless as her mercurial temperament dictated, and when it seemed she was going to be aggressive again Rain and Oliver drove away, swinging in sunlight around corkscrew bends and watching white clouds hang in the gorge below them.

'We knew Sabine Jourdain used to work on Durance's canvases in the past, but it seems she quietly continued doing so,' Rain said.

'It's the "quietly" that makes it wrong, isn't it? If the buyer is paying for a Durance then he ought to know how much Durance he's getting.'

Rain believed he was right but it seemed a curiously moral viewpoint for somebody who had been tempted to steal a head of Madame Alègre.

Oliver was thinking about supper. 'We could go straight to the restaurant I liked in Antibes.'

'I'd rather shower and change first. It won't take long.'

It should not have done, but when Rain and Oliver opened the street door leading to the flat, two men stepped out of the shadows and confronted them.

79

9

'**R**ain Morgan?'

'So I am.'

She was afraid there was a tremor in her voice. She felt for Oliver's arm in the darkness but he was just out of reach.

The black shapes of the men leaned over her. They wanted her, not Oliver. She heard Oliver snap: 'What's this about?'

One of the men thrust a document into her face. 'We're police officers. We wish to talk to you.'

She repeated what Oliver had said. 'What's this about?'

The other man said: 'The death of Sabine Jourdain.'

'But I've told the police all I know.'

The first man said: 'We don't think so, Miss Morgan.'

She did not care for their tone. 'Come up to the flat. We can't talk here.' She did not want to return to the police station.

The men had drawn attention to their presence. Neighbours in the other flats peeped around doors to see what was happening.

Rain took a bottle of wine from the fridge, and put it

on the table with four glasses and sat down. She had her first good look at the men. One was tall and cadaverous, his companion sultry. They were both dressed in clothes that were casual but not too relaxed, the worldwide uniform of the plainclothes policeman. And, like policemen anywhere, they made her feel foolish and likely to blurt out indiscretions.

The taller man said his name was Foucard, his companion Denis. Rain introduced Oliver but they appeared already to know who he was. Foucard said: 'Further enquiries have been made since your statement this morning about the death of Sabine Jourdain. We have also had the preliminary results of a post mortem examination. Madame Jourdain was murdered.'

Rain remembered the friendly policeman that morning demonstrating with a blow to his forehead. She half expected Foucard to do the same. He did not. His cool hazel eyes studied Rain. She broke the silence. 'Well, what happened to her?'

'Perhaps you'd like to tell us, Miss Morgan?'

Oliver, sensitive to the combative atmosphere, asked her: 'Rain, what are they saying?' He had spun his dining chair round and was straddling it, arms resting on the back.

She said: 'They say she was murdered and suggest I know what happened to her.'

'Please!' said Denis with a quelling look at Oliver.

'Oliver doesn't speak French. He wonders what's being said.' She was not sure the police had no English. It would not be surprising if they concealed it. If they suspected her of guilty knowledge they might think it worthwhile pretending.

Rain and Foucard challenged each other, Denis's jaw tightened. Oliver seized his moment. He gave his biggest and, so far, best shrug, opened the wine and poured four

81

glasses. 'To the Great Idea,' he said ironically as he raised a glass.

Rain laughed. 'The Great Idea,' she agreed, translating.

This was not what Foucard had been trying to achieve. Denis grunted and took up his glass. Foucard said sourly: 'Sabine Jourdain is murdered and you're laughing.'

The rebuke was for Rain but Denis put his glass down and tried to look as though he had never thought of sharing the toast. Foucard said: 'And what is this great idea? Killing an old woman, perhaps?'

'The Great Idea was to come to France to interview Sabine Jourdain for a newspaper feature. Instead, it's all gone wrong.'

Oliver asked what was going on. Rain said: 'I'm trying to explain an English joke. He wants to know why I laughed at your toast.'

'Tell him my toasts are always very funny. Tell him quickly or we'll be here all night. I'm starving, we ought to be on our way to the restaurant by now.'

She wondered whether he was simply hungry or anticipating seeing his friends there again. She said: 'It's not easy to hurry a man who's accusing you of withholding information about a murder.'

Oliver started to argue but Foucard butted in: 'Miss Morgan, you may speak to your friend who doesn't understand French once you have answered my questions.'

She could not remember a question, apart from the one about the Great Idea, and she did not think either of them wanted any more of that. 'I don't have answers to your questions. I told everything I know at the police station.'

'You must tell it to me now.'

Denis's pen moved rapidly over his notebook as she repeated her story. She tried to recall precisely what she had said earlier. Her motives for going to the police had been confused. She had been offering information, but also finding out what they knew so that she could telephone a few paragraphs to her paper.

As she neared the end of the tale Foucard's face assumed a sardonic expression. He leaned towards her across the table and it shook, jiggling the wine in the glass he had not touched. 'But that isn't true, is it?'

'What isn't true?'

'Quite a lot of it isn't true. You're an intelligent woman, Miss Morgan . . .' (She had long noticed that this remark was often the prelude to an insult.) 'How could there have been a row and a fight that created the disturbance of the lounge as you describe it, without people on board the *Jonquil* hearing? How could you have gone aboard, not once but twice, without someone hearing and seeing you? We're not talking about the *Mary Céleste*, Miss Morgan. We're talking about a luxury motor yacht with a crew of eight.'

'I can't tell you why it happened, only that it did.'

'When you realized a woman you knew had been taken dead from the water, what did you do?'

She sounded pathetically silly as she replied that she had run away.

'Where did you go?'

'I came here, but I didn't have the key and Oliver was out, so I sat in our hired car and waited until he came.'

'And how long was it before he came?'

'I don't know exactly. A couple of hours. Perhaps a bit more.'

'You *don't know*? Surely a woman always knows how long she waits for a man. To the very minute she knows.'

'I can't be more explicit. It was a long time and felt longer.'

'You sat in the car all the time?'

'The car was in a street nearby. I sat there for a while, then I went for a short drive and came back and parked in the square.'

'Where did you drive?'

'To the Villa Fièsole, on the . . .'

'I know the Villa Fièsole. No doubt you're going to tell me no one saw you waiting in the car and no one saw you at the villa.'

'I didn't speak to anyone. I can't say whether anyone noticed me.'

Foucard drummed his fingers on the table, an irritating tattoo. 'Hmmm,' he said. 'So . . . you tell us an unlikely story about the events at the *Jonquil* and you say you spent at least two hours sitting in a car and don't think anyone noticed you.'

She opened her mouth to protest, but he went on: 'But you are, if I may say so, very noticeable, Miss Morgan. How could it be that you spent all evening, from the time you parted from your friend until he returned in the early hours of the morning, without anyone noticing you?'

Oliver interrupted. Denis objected to the interruption. Rain said: 'It's all right, Oliver. He's got a point. He wants to know why no one saw me.'

Foucard barked at Denis who stood up and urged Oliver to follow him. Oliver did not. Denis flung open the bedroom door and waved Oliver inside. Oliver liked neither the suggestion nor the manner in which it was made. He did not move. 'I'm damned if I'm going. What you've got to say you can say in front of me.'

Denis advanced on him, came round the table and snatched at his arm. Oliver sprang up, the chair rocking. He was far taller than the Frenchman and looked down at him with contempt. Rain was arguing with Foucard that Denis was behaving unreasonably and Foucard was insisting that she explain to Oliver that he was to do exactly what Denis wanted. Rain refused. She retorted that unless Oliver stayed with her she would not discuss the Jourdain killing any further in French and that would be the end of the interview.

Foucard clicked his fingers, Denis dropped to his chair like a disciplined animal. Oliver refilled his glass and sat down again.

'I don't like this,' he breathed.

Rain said: 'Nor me, but there's not much I can do about it, is there?'

'You should have gone to the police station with them.'

'I was trying to get it over quickly so we could eat.'

Foucard asked her to translate and she did. He said: 'Then let's be quick, by all means. Let's get at the truth of what happened yesterday evening at the harbour and then you may go to your restaurant.'

Rain groaned. They could bat this back and forth a long time, with Foucard refusing to believe her. She said: 'I don't understand why I should be disbelieved.'

'Your story is not corroborated,' said Foucard.

'Because no one noticed me? The boat was empty, the people on the quay were preoccupied with the tragedy, and nobody saw me in the car.' She thought of something that had not seemed important before. 'But there was one place where I was seen. After I left the *Jonquil*, while the woman and man were shouting at each other, I went to the Bar de la Marine. I had some wine and ate some food there. I stayed about half an hour. It was quite busy, someone might remember me.'

Denis's pen was active again. Foucard's gaunt face allowed a thin smile of triumph. 'So . . . you hadn't told us everything. Who was at the café?'

She described the Americans and English people, said there had been two young Frenchmen sitting at a table

85

behind her but she had not seen them properly. She mentioned the waitresses and the Tunisian pedlar.

Denis wrote it all down and then said with suspicion: 'You noticed all that? All those details?'

'Yes. I was alone with nothing to do but watch other people.'

Foucard rewarded Denis with a nod of approval. 'They are very good descriptions,' said Foucard. 'It's as if you made sure you had them in case you were asked for them.'

'I'm a journalist, *of course* I notice the people and things around me!'

Foucard sneered. 'You're a journalist who sees everything but moves unseen.' He shut off her reply with a few rapid words to Denis. Denis closed his notebook, then his hand trailed towards the wine glass and he drained it.

Foucard said: 'We'll look for these witnesses of yours, Miss Morgan. If they are to be found, we'll find them. But isn't it strange you can offer us all these witnesses to a glass of wine and a plate of scraps in a café and not a single one for the rest of the evening?'

He pushed back his chair and got to his feet. He said: 'You won't run away, will you? It'll be necessary to talk to you again.'

'I'll be here at least another day.'

'We must make sure of it. When we meet again perhaps your memory will have been refreshed and you'll be ready to explain why anyone should have wanted Sabine Jourdain shot.'

'*Shot!* I thought . . .'

He was sarcastic. 'Yes, you thought she was struck on the head or drowned. Isn't that what you reported at the police station this morning?'

'No!' No, it was not. That was what she had been told

the police then believed. But Foucard's question was not really a question, he had finished with those and was playing with her.

He said: 'You may go to your restaurant now.' Before he followed Denis out of the room he leaned over the table and pushed his untouched glass of wine towards her. 'Bon *appétit*,' he said.

10

Oliver stood at the top of the stairs and watched the policemen leave the building. Then he made Rain tell him everything that had been said. She looked rather small and worried.

'We must get out,' Oliver said firmly. 'Right away. We'll just pack and go.'

'There isn't another flight to London tonight, and even if there were we might not get past passport control. I'm not sure Foucard didn't mean he would stop me leaving. If I try to go and I'm stopped, I really will look guilty.'

Oliver was pacing the room. The flat felt miserably like a trap. He said: 'When Foucard finds those witnesses to your visit to the café . . .'

'. . . it won't help much. They'd only prove I told the truth about eating there at the time I said.'

'Did he suggest why you might have gone to the police station with a false story?'

She picked up the telephone. 'No, but if everyone has told a different story from mine, he's entitled to be suspicious.' She dialled. 'I'm ringing the *Post*.'

'To ask Wilmot's advice?' Lionel Wilmot was the

newspaper's lawyer, employed to steer it around the libel laws but invoked at other nervous moments, too.

'Yes, I'd better speak to him before a nuisance becomes a calamity. But I expect Holly will be more use.'

Holly Chase greeted her with bubbling cheerfulness. The diary page, one of the earliest to be made up, was finished for the day and she had time to relax. Rain had no intention of allowing her to. Rain said: 'I need some information urgently, at the latest by first thing tomorrow morning.'

'You sound glum. Is anything wrong?'

'Not yet, but it's moving that way. It'll help if you can let me have something on the American art dealer Benedict Joseph and his wife, Merlyn. You could ring Renata Walsh and some of our other art world contacts.'

'Sure. What have the Josephs done?'

'I don't know, but there's been something going on ever since I arrived here and I'm sure they know what it is.' She outlined what had happened.

'I'll get on the trail right away. Anybody else to check on?'

'No . . . yes. It's a long shot, but see whether you can find anything about a man called Philippe Maurin. He owns the Maurin gallery in Nice.'

'Anything else?'

'And I'd like the name and phone number of the news desk's stringer down here.'

Holly gave a peal of laughter. 'I thought everyone in Fleet Street knew our man on the Côte d'Azur is James Cobalt! Don't you remember all those tired jokes about him filing us blue stories?'

Holly said she would phone Rain next morning with everything else but would get Cobalt's phone number from the news desk while Rain spoke to Wilmot. Some minutes later Rain had destroyed Wilmot's otherwise tranquil evening and written down Cobalt's phone number.

'Now,' said Oliver, 'we must find out whether there are any restaurants with food left.'

'I'd like to ring Cobalt.'

'*After.*'

He won. They found a restaurant and spent a depressed hour eating what, under other circumstances, would have been an enjoyable meal. Later, when Rain rang Cobalt, there was no reply.

She had a restless night, worrying what the next day might hold and whether the information Holly supplied would help her make sense of it. Oliver slept soundly and yet it was Oliver who had first warned her she might be in danger. Her mind would not let her relax and she lay awake much of the night, disliking the dark but unable to hide from it. Once she got up and went on to the balcony, listening to the susurrus of the sea and watching the hovering moon.

Towards morning she woke yet again, slipped out of bed and lit a lamp in the sitting room. She made a hot drink and curled up on a couch with her hands around the mug, not for warmth, because the night was not cold, but for comfort.

She picked over everything that had happened since she came to France. The tiresome things which had frustrated her looked like attempts to prevent her from spending time alone with Sabine Jourdain. If it were true the woman had been producing the Durance paintings, in whole or in substantial part, the risk that she would tell Rain had died.

And yet Rain's difficulties in getting people to talk had not ended. Barbara Coleman was still not answering the door at the Villa Fièsole, Durance was too shocked to talk, Joseph refused to and the police were on her tail.

In the east the sky was red and yellow, promising a hot day. She stood on the balcony, thinking of that first afternoon there with Oliver when they planned how to enjoy themselves once she had finished her work. She remembered the time she watched the children's boats bobbing obediently until the man's vigilance was relaxed.

The sea was now pallid, roofs softest russet. A solitary motor cycle went along the coast road. Gradually the colours deepened, pigeons came to parade, doors banged, footsteps drummed in alleyways. A noise behind her. Oliver.

'Couldn't you sleep? How long have you been up?'

It was long enough for the emptiness of night to be superseded by the activity of day. She looked at the kitchen clock. 'No,' said Oliver, guessing. 'It's far too early to ring Cobalt.'

'Or for Holly to ring me.'

'Quite. Come and have breakfast.'

She was not hungry, just wanted coffee. Oliver made it, made her sit and drink it while he bought newspapers. There were brief paragraphs about Sabine Jourdain in one, but in *Nice Matin* the story was given prominence. There was even a photograph of her with Durance.

Oliver asked: 'What does it say about her?'

She scanned. 'Rather less than we know. It doesn't say she was shot or that the police suspect murder.' She peered at the photograph. Oliver asked what she was looking for.

'I'm trying to make out where it was taken. The background is rather vague.'

Another picture was printed overleaf and it showed through. The person who had taken such a relaxed photograph of the couple (smiling at the camera with Durance's arm around Sabine Jourdain's shoulders) might know them well and tell Rain about the relationship.

When she got through to Cobalt she asked whether he could find out from *Nice Matin* where the picture came from.

'Easily,' said Cobalt. 'Shall I phone you or are you coming to Nice?'

'I'd like to drive over later this morning. I have to make a call here first. Does that suit your plans for the day?'

'My *what!*' said Cobalt with a laugh. 'Come any time. Got a pen? I'll give you the address.'

Rain wrote down an address in the rue de Rivoli which Cobalt said she could not miss because it ran off the Promenade des Anglais at the side of the Hotel Negresco, and no one who had been to Nice had ever been known to lose the Negresco.

'I'll find you,' she promised.

'And I'll find the information you want.'

Rain waited fretfully for Holly Chase to ring. She tried Holly's home number and got the unobtainable signal. She fretted some more.

'If Holly's line is out of order she'll have to get to another phone,' Oliver said. 'Give her time.'

At last the call came. 'Hi!' said Holly. 'They've dug up the road at Spinney Green and they've dug up my telephone cable with it. Aren't gas boards wonderful?'

'What other news?'

'I'll dictate what I've found out and you can ask questions afterwards. OK?'

'OK.'

Holly read out notes on the life and loves of Benedict Joseph. He was born in New York, the son of a Jewish tailor. There were three brothers, the elder two became doctors but Ben did not do well at school and was destined for the tailor's shop. He had other ideas and got himself into art college. He was talented enough to stay the course and clever enough to know he had no future as an artist.

By that time his father owned a retail shop as well as a business making men's clothes. Ben tried to persuade his parents to put up the money for him to open an art gallery. They, not surprisingly, viewed that as a certain method of losing money and would not help. There was some conflict with the two brothers over the matter and Ben broke with the family.

'By the way,' said Holly, 'he started off as plain Benjamin. The Benedict came later. I suppose he thought it had more cachet.'

'Never mind the cachet, let's concentrate on the cash. How did he get rich?'

'He married money. He shared a studio with a couple of other artists, one of whom was fairly successful. Peter Leary—remember that name. Through Leary he met his first wife, Elspeth Paget, daughter of a small-time collector. Paget owned a lot of property.'

'Joseph had a rich wife and could start dealing.'

'Yes, he began buying on behalf of his father-in-law. Very cosy. However, Elspeth Paget seems not to have appreciated that a dealer must go to the market place. One day when he came home from Europe with his latest batch of goodies he found the proverbial letter on the mantelpiece saying she'd left. She ran off with Peter Leary.'

'Weren't there children?'

'Four. Elspeth took them, Leary made her send them back.'

'And you're going to tell me what the notes she tied around their necks said? This is so detailed—are you sure you're not making it all up to please me?'

Holly gave a whoop of laughter. 'Renata Walsh's grasp of gossip is unflawed.'

'And she tells you there was a divorce and Benedict married Merlyn?'

'Not quite. They were heading for divorce when Elspeth died. There was a lot of legal fuss about how much of her money Benedict ought to get. In the end, the answer was not much. His children were rich but he didn't have access to the money of the youngest, and the others were grown up. No, the marriage to Merlyn came later, after a number of liaisons which foundered before actual marriage.'

'Merlyn says she was a film actress. Is that right?'

Holly laughed again. 'Strictly true, I suppose. My source insists she got as far as a television commercial with Michael Caine, spent some months resting and then married Mr Joseph. There was a brief, early marriage to an actor. She's thirty-two now, younger than two of Joseph's children.'

'Was she rich, helpful to him in that way?'

'Nothing suggests it. Oh, and her name wasn't Merlyn. She was an Arlene which she decided to change for something smoother.'

'I thought a merlin was a bird of prey. Perhaps she doesn't know that.'

'Despite the soft and cuddly name she's at least as tough as he is. Since her arrival in his life, about five years ago, he's been spending like a rich man. Nobody can account for it. And that,' said Holly, 'is all I have to report. I had no luck with Philippe Maurin. Renata can't find anyone who's heard of him and says he must be very small fry.'

'But quite beautiful,' Rain said.

'Then you won't mind seeing him yourself to sniff out the details.' Before Rain could object, Holly rushed on with the news that Dick Tavett was going to phone her to chase up the story of the missing Tarquin Poulteney-

Crosse. 'Dick's convincing himself Tarquin's been forgotten.'

'He's not forgotten, he's just slithered down my scale of priorities.'

Rain relayed to Oliver what Holly had said. 'She's excellent, 100 per cent reliable.'

'And 100 per cent ambitious and trying to snatch your job.'

'Nonsense. The *Post* isn't ready for its first black female gossip columnist.' It was cruel and true.

Oliver would not drop the subject. 'You're exploiting her. You're confident she can't replace you and so you let her slave away proving she's capable of it.'

'She isn't proving anything to me. Holly proves things to herself.'

There was a pause. They had been around this course before. Oliver said: 'Doesn't it bother you, in the way it bothers you that Sabine Jourdain was forever playing second fiddle to Durance?'

'I don't see the parallel.'

'Oh yes, you do. You believe it was demeaning for those women to live under the shadow of Durance, and now we've found that she was actually contributing to the work that appeared under his name.'

'But that isn't the same at all. The gossip column appears under my name but one journalist couldn't write and research all that material every day. Durance exercised a hold—sexual or whatever else it was—over those women. I don't have a hold over Holly, she can do what she likes. I'm very lucky she works with me, but she could decide to take off tomorrow and I wouldn't have a way of stopping her.'

'Very persuasive,' said Oliver, unpersuaded. 'Holly isn't going to risk moving to another paper. The *Post* has given her a chance that no other paper would. That's what holds her. She has no more choice than Sabine Jourdain had about staying with Durance.'

Rain sighed. 'I may never know the truth about Sabine Jourdain, but I do hope you're wrong about Holly.'

The telephone rang. Joseph. 'Rain, I was afraid you might have gone out. Would you come to the *Jonquil* this morning? There's something I want to talk about. No, not now. We'll go into it then. You're sure you don't mind?'

Rain put the phone down with a bemused smile. 'Life isn't always so convenient. I meant to call on the Josephs and wondered how to say I was "just passing" when I couldn't possibly have been.'

'Will you be all right going alone?'

'Why ever not? It's broad daylight and I wouldn't be surprised to find a policeman tailing me.'

'If one tails me he'll find himself on the beach,' said Oliver and picked up *Bludgeon* and went there while Rain walked to the boat.

Joseph was looking out for her. He waved, calling an enthusiastic greeting. She could not think why he was so jovial. The last time they met he was very worried. He helped her on board. 'Come on inside and we'll find something to drink.'

'Coffee will be fine.'

'Sure, we'll have coffee.' He signalled to Ross, the steward.

'On deck, sir?'

Joseph raised his eyebrows at Rain. She chose to be outside. The slap of water as a launch set out from the quay and the blue arc of the Alps were not to be exchanged for the coolness inside.

Joseph offered her a chair near a bamboo table, then drew one up opposite for himself. It was to be a serious discussion, then. She felt her stomach tense. Frightening

96

things had happened on board this yacht. Some of them had happened to her. And here she was again, curiosity leading her into more potential danger.

She took a deep breath and told herself not to be foolish: it was day, she was in public view, she had no reason to be afraid. There might even be a French detective keeping an eye on her. She wondered whether, subconsciously, the idea of the French detective had persuaded her to opt for the open deck.

Coffee came. Joseph sugared his, took a sip, lowered the cup. 'Er . . . Rain . . . er . . .' He was demonstrably anxious. 'Yesterday . . . you said the police would come here, because of . . . that awful business.'

She stirred her coffee, watching him. He was quite unlike the man who had exuded *bonhomie* that first evening when he and his wife appeared in utter control of everything and everyone. That first evening, when Sabine Jourdain was still alive.

She said: 'Didn't they come?'

'Sure, they came, but they didn't ask the sort of questions I was ready for. I didn't go to them first. Oh yes, I know I said to you I thought I might do that, rather than have them come on board and upset the crew . . .'

They both realized it was not the crew who would be upset.

'Why did you change your mind?'

He grimaced. 'My French. I mean my lack of it. What was the point of going to see them when I've never been able to manage more than that stuff about pens and aunts?'

'I see.' She did not know why she did not tell him of the rabbit-faced senior officer with the impeccable English. He might still need him, but she did not tell him.

'They came and I can't say I was pleased to see them. They came in a car and . . . I'll swear if they'd come aboard waving handcuffs at me they couldn't have made themselves more obvious.' He wiped a hand across his brow. 'The trouble is, they don't believe what I told them.'

'You spoke English to them?' She wondered who they were.

'Yes, they had enough for a simple conversation and then I called in Ross. He's quite a linguist.'

'Do you remember the names of the policemen?'

Joseph looked irritated by the question, it was clearly off the point as he saw it. 'Yes, there was a tall one called Foucard and a dark, mysterious guy called Denis.'

So she had been right. The inability to speak English when they had called on her had been a deception. It pleased her that she had been careful enough to suspect. She said: 'Why do you think they disbelieve you?'

'Because they more or less said so. I was asked to tell them what happened here on the night Sabine fell into the harbour and drowned. Well, of course, I explained I wasn't here and neither was Merlyn. When we got back it was very late and we went straight to bed. Foucard insisted there was trouble on board and Sabine was injured right here. I don't know where he could have got that idea from.' His eyes avoided her.

Rain thought fast. She could tell him she was the source of the story of the fight on board, and then get him to challenge the crew in her presence because someone had cleared up the mess even if they had not known what caused it. If Joseph was being honest with her now, then at least one of the crew knew the truth.

But on the other hand, perhaps Joseph was not being frank, and was merely trying to find out how much she knew. She used the same delaying tactic he had chosen and raised her cup and sipped. A gull alighted on the rail of the boat and they both pretended to let it hold their attention for a moment. It cried and glided out to sea, sending her thoughts back to the escaping children's boats. A moment's inattention, that's all that's needed for someone to take advantage of you. And she heard in her mind Oliver's words: 'Haven't you thought you might be in danger?'

She shook her head as though clearing it, gave Joseph her most disarming smile and said: 'Forgive me, I was dreaming. I've forgotten what you said.'

He returned her smile. 'I asked whether you'd heard or seen any sign of trouble on board on the night Sabine died.'

'What sort of trouble?'

'Oh, you know. A couple of people shouting, having a fight. Some chairs turned over . . . that sort of trouble.'

'Did the police say they believed that had happened?'

'They'd heard a story about it. I said they'd got the wrong boat, nothing like that could have taken place here, there'd have been too many people around for it to go unnoticed.'

Rain reasoned that if he were seriously interested in finding out he would have asked the crew, or pressed the police to say where the story had come from. As he was asking her he was most likely trying to find out how much she knew. He raised his cup again, then looked beyond her and into the cocktail bar. Merlyn was coming towards them wearing a loose silk robe.

'Rain, how lovely to see you.' Merlyn held out a jewelled hand which Rain had no option but to take. Ross appeared at her elbow and Merlyn asked for wine. She wandered around, tipping her face to the sun. 'Don't you just love this weather?'

Rain murmured. Ross put a glass of wine on the table and Joseph called Merlyn's attention to it. She sat down, angling her chair slightly so that she and her husband were now both facing Rain. She watched Rain over the rim of her glass as she drank. Then: 'You've heard we had the most awful policemen here? I don't know how we can explain that to the crew. I'm sure none of the other people who charter this yacht have the police running about asking impertinent questions.'

Joseph cleared his throat. 'They weren't such impertinent questions.'

'Oh, I think so, Ben. How about asking how much we'd had to drink that evening? I don't think they'd any right to ask that sort of thing.'

Rain wondered how much Merlyn had already drunk this morning. She returned to the topic that concerned her most, saying she wanted to write an appreciation of Sabine Jourdain's work.

Merlyn interrupted with a dismissive wave of the hand. 'Nothing to appreciate, isn't that right, Ben? Sabine was an acolyte, Durance the master.'

'That's right,' Joseph said eagerly. 'She can only be discussed in relation to Durance. Now his work . . .'

Rain butted in: '. . . seems to have been done by Sabine Jourdain.'

There was a terrible silence. Far off a voice called across water. In the bar a steward was clinking glasses. Flags stirred in the breeze. For all that, there was an uncomfortable, enduring silence.

Joseph cleared his throat. When he spoke his voice was a husky whisper. 'Are you crazy? Sabine Jourdain paint Durance's pictures for him?'

Rain relented with a cheeky grin. '*Part* of them, let's say. Isn't it true she worked on the canvases with him?'

Joseph recovered and gave a roguish chuckle. He thrust out a clenched fist as though he were going to punch her playfully. He stopped short. 'Sabine was always a pupil, she studied with him, learned her technique from him and was privileged to help on his canvases. But that was in the old days, when they were . . .'

'Lovers,' said Merlyn languorously.

'Yes,' said Joseph with a sharp glance at his wife. 'He was working on a bigger scale then. It's quite usual for artists to have help in that way.'

Rain was still smiling. 'Yes, of course. How much work did she do on his recent canvases? During the last five years?' She had cornered the Josephs. They would either have to deny flatly that Sabine Jourdain had been exploited to promote Durance or else they would have to confess that much of Durance's recent work had been done by her.

Merlyn sat unflinching. Joseph saw an escape route and took it. He shrugged. 'Who's to say? I buy paintings from Marius Durance. If he tells me he's painted a picture I don't challenge the guy about every brush-stroke. Does it matter if he has help? He's a very old man. If you want precise details of how he paints you'll have to get them from him.'

Merlyn swirled the wine in her glass. 'He's very old,' she echoed. 'It would be criminal to go upsetting him with this sort of nonsense just for a newspaper article. He's stunned as it is by Sabine's death.'

She emptied her glass and called in the direction of the bar for more wine. At the second time of shouting, Ross came. He looked enquiringly at the other two but Rain said she must leave and Joseph deliberated before asking for wine.

'Do you really have to go so soon?' asked Merlyn, but it was a formality and not an expression of disappointment.

'I have to call on someone.'

'You're still trying Barbara Coleman?' asked Merlyn.

'You won't get much sense from her. She's an oddball.'

Joseph came in with: 'She paints and likes to be alone when she does it.'

'Doesn't answer the door, that sort of thing?' Rain helped him.

He accompanied her to the gangway. To her astonishment he said: 'We'd be delighted if you and Oliver came to supper again. We never did get much of a chance to talk. Why don't you come this evening?' He suggested a time. Rain heard herself accepting, without in the least wanting to.

He waited by the rail. When she reached land she turned to wave to him. And all the while she was remembering the time someone had crept aboard on the night Sabine Jourdain was killed. Not drowned, as Joseph said, but shot.

Rain made the slight detour to the beach to tell Oliver about the invitation to the *Jonquil* but there was no one there. She hurried back to the flat to leave a note for him instead. Despite the warmth of the day she felt chilled. She was not fooled by Joseph's speech about the provenance of the paintings. If she were right that Sabine Jourdain had painted them, then she was equally right that Joseph knew all about it.

11

After the great sweep of the bay the rue de Rivoli is a mean street. Rain Morgan reached the number Cobalt had given her, and looked up. Dull stucco, long unpainted. Uncared-for shutters weathered grey. The simplest of metal balcony rails.

She thrust open the green doors. There was a stale smell and an old-fashioned lift, the open cage type where small boys would strain to peer up skirts. But there were no small boys, no sound or sign of anyone.

She summoned the lift. Nothing happened. She tried again, pressing the button more insistently. But the cables she could see through the iron and brass rails were unmoved. Rain stared up the stairs which spiralled around the lift shaft, sought a light switch, found it, and there was an ungenerous glow from somewhere above. She began to climb.

The stairwell light went out. She fumbled along a wall in the dark. There was no switch to hand, only a door leading, presumably, to a flat. She edged forward, feeling with her outstretched foot for the first step of the next flight. She found it, mounted, tried to remember how many steps in the flights. She got it wrong and tripped, bumping against the wall and grazing her hand.

Somewhere on her left there must be a door, on the door there ought to be a number. She felt along the wall, discovered a door, passed her hands over it as carefully as a blind woman getting to know a stranger's face. There were no numbers. She tried the wall near the door, touched a light switch. The lamp it worked was directly above her head. The number of the flat was painted on the wall. In the dark she would never have found it. Two more doors to go and she would be at Cobalt's flat.

Running, to get there before the light forsook her again, she arrived breathless on the second-floor landing and rang the bell. The stair light extinguished itself, so when she first saw Cobalt he was backlit by the poor daylight in his passage. The light flattered him. He looked young, unlined, his slight stoop was not obvious.

'You made it up those stairs in the dark, then?'

She ignored her stinging hand and said yes, and followed him inside.

'The landlords call it economy, I say it's inefficiency. It ought to be an event in the European Games—trying to make it to the second floor before the light goes.' He led her into an untidy sitting room.

She saw him properly. Straight, shining, ginger hair which fell across his forehead; slightly bulging, palest blue eyes; a few freckles. Not a complexion to enjoy the Mediterranean sun. He went to the floor-length window which stood ajar and pulled it wide open. Exterior shutters were already folded back on the balcony. He let in the maximum light and fresh air, and the maximum noise from the street below.

'My apologies for the fug. I had a couple of friends round last night.'

He was right about the fug. Stale smoke, stale cooking

smells, something rank and unpleasant about the place. Rain went on to the balcony. There was just space for a couple of chairs to face each other, maybe a very small table between them. She leaned out.

'Yes,' said Cobalt behind her. 'You *can* see the sea. Got it? That block of blue at the end of the street, the Hotel Negresco on this side of it and . . . ?' He laughed and the laugh turned into a chesty cough.

Rain waited until he recovered, waited on the balcony with the hubbub of the rue de Rivoli rising to entertain her. She listened to a couple of Italians arguing, some Germans trying to park their car in a bad place and refusing to take the voluble advice of a Frenchwoman with two dogs. While the woman shouted that what the driver was doing was against the law, one of her dogs fouled the pavement, which was also against the law.

Rain went indoors. Cobalt had left the room to fetch a pot of coffee. He cleared a space on a dining table, shoving a typewriter and papers aside with the tray. Rain went to help. He said: 'This is the trouble with living in the shop. There are no demarcation rules to separate work and domestic life.'

She ran her eye over the typewritten pages. 'Who do you work for, apart from the *Post?*'

He reeled off the names of several British and American newspapers and magazines. 'But that . . .' he nodded towards the typed pages '. . . is the Great Novel.'

She had immediate doubts about the future of the Great Novel. If Cobalt's literary style was anything like his newspaper style, he did not stand much chance. As a stringer for papers who did not want the expense of their own staff in a place, he was more than adequate. He did not let them down. If a mermaid came out of the bay on to the Promenade des Anglais, Cobalt would be sure to know about her before her scales were dry, and he would see that his papers did, too. But he had never mastered writing to length, rambled so that sub-editors had to scythe through his copy to create the snappy story he ought to have filed. If he had been promising the Long Novel, Rain would have believed him.

Cobalt poured. 'I got what you wanted. That picture in *Nice Matin* was taken last year in the garden of a villa in Antibes. The Villa Fièsole, it's called. The photographer was someone with the initials B.C., a friend of Sabine Jourdain and Durance.'

'Barbara Coleman?'

'If you knew she took it, why didn't you say?'

'I didn't know, James. The Villa Fièsole is where Barbara Coleman is supposed to live.'

'Supposed? What kind of word is that for a journalist to use?' There was a mischievous smile in the pale eyes. She started to say something but he interrupted to apologize that there was no milk.

She helped herself to sugar. She said: 'I'll explain "supposed".' And did, telling him how she had failed to find Barbara Coleman. Then: 'Did the paper tell you how they acquired the photograph?'

'They said it was left at their office. There was no note with it, but on the back were the names, a date and a line about "B.C." taking it. We can collect a print of it.'

'You arranged that?'

'One of the men who works in the darkroom is a friend. I buy him the occasional drink and he does me the occasional favour.'

Rain could see how it worked. A good picture the paper had taken or bought could be copied and slipped to Cobalt who would wire it to the papers and magazines he served in other countries. Probably plenty of people knew what was going on but nobody bothered to stop it.

The loser would be the person who owned the copyright, perhaps the paper itself or perhaps a freelance photographer. They could lose hundreds of pounds of income every time it happened.

A telephone rang in another room. Cobalt crossed the passage and pushed open a bedroom door. There was an unmade bed, trousers sliding off a chair, a heap of clothes on the floor, an empty glass.

Rain strolled around the sitting room, trying to ignore the smell. It was threadbare, could not have been decorated for fifteen years judging by the pattern of the wallpaper. She wondered how long Cobalt had lived there, why he did not smarten the place up.

'You're asking yourself why I don't get this place cleaned up,' he said coming back.

She looked guilty. He said: 'Everyone asks sooner or later.'

'How long have you lived here?'

'Eleven years? Twelve? I did my turn in Fleet Street, came here for a holiday and decided to stay.'

'Just like that?'

'I'd got the sack. So, yes, just like that. Nothing to go back for.'

'It's worked out well, though.'

'I get by. I do as much as I want and when I want.'

She knew he was being modest. He never let them down. 'And when you're not working?'

'I get drunk.' He repeated the mischievous smile. She believed what he said. He continued: 'You asked me about "plans" on the phone. I've invented one: we call at a bar where an envelope will be waiting for me. It'll be addressed to J. Blue. My friend the printer has to be very careful.'

Rain laughed, the charade was preposterous. Cobalt said: 'And on the way you can tell me about the murder of Sabine Jourdain and whom the police believe is guilty. After all, we're both more interested in her murder than in what her friends, if we could find them, might have to say about the way she lived.'

Cobalt, even with a hangover which the unkind sunlight made more obvious, was nobody's fool. Rain pigeon-holed him as one of those hard-drinking journalists whose mind was soberly focused immediately there was work to do. His sense of decorum might sag when he drank too much, but his nose for news never deserted him. So she was guarded as she told him the little she wanted to. Her purpose was to gain information, not give it.

'There's a detective called Foucard,' said Cobalt as they crossed the rue de Rivoli. 'Watch out for him. He doesn't trust a soul. But if you can get him to talk he'll tell you the truth. If he refuses to talk there's no way of persuading him.'

As they walked and talked Cobalt broke off to exchange greetings with a number of people, very different sorts of people. Rain thought Cobalt could be pigeon-holed in another way, too. He had that instinct for looking acceptable to everyone—not too smart to be on terms with the working class and not too scruffy for the higher echelons. She tried to remember which of her Fleet Street colleagues once summed up that being a journalist was having expensive champagne spilled down your only suit. Cobalt would have known precisely what was meant.

He stopped abruptly at a café, indicating where Rain should sit. The waiter welcomed him, Cobalt was a regular customer. He ordered beer and Rain asked for wine and something to eat. She had eaten nothing that morning. Cobalt said that neither had he but he never did.

'This is a good place,' he said. It was not the most

appealing of the cafés in the street and it was not the busiest but it was a good place to sit unobtrusively and watch the world go by. Cobalt had the knack of watching everyone and everything without making it apparent. While he watched, Rain asked him about Maurin.

'A member of the charmed circle,' said Cobalt. 'Nothing ever goes wrong for him. Maurin *père* was a banker and set Philippe up in business. I think it was some other line to begin with, but later he opened his gallery. Not any old gallery but a gallery with a good address, rich clients and top flight artists.'

'Including Durance.'

'He took him from under the noses of the others, so he isn't universally loved. But then, who is?'

'Can you name the people who resent him?'

'No, and I didn't say they were in Nice. Ask around Paris, New York, London . . .'

'Is there a Madame Maurin?'

'She was also the daughter of a banker. The perfect match, you might say, but the marriage appears a rather loose arrangement. I see her around with another man more often than with Maurin.' A movement of the hand and he ordered another drink. The waiter had been ready, it was their daily routine. Cobalt said: 'What else can I tell you about Maurin?'

'I'm not clear why I'm curious about him. Perhaps I was hoping there was something shady.'

'Shady? Maurin doesn't need to be shady. Life's handed him everything he wanted. I'm told the women find him irresistibly attractive. Are you thinking of going to see him?'

Rain did not care for his ambiguous smile. 'I've met him twice. He bought me lunch, and he was perfectly resistible.' She did not spoil it by saying Oliver had been there. Cobalt had not asked her whether she had come alone to France and she had not mentioned Oliver at all.

In a while they went to the bar where a brown envelope was waiting, addressed to J. Blue. In the street Cobalt tore it open and took out two identical black and white prints. He gave her one, which she put in her bag. She knew what would become of the other.

She waited for him to make his next move. He did. They were nearly at the rue de Rivoli again when he said casually: 'You're not going to bother with the Jourdain murder story any more, are you? I'll ring the *Post* news desk and tell them I'll look after it. You'll want to get back to the glamour of the gossip column, won't you?'

Rain concealed a smile. 'Oh, it would be a pity to rush back to London. Do you realize it's still winter there?' But she had not finished with Cobalt. There was something else he could do for her. 'You haven't come across a young man called Tarquin Poulteney-Crosse, have you? He's faintly related to a duke and the features editor has asked me to look for him while I'm here.'

'What's he done?'

'Not much. He's given up going to school, allegedly taken some of the family treasures and come to the South of France to lead the carefree life.' She gave him a mocking smile which was a good match for one of his own. 'You know how it is . . .'

Cobalt acknowledged her triumph with a laugh which became a cough. Then he confessed to never having heard of Tarquin Poulteney-Crosse and having no sensible ideas where to start looking for him. 'If you haven't snared him by the time you want to leave for London, let me know and I'll see whether the *Post* want me to try.' Like all careful freelances he wasn't going to embark on a job no one had agreed to pay for.

When she reached her car, parked beneath palms on the Promenade des Anglais, Rain wrote in her notebook everything Cobalt had told her. She wished she had got him on a better day when it was not so ruthless to prod the hangover. But she was not confident he had better days.

Then she looked at the photograph of Durance and Sabine Jourdain in the rear garden of the Villa Fièsole. Durance attracted attention first, but shifting to the woman Rain recognized the merriment she had seen on her face during a brief moment of laughter around the dining table on board the boat.

She tried to calculate how long ago the photograph had been taken. With a younger woman she might have worked something out from the style of the clothes—an inch on a hemline, a neckline shape, a mere detail which was fashionable one year and not before. But the clothes were no help. It was just a snapshot of a couple of old friends in a garden, taken with no thought of publication. A sub-editor had cropped it to get a reasonable shape for the column format, but had been obliged to keep extraneous material in, and then there had been the mistake of printing a much darker picture overleaf.

Rain turned the ignition key and headed west. The newspaper office identified itself by the words *Nice Matin* in tall blue letters spelled out against the sky. She wanted to see the original print. The writing on the back of it was probably more important to her than the picture itself.

12

The day a photograph appears in a publication is the worst time to ask anyone to put their hands on the original. It will not have been filed in the picture library by then, it could be anywhere in the building, and if the production centre is away from the editorial offices it might not be in the building at all.

But Rain was more fortunate than she had any right to expect. She talked her way in and told a very young reporter she wanted to look at the photograph as it had not printed well in the paper. Her explanation that she was a fellow journalist was enough.

He went in search, backing a mysterious hunch. After a while he returned to say the hunt would take a little longer and asked her to call back in half an hour. Half an hour later, he gave her the picture to look at.

She took it to a window, pretending to need more light. Her unsuspecting colleague was accosted by a reader with a story. Rain flipped the picture over and saw handwriting on the back. Checking in the window reflection that she was not observed, she swapped the original for the print in her bag.

With a word of thanks she handed over the print, and the reporter put her out of his mind. His caller was telling him a story which might make that night's paper. Rain blessed the single-mindedness of newsmen and left. Antibes lay away to the west but she drove east.

May Radley was still in the Galerie Bellandu, although the door was locked and a sign said 'Closed'. Rain tapped on the glass, relying on Mrs Radley recognizing her. The door opened.

'Rain Morgan!' Mrs Radley, from Harpenden, threw up her hands in a rather French gesture. Rain remembered Madeleine Corley and her dramatic movements, Oliver and his shrugs.

She said: 'I'm sorry to make you open up again, but it's rather urgent. I need your opinion.' She offered the photograph.

'Sabine and Durance. That was the picture in the paper today, wasn't it?' They both said how shocked they were at the death and May Radley wondered aloud how Barbara Coleman was coping with it. She said she had written to her sympathizing.

Rain asked her to turn over the photograph. 'Do you recognize the handwriting?'

May Radley considered. Rain's spirits drooped. If May Radley did not have the answer she did not know who else to ask. There was a doubtful: 'Well . . . I can't say that I do . . . ' She looked at Rain enquiringly. 'I'll need a clue, Rain. Who do *you* think it might belong to?'

Rain gave her the clue. 'Barbara Coleman.'

'It could be. I've seen her handwriting and I don't remember anything distinctive about it.' She recited the words in front of her: ' "Marius Durance and Sabine Jourdain in the garden of the Villa Fièsole, taken by their friend B.C. in March." ' There was something else, which they agreed was the year, but the words had been written with a fountain pen and the last one was badly smudged.

Rain said: 'Do you have anything written by Barbara Coleman to compare it with?'

The answer appeared to be no, but then May Radley said: 'She sent me a note to say she'd bring some more pieces if I wanted them. Let's see whether I kept it.'

From a desk drawer she took a book recording all the items purchased and sold by the gallery. Beneath it was a sheaf of papers and amongst them May Radley found it. 'I'm such a squirrel, anyone else would have thrown this away months ago. Yes, you see she's offering to bring me some more of Sabine's work. Other people's, too, but it was Sabine's which interested me.'

Rain held out the photograph, May Radley held out the brief letter. Together they compared the handwriting. Rain said: 'It looks very much like the same hand to me.'

'And the same pen, a thicker than usual nib for a woman's pen, don't you think?'

Rain said: 'Did Barbara Coleman ever mention taking a snapshot of Durance and Sabine Jourdain?'

'I don't remember it.' She checked the time. 'Forgive me, Rain. I have an appointment shortly with an artist I hope will let me handle his work. It creates such a poor impression if I'm late.'

Rain asked whether she could keep the note.

'Yes, it's of no use now.' She replaced the other things in the drawer. They went out together and May Radley locked up. 'You might wonder why Barbara and I write to each other. It seems a shade formal for people who've known each other for so long, doesn't it? Well, the truth is Barbara hates the telephone. She says it's only the French telephone system she can't cope with but I think that's a bit of face-saving nonsense. She's one of those people who're very awkward on the telephone and avoid using it.'

Rain thought about that on the way to Antibes. It explained why Barbara Coleman had never phoned her about the muddle over the rendezvous at the villa, although Rain had given her Antibes address and phone number when she made her arrangements to come to France. But it did not explain why she had not written.

She crossed the river Var, the boundary between Provence and Nice when neither was France. An airplane took off from Nice airport, its winking lights soaring into the distance. Rain envied the passengers, she wished very much that she could go too.

Instead she had to track down Oliver, who would have spent a happy day with his new friends and hardly have given her a thought. She might get an impatient phone call from Lavett grumbling that she had not succeeded in the wild goose chase he had given her. She would have to pretend to enjoy the Josephs' hospitality when, in truth, the *Jonquil* and all its associations depressed her. And perhaps the police would want to interview her again.

She rounded the curve of the bay, left Villeneuve Loubet Plage behind and began the straight run on the coast road almost due south to Antibes. Her thoughts were growing gloomier. Supposing she could not find Oliver? She did not want to walk through the harbour in fading light, it frightened her to think of it. Supposing Foucard took her to the police station and kept her there? She was tempted to turn the car and strike out in another direction, escape from the intrigue and unpleasantness.

The cobbled square was full, so she parked some streets away, the alleys that were attractive in daytime now sombrely shadowed. There was a light on in the flat and her steps quickened. But Oliver, maddeningly, was not there. He had left her a note. It was timed at 6 p.m. and said he was going to his friends' villa but would fall in with the plan to have supper with the Josephs. He would meet her on board.

There was more. He had taken a phone call from Tavett. Tavett, he said, was 'twitching', and she was to ring London. She did not. She looked in the fridge and found Oliver had left her the local version of a sausage roll. After eating it she showered and changed into a dress, and while she was doing so sketched out in her mind the feature she would write on Sabine Jourdain. Then she took a pad of paper and wrote the first few hundred words. And the whole time she was conscious of forcing herself to keep busy to avoid anxiety.

There came a point where she had to choose how much detail to give about Sabine Jourdain's death: the bald fact, or the information that the woman had died violently, or that the police said she had been shot? She opted to include most of what she knew. Every jot of information about Sabine Jourdain was precious, too much of the feature was about Durance because she had only ever been discussed in relation to him.

Rain duly recounted the death and the subsequent police investigation. She did not mention how she had seen the body on the quayside, nor the row on board the yacht, but she did say that when Sabine Jourdain died they ought to have been having supper together.

Writing made her analyse more coolly than she had previously done. And there came the creeping realization that her own arrival in Antibes had been the catalyst which led to the decision to kill Sabine Jourdain.

She set her pen down, not noticing how it rolled off the pad and across the table, coming to rest dangerously near the edge. She and Oliver had discovered the secret that the woman was responsible for an important part of the work being sold, very expensively, as Durance's. A number of people would have cared very much if that information had got out and would have feared that once Sabine Jourdain broke her silence about the past, she might also talk about her up-to-date relationship with Durance.

Durance was a very old man who lived modestly and had long since established a great reputation. The real loser would have been the entrepreneur who had grown rich promoting him: Benedict Joseph. His reputation as a dealer would have been destroyed if it were shown he had known about the deception. But if he could have proved that he, too, had been deceived, his judgement as an expert would never have been trusted again. If Sabine Jourdain had announced to the readers of the *Daily Post* that Joseph had been passing off her work as Durance's, then Joseph was ruined.

Rain imagined what might have happened. Jilly Poynter's lack of French had hampered her book. Probably she and her researcher had been given the same excuse as Rain and May Radley for keeping away from the Villa Souleiado. A reclusive artist was no phenomenon, but the truth seemed to be that visitors were kept away because of the paintings. Only half-crazed Madame Alègre was allowed.

And when the Women's Word book appeared to have foundered, Rain Morgan had come. Despite the refusal to let her visit the house, Joseph had taken no chances. He had orchestrated Rain's visit so that she was allowed no time alone with her subject.

It was Joseph who had sent the note saying the rendezvous was changed, and he must have found means of keeping Barbara Coleman out of Rain's way. Yet Sabine Jourdain had been invited to the *Jonquil* to meet Rain a second time, which suggested she had promised not to reveal the truth about the Durances after all.

Rain knew it was not Joseph threatening Sabine Jourdain the night she died, for one thing he spoke no French. Perhaps he had used someone else to bully her into agreeing to keep silent about the deception, perhaps there had been a last-minute attempt to do this before Rain arrived and Rain had been in time to overhear that it had gone wrong. The more she thought about it the plainer it became: Joseph and his wife had stayed away from the yacht until the early hours because they had known something would happen and wanted an alibi.

Rain looked at the clock. She was late. There were details to slot into place, but that would have to wait. It was time for her to go to supper with the man she was convinced was responsible for Sabine Jourdain's murder.

13

Candlelight glowed on the deck outside the cocktail bar. A group of figures was there, talking, laughing now and then in the polite and unconvincing way of people who are not relaxed in each other's company. Another figure, one of the crew, waited near the gangway to welcome Rain aboard.

There were lights on in various parts of the yacht, there was music. The bar was staffed, and in the background other crew members went about the business of caring for the Josephs and their guests. Rain was surprised to see who the other guests were: Maurin and Durance. Oliver was there too, sitting close to Merlyn. Merlyn wore a flirtatious air and a clinging silk dress that would not have disgraced Fortuny. She did not stir from her chair as Rain approached, but Maurin and Joseph were immediately on their feet.

'Rain, we're delighted to see you. You had a busy day?' Joseph promised to be as effusive as on that first evening.

'I've been writing. I rather forgot the time.'

Maurin smiled a welcome and held her hand in his,

a moment too long. Joseph said: 'Who says you're late? There's no rush at all, we can sit here as long as we like, isn't that right?' His appeal was general. Maurin murmured agreement; Merlyn simpered above the rim of her wine glass; Oliver watched Merlyn; and Durance sat, head bowed, taking no interest.

Maurin and Joseph were quick to offer Rain a chair, quicker than the steward who also had ideas about where she ought to sit. Maurin won. 'Was your search for Sabine's work successful?' he asked, and she told him about the Galerie Bellanda. She drew Oliver into the discussion, saying he had admired the heads of the woman and boys.

Merlyn asked: 'Was she any good as a sculptor?'

Oliver began to say he thought her work admirable, but Joseph was saying: 'Oh, you know, Merlyn . . . she had the rather old-fashioned approach. It's not what I can sell. What's the use of offering my clients a head that looks like a head?'

'Are none of your clients keen on the representational?' Rain asked.

'Oh, sure, but it's no good if a head represents a head. If they could believe it represented something else, preferably an abstract concept, they'd buy. A head's got to be cerebral but it has *not* got to look like a head.' He shook with laughter at his joke. Merlyn smiled at it like a woman recognizing an acquaintance.

Oliver said: 'I don't mind a head looking like a head if it's well done. In fact, I'd very much like to own a head of Madame . . .'

Rain leaped in. '*Was* she called "Madame" Jourdain? I'm not sure whether she married, or whether that was a courtesy title. They used to do that in France, didn't they?'

'Ladies of a certain age,' said Merlyn. She looked

where her husband was looking, at Durance. The lion head was still bent, the shrunken figure slumped. Merlyn felt he needed to be brought into the conversation, not allowed to mope like that. She asked Maurin to say on her behalf: 'We were wondering whether Sabine ever married.'

Durance jerked to attention. His hand went out to the bamboo table in the centre of the group and he lifted his glass. 'Married? Yes. When she was very young Sabine was married. That was the scandal, you see. She left her husband and she left her baby to . . .' His voice, at first strong, weakened and trailed away. Maurin translated for Oliver and the Josephs.

'Do you know,' said Joseph unnecessarily, 'I never knew that.'

'Leaving a husband I can understand,' said Merlyn, who had. 'But leaving a baby . . .' She shuddered. She took another gulp from her glass. 'If a woman's been to all the trouble of having a baby, you'd think leaving it would be the last thing she'd get up to.'

Rain, remembering Holly Chase's story about the first Mrs Joseph sending her four children back to her husband on her lover's say-so, gave an attentive look in his direction. Joseph's face was impassive. His eyes were on Durance, and Durance was watching Maurin and waiting for a translation. Maurin made a faint gesture to indicate there was nothing worth repeating. Then Maurin asked Durance: 'Was Jourdain her married name?'

Durance nodded. 'He was a fool, that Jourdain. An electrician and a fool. She was pretty when she was young, so full of fun and life.' His voice quavered again. He drank. No one knew how to go on and it was left to him to pick up the thread. 'Jourdain didn't understand about artists, about the things which matter to us. He wanted a little electrician's shop of his own, with Sabine behind the counter. A little shop in a provincial town, that was the sum of his ambition.' Maurin offered a faithful translation.

'Did he achieve that?' asked Joseph who had wanted more, much more, and got it. Maurin relayed the question.

Durance replied: 'Three, or was it four shops? She would have had a comfortable life if she'd stayed with Jourdain, but a comfortable life isn't what an artist, a passionate being, needs.' His hand was unsteady as he put the glass down. He knocked against a candle and it toppled. Oliver snuffed the flame. The smoke rose acrid, and there was a shadow where moments before there had been Durance's sad eyes.

A steward sprang forward to replace the candle with one in a more stable holder, but the moment was too poignant to be forgotten. Awkwardly, the conversation restarted. After another round of drinks dinner was announced and they trooped through the cocktail bar and down to the dining room.

The talk dipped in and out of French and English. Rain sat near Durance although it was little pleasure as the old man told rambling and disjointed stories. The Josephs tired of waiting for translations and talked together and to Oliver.

If the Josephs had thought inviting Durance would cheer him up, it was a mistake. His half-eaten food was cleared away at the end of each course and his glass never needed refilling. Eventually, with Maurin's help, Rain got him to talk about his work, especially the work during the years when he made his name. He was far happier talking about the long ago.

Rain was seeing another side of Maurin. He was gentle with Durance, sensitive to his hurt, and understood that although Durance wished to withdraw from sympathy, it was important that people showed concern for him.

Merlyn and Oliver covered a number of topics, accompanied by Merlyn's flirtatious smiles which Oliver saw no reason to discourage. Joseph's eyes flicked repeatedly towards Durance. Rain fought down the inclination to prod the Josephs for information which might confirm her suspicions of their guilt.

Suddenly Oliver, with no finesse at all, was asking them whether the police had checked up on their alibi for the murder night. He appeared not to notice the effect this had. If Merlyn's suntan had allowed it she might have blanched. If Joseph had not swallowed quickly he might have spluttered his wine.

'Alibi!' said Merlyn with a croak. 'What do you mean "alibi"? We don't need an alibi because that business was nothing to do with us!'

'That's right,' muttered Joseph, dabbing his mouth with a napkin.

Unabashed, Oliver tried to find a polite way of pointing out that an alibi is not an excuse or a deception or a red herring, that an alibi literally means being somewhere else. He did not find a polite way, he made a mess of it.

Rain prepared to intervene, Oliver's tactlessness was famous. A cartoon idea flashed through her mind: she and Oliver being made to walk the plank as punishment for gross rudeness at the *Jonquil* dinner table. She knew she ought to hurl herself into the conversation immediately and drag it off in another direction, *any* direction. After all, she had been warned that Oliver was at his clumsiest when he nearly gave away that they knew about Madame Alègre.

On the other hand, she rather wanted to know where the Josephs had been when the boat was deserted except for the dead woman, herself, and the murderer. If anyone had the gall to ask them straight out for an explanation, it was Oliver.

He did, quite insensitive to the implications. 'We went to see a friend down on Cap d'Antibes,' said Joseph, recovering the good nature he liked to show the world.

Oliver didn't exactly say: 'Who?' in a challenging tone, but he got them to expand. Joseph said the man was an American painter he had known since his youth. And Merlyn said: 'Maybe you've heard of him? His name's Peter Leary.'

Oliver said he had, but could not think where. Rain could. She attempted to look as though she were concentrating on the discussion between Maurin and Durance, but it was increasingly difficult, not only because she had to be careful what disasters Oliver might cause but because her French was being strained. With relief she saw Ross offer coffee and heard Merlyn say they would like it in the lounge.

This time there was no ploy to take her to the study. When they were seated in the turquoise chairs and Merlyn was languidly using the purple footstool, Rain asked Joseph: 'Have you found a buyer for the new painting yet?'

A faint frown came before he realized what she meant. 'I'm going to keep that a while. I told you I might.'

'You're taking it back to the States with you?'

'There should be a lot of interest in the painting there. The artist is a big name, paintings like that can only make it bigger.'

But Durance himself was looking diminished. Before long it was suggested he be taken home and there was the Josephs' offer of a chauffeur driven car and Maurin's preference to take him himself. Durance went with Maurin, and as half the guests were leaving, Rain chose to live no longer with the threat that Oliver might say something dreadful. They left soon after.

Rain slipped her hand in Oliver's. 'I'm glad you're here. I hate this place in the dark.'

She told him she suspected the Josephs were involved in the murder, and told him why. Oliver said that nothing would surprise him, and repeated that he and Rain should leave for London.

'Durance is on the way out.' Oliver was quite unsentimental. 'I've seen that before. They get old, they get a shock, and they give up. I doubt if he'll live more than a month or two.'

They went on in silence, Rain regretting that it might well be true.

'By the way,' said Oliver with a complete change of tone. 'I have some good news for you. I've found Tarquin Poulteney-Crosse.'

14

'The funny thing,' said Oliver, explaining how he had found Tarquin Poulteney-Crosse, 'is that I met him days ago.'

'And you didn't think of mentioning it?' Rain did not believe even Oliver could be so obstructive.

'I didn't recognize him.'

'What has he done? Disguised himself as a Tunisian pedlar?'

'No, but he's never known as Tarquin. He was introduced to me as "Tim".'

'Tim Poulteney-Crosse? And you didn't make a connection?'

'Tim Nothing. In the circles he's moving in you can go all year without using your surname. It's very casual. People just come and go, stay for a while and wander on when the spirit moves.'

'Or when the cash from melting down the family silver runs out. Is he carrying around a bag marked "swag"?'

'If so it's a very small one and I haven't noticed. You can see for yourself tomorrow.'

'Yes, please. Apart from meeting your friend, Tim,

I'd like to see this villa you've been sneaking off to.'

'He's not staying there. I told you, it's very casual. He's sleeping on the beach.'

Rain shivered. 'That must be chillier than an English stately home.'

'Don't be silly, he has a sleeping bag.'

When they reached the flat they sat up late, talking about Rain's visit to Nice, the deepening puzzle about Barbara Coleman and the suspicious behaviour of the Josephs. The frequency of Oliver's yawns increased and eventually he persuaded Rain they ought to go to bed and forget it. 'You can talk to Tim tomorrow morning, which will keep Tavett happy, and then we can pack and fly home on the 1.30 p.m. plane.'

'You're forgetting Monsieur Foucard, aren't you?'

'No, but if the police wanted to see you again they've had ample time. They haven't charged you with anything yet . . .'

'I should hope not!'

'. . . and they can't compel you to stay. Wilmot said so. We'll fly home tomorrow.'

Rain gave him a quizzical look. 'But you were the one who was determined to stay.'

'That was before a lot of unpleasant things.'

Next morning Foucard and Denis came to try again to shake Rain's story about the night Sabine Jourdain died. The waitress and a customer at the café had confirmed she was there at the time she said but, as she had warned Oliver, that did not help her at all.

'So you see, Miss Morgan, there's still no one who saw you before the woman's body was discovered, and the people at the café saw you for only a short time after that. The Josephs and some of the crew saw Sabine Jourdain on board the yacht and we're told she was alive at 8.30 p.m. when the Josephs left her there. Two hours later her body was taken from the water.'

'Somebody *must* have seen or heard something.'

'No one has corroborated your story about the shouting and the disarrangement on the boat, and no one has explained what you were doing later. Also, no one remembers seeing you on the quay when the body was taken from the water.'

'But a man in a beret spoke to me.'

'A man in a beret? Who was this stereotype Frenchman?' Foucard's sarcasm made Denis smile.

Rain struggled not to show her exasperation. 'The man said something to me about a doctor, but . . .'

Foucard's eyes were hard. 'But what?'

Her next words sounded lame, she could see how useless the man in the beret was to her. 'He thought I was someone else. He spoke to me over his shoulder, he didn't look round.'

'Ah, I see.' Foucard had his elbows on the table, he pressed his fingertips together. 'So, we have a new witness that you have never mentioned before, and this turns out to be a comic Frenchman who wears a beret and speaks over his shoulder to a woman he does not see. What use is a witness who has seen nothing?'

Rain was inclined to ask what use was a policeman who harried the innocent while a murderer was at large. It seemed best to resist the inclination. Denis filled a few more pages of his notebook with Foucard's questions and Rain's answers. But he could not record how the tension between Rain and Foucard ebbed and flowed, how they fought for control of the interview and how they were each at times skilful at gaining it. Oliver, understanding none of the conversation, was keenly aware of this battle and sat silent, not daring to intervene even when he saw Rain falter.

At last it was all over, but the policemen did not go

immediately. Foucard opened the doors of the other rooms and gave each a cursory glance. Rain determined she would resist a search until she had found out what the legal position was. But Foucard said nothing about a search, told her to expect to see him again and left.

She stood on the balcony for a while, leaning on the rail and feeling the sun. Oliver brought out coffee. He said: 'Now you can tell me what all that was about.'

She did. At the end she said: 'I can't believe the Josephs are being subjected to this sort of treatment. Foucard is trying to break my story, and that suggests he's accepted theirs. If the stories are substantially different they must be lying.'

'The Josephs are rich.'

She laughed. 'However rich they are, Foucard doesn't look like a man who'd be bribed.'

Oliver said that was a crude interpretation of what he meant. 'I can't imagine them speaking to the extremely rich tenants of the *Jonquil* in the way they speak to you. Even the surroundings of the yacht must intimidate them a bit.'

Rain was thoughtful. He said: 'Let's stroll down to the beach and see whether Tim's awake yet. After you've talked to him we can quietly pack and fly away and leave Monsieur Foucard to his own devices. Then he'll have no alternative but to concentrate his efforts on the Josephs.'

'I'd like to do something else before we leave. It won't take long.'

Oliver opened a wary eye. 'I recognize an ominous tone.'

'Which one?'

'The scheming one.'

'I confess. The scheme is that if Foucard won't check out the Josephs' alibi, I will. I'm going to drive down the Cap to call on Peter Leary.'

'With what possible excuse?'

'I don't need one. I'm a journalist and he's an artist and everyone knows I'm here writing about artists.'

Merlyn had given Oliver the name of the villa and that was all Rain had to go on, except that there was a road of the same name and this suggested a good starting point for her search. Rain and Oliver called at one tucked-away house after another until someone gave them directions and they found Leary.

'Do you want me to come in?' asked Oliver as Rain parked the car. He was disappointed with the Cap, which was a pinewood peninsula from a distance but in reality the same suburban sprawl which marred much of the coastline.

'No, wait here. You can be my excuse for getting away quickly. I'm going to say I want to fix an interview with him, that sort of approach.' She put her diary in her pocket so she could go through the motions of making an appointment. She was going to slide into their conversation the fact that she had seen Benedict Joseph in Antibes, and she would ask whether Leary had. From there it should be simple to discover whether the Josephs were with Leary on the night of the murder. Later, she would have to telephone Leary and cancel the appointment, because later she would be on a flight home.

There were flowers climbing the walls of the villa and sounds of activity indoors. After a few minutes a bronzed man with a balding head came to the door. 'Peter Leary?' Rain asked with a practised smile.

An equally practised smile in return. 'What can I do for you?'

She explained herself. Leary said: 'Sure, when shall we do it?' His smile now looked genuine.

Rain felt ashamed of the deception. She promised

herself she would make it up to him, arrange for some other coverage of him in the paper before long. She opened her diary. 'Tomorrow?'

He stroked his chin with his hand. 'The fact is I'm busy tomorrow. I have someone coming to see me that I haven't met in years. And there's going to be so much to catch up on, I said come in the morning and make a day of it. You know how it is.'

Rain nodded. 'We'll pick another time. What about the day after?'

'That sounds better.' They agreed a time. 'You can be the first to see the work I've done since I came over in the fall.' He snapped his fingers, recollecting. 'No, that's wrong. You'll have to be second. My friend will want a good look tomorrow. If you write about art perhaps you know him. He's a dealer—Benedict Joseph.'

Rain said she did, and remarked what a coincidence it was that two old friends had to come from the States to be reunited in the South of France.

Rain said to Oliver as she turned the car and headed up the Cap: 'Leary did *not* see the Josephs on the evening Sabine Jourdain was killed. They lied. I knew it all along. But where were they?'

'Who cares? We're going, and that's just as well because by tomorrow the Josephs will know you called on Leary and he gave them away.'

Rain admitted he was right: the sooner they went the better. But one day someone else, perhaps Jilly Poynter or perhaps Cobalt, would tell an unsuspecting world that Sabine Jourdain had been painting Durance's pictures for him. She drove on, anticipating how self-critical she would feel when that happened.

Oliver patted her thigh. 'Let's go to the flat first and pack. Then we can take Tim for lunch and go to the airport afterwards.'

It sounded a sensible plan, but when they got to the flat she found a very good reason to change it. Waiting for Rain was a letter from Barbara Coleman.

It bore no date or address and rushed straight into an apology for not contacting Rain sooner, followed by the hope they could meet in Nice that afternoon. Rain was asked to enquire for her at the Hotel Negresco.

Oliver spluttered in disbelief. 'She's been hiding in the Negresco all along! Leaving you standing outside the Villa Fièsole and finding blood in the garden and . . . and all along she's been living in luxury at the most famous hotel in Nice!'

Rain fetched the letter May Radley had given her and checked the handwriting against the new one. There were differences. The first letter was written with a thick-nibbed fountain pen, the second with a ballpoint. The writing in the letter to Rain was shakier and more nervous. Despite the differences, Rain was sure both were by the same hand.

She said: 'I imagined all sorts of fates for her, but staying at the Negresco wasn't one of them. I'm going to set off for Nice straight away and delegate Tim to you.'

Oliver protested. 'I'm not Holly Chase to be exploited, you know.'

'You can ask Tim what he's done with the family silver as competently as Holly or I can. And you can buy him lunch and wheedle his life story and his plans out of him *more* easily because you already know him.'

'Yes, but . . .'

'And you can designate a restaurant where the three of us can meet this evening.'

Oliver looked unwilling. 'I don't like this at all.'

'I'm sure you don't, but if you'll co-operate we can catch the lunchtime flight tomorrow.' She was already letting herself out of the flat before Oliver gave his reluctant approval.

She drove off at high speed, feeling annoyed with him. Anyone else, she reasoned, would have been keen to help, but not Oliver. He had to be urged and bullied. However, she had won and was free to pursue Barbara Coleman without fearing that Tarquin Poulteney Crosse would roll up his sleeping bag and wander on because the spirit had moved. Whether she came face to face with Tim or not, Dick Tavett would get his diary item.

She had driven a good part of her journey, thinking along these lines, before it occurred to her that Oliver's protest had not been prompted by laziness or selfishness. He was afraid for her.

15

When Rain Morgan asked for Barbara Coleman at the reception desk of the Hotel Negresco she was handed an envelope. The note asked her to be at the Chagall Museum between 4 and 4.30 p.m.

The museum stood back from the road in a suburb on a hill. Rain was early, she had time to look. Hurry and impatience drained from her.

Through a doorway she glimpsed suffused blue light. Visitors, reverentially quiet, moved into the blue and disappeared from view. The theatre was gently raked, seats leading down to a dais with equipment for a lecture. But the furnishings were scarcely noticed because the beauty of the long glass windows captured attention. The richness of the blue was overwhelming in its intensity.

Rain stood inside the doorway for a moment. Gradually she moved forward, remembering her instructions. They did not lead her towards the magnificent windows but to the least noticed part of the room. No one was sitting there.

She took the seat she had been asked to take and

waited, unmindful of the time, happy merely to rejoice in Chagall's colour. In a leaflet picked up in the entrance hall she read his words about the museum: 'Perhaps in this abode one will come and seek an ideal of fraternity and love such as my colours and my lines have dreamt.'

She had always loved colour but she had never seen colour to equal this. She knew it would be a wrench when it was time to leave and she knew she must find a way of returning.

When there was a gentle footfall behind her, she did not notice. When a figure leaned towards her, she did not sense the proximity. Her realization that Barbara Coleman had come coincided with the woman's whisper. 'You must be Rain Morgan?'

'So I am. Barbara Coleman?'

'Yes. Don't look round, we must not seem to be together. I have to be very quick. Thank you for coming, I was afraid you mightn't. What I want to tell you is this. Sabine Jourdain was murdered.'

Rain, her eyes still on the windows across the room, said softly: 'The police think so, too, but who . . .'

'Benedict Joseph. Nobody else has a reason, but he has. He wanted to stop her talking. After all those years she suddenly intended to talk about the old days. He came to see me and said she must be stopped. I said: "But what do you expect? Older people think very much about the old days." '

There was a silence during which Rain imagined the woman had vanished. She edged round in her seat. Barbara Coleman said: 'Please don't look round, my dear, we mustn't be seen talking.'

Rain said: 'Why would it have mattered if she'd talked about the old days? It was all so long ago, and some of the others who were there have talked.'

'Gossip. I know what they said. But Sabine was different, she was with Durance almost all her adult life. She knew everything there was to know. If she talked about him it would all have come out, about him forcing her to leave her husband and her child and the wretched life he gave her afterwards. She thought when she went to him she was going to live a life of freedom, but she was not free. Never. She made herself his slave and the pity is it took her so long to see it.'

Rain remembered the electrician, Jourdain, and the three or four electrical shops, and wondered how free the wife of an electrician would have been. She said: 'Why didn't she leave?'

'To go where? Besides, her life was over by the time she realized how she'd wasted it when she might have been doing things for herself. He took everything she had: family, talent—she always worked on his paintings for him. Have you seen his hands? Do you think those are the hands of an active painter? He's had arthritis in those hands for years.'

Rain saw in her mind's eye the clumsy hands that Durance had rested on the dining table on board the *Jonquil*. She thought of the studio where everything was too neat, too pat. The studio where, the caretaker had explained, Durance did not go very often because of the several flights of steep stairs. She said: 'Are you saying Sabine Jourdain did all his recent work?'

'No, I don't think all. But, you see, she'd always worked under his direction. It was a matter of degree. In the end she realized to what ridiculous lengths it had gone. She decided to . . . what's that word they use now? *Assert* herself.'

'How did Durance react to that?'

'She said he saw it was inevitable, he accepted it. But Benedict Joseph was furious.'

'Why did he kill her? Once she was dead there could

be no more work by her hand or Durance's.'

'Joseph is a rich man now. He wasn't when it began, when he took up Durance. Until then there wasn't any money in it. Durance had a bit from his family, but he was always useless with money. Joseph had to choose whether to risk her besmirching Durance's reputation and his own by casting doubt on which was Durance's work and which was hers. He's rich enough now to be able to choose to destroy her, knowing there can be no more paintings from the studio of Durance.'

Rain said: 'It seems too extreme, to kill her for that.'

There was urgency in Barbara Coleman's voice. 'Believe me, I know he did it.'

'But where have *you* been? Did Joseph force you to leave the Villa Fièsole so that you couldn't talk to me?'

'Yes, he made me leave Antibes. He was angry because I talked to a woman called Jilly Poynter who was going to write a book about Sabine. Just by chance he came to the villa as she was leaving. They passed in the garden. He made me tell him what she wanted and he was very cross about it. He said I wasn't to help her and she was not to meet Sabine.'

'*Did* they meet?'

'No, I'm sure they didn't. Miss Poynter went back to England and a French girl from Cannes came afterwards and said she was working as a researcher on the book. I'm afraid I wasn't very kind to her, I said I'd changed my mind and couldn't tell her anything.'

'But why not? If Sabine wanted the book written, why wouldn't you help?'

'Because Benedict Joseph had frightened me. He threatened he'd turn me out of the villa. He owns it, you see, my dear. It used to be Durance's but Joseph bought it off him. He talked about using it instead of the yacht when he comes over from America, but it needs a lot of work and he hasn't done anything. He calls in sometimes, and he keeps some of his things there.'

Rain asked: 'Did the coterie break up after Joseph bought the villa?'

'Yes, that was the end of it. I think Durance expected everything to be just the same but it never was. People drifted away and now there's only me. I look after the house and I do my own work there.'

'Did Sabine leave at the same time as the others?'

'She stayed on for a while. She and Durance worked in a studio together upstairs. And then quite suddenly Durance moved out and Sabine said she was going to a quiet place in the country to sculpt. I was told that when people asked for them I was to say I didn't know where they were.'

'But you did know.'

There was a faint laugh. 'Well, you can't lose a famous man like Durance in a place the size of Antibes. Yes, I knew where he was living although when I called on him sometimes he got the caretaker to say he was too busy to see anyone. Sabine wrote to tell me where she was. It was an old house Durance still owns. It's a wreck now but at one time we all lived there, nearly twenty of us and most of us from England. And then . . .'

She broke off and looked round cautiously. A man came tiptoeing towards them but stopped some rows away and sat down. Barbara Coleman said: 'Sabine told me she'd returned to the Villa Souleiado because she wanted peace to get on with her own work. Well, I wrote back and said: "Sabine this is nonsense. You're hiding away up there because you don't want anyone to know you paint Durance's pictures for him." There! That's what I said to her. She was a dear friend but I'd never dared say anything about it before.'

'Was she angry?'

'She wrote me a very emphatic letter saying I was never to repeat that accusation and that she'd destroyed my letter. But, you see, she didn't deny it. I've wondered whether my letter didn't help her towards her decision to give up the Durances. What she wrote at the time was that she'd faced many difficult decisions in her life and working on the paintings wasn't one of them because she'd always been involved in Durance's work. She said their lives and their work were indivisible.'

Barbara Coleman sighed. 'Oh dear, there's so much I want you to understand and so little time. I have to get back.'

'Where are you staying?'

'In Nice. Oh, not at the Hotel Negresco, please don't think that. I happen to know a young man who works there and it was convenient to get a message to you that way.'

'So where . . .'

'In Nice, I don't want to say any more. Someone has loaned me a room for a few days, it's really only until you leave . . .'

'You're being kept out of the way until I go home? Is Benedict Joseph doing this to you?'

'I'm afraid so. He was so angry that Sabine had agreed to see you and he blamed me for putting her up to it.'

'But you had nothing to do with it. I wrote to her at the Villa Fièsole because that was the only address I had for her.'

'Benedict Joseph doesn't believe I only forwarded your letter to her, especially as she planned to stay at the villa and talk to you there. She told him outright, you see, that you were coming to write about her. He'd arrived on some other business and found her there. It was a very unfortunate coincidence. We'd had lunch and we were sitting and talking and waiting for you to arrive. And in he came.'

She stopped and Rain asked: 'What then?'

'It started off pleasantly enough but when she asked me to say why she was there—she didn't have much English, as you know, and his French is almost non-existent—he flared up. I was very uncomfortable about it, having to translate for them in turn as they argued. He was saying she was being disloyal and foolish, and she was saying it was none of his business. Suddenly he rushed out of the house and we laughed and thought he'd gone. But no, he came back and he had Philippe Maurin with him.'

'Maurin!' Rain was surprised at her degree of disappointment that he was involved.

Barbara Coleman did not notice and went on: 'Sabine was driven away in Joseph's car and Philippe told me to get into his. I thought I could escape. I let him walk round the car and get into the driving seat and then I had my door open and was running for the garden gate. I shot the bolt and ran towards the house but the doors were locked. Then I saw Philippe coming over the wall and I knew he had caught me. I tried to hide from him but, naturally, he saw me, and he's much younger and faster than I am. When he had me he dragged me back to the car.'

Rain was having difficulty imagining the scene, it didn't match up with her impressions of Maurin. But all she said was: 'Did you hurt your hand?'

'He dragged me across the veranda and I fell by the steps and cut it. How did you know?'

Rain told her. Then: 'Did you ever see Sabine again?'

'Never. Philippe locked me into an apartment outside Antibes. It's the sort of place people let for holidays, rather spartan but adequate. He said I'd be there until late that evening and there was no point in making a fuss because no one would hear me. He was right about that. The place was the top half of a restored cottage at the far end of the garden of a big villa. We got to it down a track. No one came near it, all the time I was there.'

Rain said: 'You must have been terribly frightened.'

'Not then. Once it got dark and I realized there was no electricity connected I began to think I'd been too docile and I ought to have forced my way out. But, you see, there was a large dog in the villa garden and I'm very nervous of dogs, my dear. If I'd got free I couldn't have gone anywhere because of that.'

'When did Maurin return?'

'Quite late. He said you'd all had supper with Sabine on the *Jonquil* and she'd been driven to the Villa Souleiado. I said: "Good, so I can go home, can I?" I was being a bit sarcastic, you see. But he said: "Not yet, Barbara. You're what the English call a chatterbox and Benedict Joseph calls a damned nuisance. I've got to keep you out of the way for a couple of days." If I'd known what was going to happen I'd have been terrified, but at the time it was a silly adventure. I hardly minded at all. I could see we were heading round the bay towards Nice and I thought: "Well, there's plenty to occupy me there. It's a long time since I've spent a couple of days going round the art galleries." '

'But he didn't let you do that?'

'No, there's a poky little flat and the couple who live there have orders not to let me out. But the woman is out sometimes and her husband goes to work and I've found where a spare key is kept.' Once more she looked nervously round. 'I must go, if they find out I slip away . . .'

Rain said: 'Why go back? You're free, you could . . .'

'What could I do? Go back to the Villa Fièsole and

have Benedict Joseph turn me out of the only home I've got, or else kill me like he killed Sabine? Or go to the police with this story which I can't prove? Or try to run away somewhere when all my personal belongings and my little money are in the villa? No, I must go back to the flat. Once you've gone away I'll be freed and I'll have a home to go to and that will be an end of it. Philippe Maurin promised me that.'

Rain was sure that would not be the end of it and that Barbara Coleman must surely realize it. She said: 'Before you go, tell me about the photograph. Did you send it to the newspaper?'

'My handbag was the only thing I brought with me when I left the villa. I always carry the photograph in there. I took it last summer in the garden, it was one of the last happy times the three of us had together. After that Sabine said she meant to give up the Durance paintings altogether and sculpt. I suppose I encouraged her, taking her pieces to a gallery in Nice for her. Once I persuaded her to come with me and meet the gallery owner. I was trying so hard to help.'

There was the sound of a stifled sob. Then Barbara Coleman said: 'I think Sabine appreciated what I was doing, but Durance was unhappy. He wasn't angry in the way Joseph was angry, he was just sad and resigned.'

Rain heard her move. The woman said: 'I have to go now.'

'You haven't explained about the photograph.'

'I got someone to take it to the newspaper office after I heard on the radio that Sabine was dead.'

Another movement. Rain said: 'Why did you want the paper to have it?'

'I suppose I just wanted to share my memory of the two of them happy together. I'm going now. Don't follow me. Give me time to get away.'

They whispered goodbyes. Barbara Coleman added some final, chilling words and then there was silence.

Shadowy figures came and went across the room in front of Rain but she was unaware of them. She sat there for several minutes, revelling in the colour. The windows had been made to take the Mediterranean light, the room had been built to take the windows. It was the most extraordinary and distracting place for the meeting which had just taken place.

Rain snatched up her bag and ran from the room. Eyes followed her as she sped through the gallery. There were people outside, either in the garden or the road leading from it. Several of them were elderly women, almost any of those could have been Barbara Coleman. There was a bus stop and a group of people waited by it.

Rain reached her car. Casually, not appearing to be searching, she looked over the people in the queue. Rain chose to assume that Barbara Coleman's story was substantially true. If it were not, then the woman might have gone anywhere, but if she had left most of her money in Antibes and slipped out to the museum on her own, then it was probable she was going to catch a bus.

The bus arrived, took passengers on board, and began the downhill drive to the centre of Nice. Rain gave it a head start and then followed.

People alighted at various points on the way. The roads got busier and it became more difficult to watch both the traffic and the bus passengers. Eventually Rain had to pass the bus when it made one of its stops. Soon she left it behind at traffic lights. If Barbara Coleman was on board, Rain had lost her.

She groaned. She had been bewitched by Chagall and let a foolish old woman walk away to danger. If she had kept her wits about her, she would have ignored the silly rules Barbara Coleman had imposed on the meeting, she would not have let her suffer any more mistreatment. Barbara Coleman's final words rang in her mind: 'Sabine Jourdain was killed because of us, because of what I knew and what you might find out.'

16

Tarquin Poulteney-Crosse sat across a table from Rain Morgan in a restaurant in the rue de Sade in Antibes and gave her his boyish, lopsided smile. 'The police really believe I stole the family silver?'

'So I'm told. Didn't you take it?'

He ran long fingers through fair hair. He kept smiling. 'Did they say that a silver tureen was stolen? And a teapot, a teapot made for the family by Paul de Lamerie?'

'I didn't hear any details.' Out of the corner of her eye she saw Oliver showing smug amusement.

The fingers ploughed through the hair again. The smile broke into a triumphant laugh and people at other tables looked round.

Rain said: 'I'm not about to make a citizen's arrest. You can tell me whether you helped yourself to the loot or not.'

Oliver refilled three wine glasses. He had eaten an excellent *daurade au fenouil* and was feeling lazily content. He said: 'I don't see why you should tell anyone, Tim. It's not as though it's anyone else's business but yours and your family's. Only yours, really, because if you hadn't disposed of the things now you would have inherited them some day.' He raised his glass to drink but was stopped short by a rapid switch in Tim's manner.

'Now, just a minute.' Tim was thrusting his face angrily towards him. 'I don't mind a joke. If the police back home have decided I've stolen the silver then that's a joke. It just shows how hopeless they must be. But I'm not going to be accused by you or . . .'

Rain put a restraining hand on his arm. 'Oliver doesn't really believe you did it, it's just that you've been a long time discussing it without actually denying it.'

Tim drew his arm away, disguised the movement by lifting his glass. His reply was delayed by the interruption of a small Algerian boy going from table to table, restaurant to restaurant, trying to sell flowers. Tim set the glass down again without drinking. 'All right, then. I'll deny it. If the stuff vanished when I ran off then it was coincidence.'

Rain said: 'And you were just guessing about the tureen and the teapot?'

'Yes.' The lopsided smile made a tentative reappearance. 'Look. That tureen is this size.' His outstretched hands made a space nearly three feet long. 'What's more, it's hideous. Now, what do we do with a thing like that? We don't display it because the average frying pan would look more fetching, and we don't use it because we don't go in for banquets any more and if we did we would need a crane or a whole estate of serfs to lift it. You get the point?'

Rain said she did. 'Someone with an eye on the family silver would steal something more portable, and the family wouldn't be grieved if they never saw the tureen again.'

'They should have melted it down years ago. They were always talking about it.'

'And the teapot? You aren't going to convince me a teapot by Paul de Lamerie is so ugly it ought to be melted down?'

'No. Whether it's really by Paul de Lamerie is a matter of contention, but in use the handle gets red hot. If I had a say—*when* I have a say—I'll sell off all the useless things like the tureen and the teapot and spend the proceeds on a weatherproof roof.'

'Too late,' said Oliver, 'if they've been stolen.'

'Never mind, I don't expect to live there. I was only planning to sell the house and spend the rest of my life in the sun.'

'Sleeping on the beach?' Rain enquired.

'Whenever I feel like it. That's real freedom, the best I've found. While everyone else is acquiring things, I'll sell everything I have no need for and do whatever I feel like, wherever I feel like.'

Rain was annoyed that Oliver was looking wistful at this. She said: 'Your sleeping bag doesn't appear to be a bed of roses, if I may put it like that. Didn't I see someone waking you with his foot one morning? There seem to be infringements of personal liberty even on the beach.'

It was a lighthearted comment, and she was surprised that Tim's face clouded. He said: 'Where were you?'

'Across the beach. I was going to interrupt Oliver's sunbathing. There was a pedlar, selling leather bags. He seemed very anxious to talk to you.'

'Oh, yes,' said Tim quickly. 'He's always around.' He gulped his wine, then said: 'I'd rather you didn't say anything about the family silver when you write your piece for the *Daily Post*. If we can agree on that, I don't mind telling you the rest.'

Rain, who had never proposed to libel him by hinting he was a thief, solemnly accepted his terms and then listened to him on freedom of the individual, the lure of the Côte d'Azur and a garbled version of the life and philosophy of Scott Fitzgerald. The Fitzgerald thing could be blamed on the combined forces of a television series about Fitzgerald's life and a cinema remake of *Tender is the Night*. The British viewing public now had fact and fiction as hopelessly entwined as Fitzgerald himself had done.

Before Tim's speech was over Oliver had several times had to mask yawns and Rain was ill-wishing Dick Tavett for forcing her to listen to it. Unfortunately it slipped out that she had actually read some Fitzgerald, apart from the excerpts the newspaper colour supplements had published to accompany pages of photographs of the filming. Tim pounced on this fact. He had a battered but new copy of *Tender is the Night* in his bag and intended to visit all the local places where Fitzgerald (or Dick Diver, it was all the same to him) had been.

'I want to stand above that beach where Fitzgerald blessed the sunbathers,' he said, getting it wrong.

'Plage de la Garoupe,' said Rain and consoled herself with another glass of wine and did not argue.

A man carrying a cartoon portrait of himself entered the restaurant and tried to sell watercolour scenes to the diners. Tim leaned forward to Rain and whispered that he had been told the man was only posing as an artist, the paintings were not his own so he was just a salesman fooling the customers. The man sold nothing and soon after went away. Tim returned to his theme: 'I want to go to the Hotel du Cap, just to sit in the bar or something like that, so I can say I've been there. Of course, I know that was really the Murphys' place, not the Fitzgeralds', but Scott and Zelda did stay there.'

'What for?' asked Oliver, meaning why did Tim want to say he had been there.

Rain answered the other question. 'For one of Zelda's suicide bids.'

Tim let that go by. The cruel facts of the Fitzgeralds' existence interested him less than the sunshiny glamour, and that, Rain thought, was how it was with the remake of the film and how it must have been half a century ago when the Fitzgeralds lived it. Tim talked about the writing as well as the locations. He had been through the books with his magpie brain snatching up quotations. He challenged Rain to identify where lines came from, ruling out Gatsby's green light at the end of the dock and the rich being different from us, and all the other easy ones.

Oliver yawned when Tim mentioned: 'There are only the pursued, the pursuing, the busy and the tired,' and yawned again when he said: 'If life isn't a seeking for the grail it may be a damned amusing game.'

Oliver was not amused. He tried to get them to talk about *Bludgeon*, pointing out that its author had also visited the Côte d'Azur. No one was interested and he made Rain get the bill. They strolled along talking, Tim on his way to the beach and his sleeping bag and Rain and Oliver taking a circuitous route to the flat.

Surprisingly, Oliver suggested stopping at the Bar de la Marine. He tried to talk again about *Bludgeon*, the millions of dollars it had earned, the rumours that its author had hired a hack to write it for him. But it was no use—over another glass Tim found new vigour to talk about Fitzgerald. He remembered that 'all good writing is swimming under water and holding your breath' and he argued about the relevance of the italics some sources gave some of the words. Rain wondered whether Tim was deliberately being boring.

In fact he was so trying that the interruption of the Tunisian pedlar and his half-hearted attempt to sell her a new shoulder bag was a welcome diversion. The Tunisian then concentrated on Tim, who told him to go away. The man persisted, holding out one of the bags even when Tim resumed talking. Rain saw Tim's eyes drop to the bag, the pedlar would not take it away. Tim carried on speaking to her, and eventually, using the back of his hand, he brushed the bag aside. The pedlar went away wordlessly, his robes flapping as he turned the corner out of sight.

A couple of Tim's beach friends, older and scruffier, came by, and Tim called them over. Jock and Tony didn't sit down but stood near the table for a while, joking and talking, making much of Tim's invention that the *Daily Post* had sent Rain Morgan all the way from London to check up on him. Jock offered spoof questions about Tim, Tony preferred to lampoon Jock, and the waitress preferred them to move so that she could attend to her customers.

Tim got to his feet. 'We'd better go, before we get thrown out,' he said to Jock and Tony. 'I don't want any stories like that appearing in the paper.'

The joke was batted around as Tim and his two friends edged away from the table and called their goodbyes. Rain asked the waitress for the bill.

Hurrying with it, the woman gave an exclamation and bobbed down to pick up a man's wallet. 'Your friends have left this,' she said. Oliver flipped it open, revealing a driving licence. He said: 'It's Tim's. We'd better catch up with him.'

But the waitress was interrupted before she reached the till with the money Rain had given her. Rain said: 'She's going to be ages. Will you wait here for the change while I run after Tim?'

'Did you notice which way he went?'

'Yes, to the right, towards the beach. Jock and Tony

went in another direction. Don't stray, I'll see you back here.'

Oliver smothered another yawn. He did not look as though he had the energy to stray. Rain squeezed between tables and ran down the street towards the beach. She went through the arch with the anchor, had to go a short distance along the harbour to her right and then through another arch to the beach. After the brightness of the café it was difficult to see. The sea was a dark sheen. A motorcycle on the coast road split the silence. As its noise died, she made out shapes across the beach, near where she had once seen Tim's head protruding from a sleeping bag. She set off in shadow towards the shapes she believed were people.

Her eyes grew used to the lack of light. She was confident the young, slim figure moving away from her was Tim. She did not want to go further, sand was grating in her shoes. She took a breath, ready to call out to him and bring him back to her.

But before she made a sound another figure came out of the shadows to her left, a tall, erect figure. Tim recoiled from it, but then stood his ground. Rain was certain the second figure was the pedlar.

Rain saw angry gestures from both and then Tim strode towards the rocks. But the pedlar caught hold of him and there was a scuffle. Some of the bags slipped from the pedlar's grasp and became black lumps on the night-grey sand. Tim darted forward. The pedlar was not swift enough, Tim snatched up one of the bags and backed away with it.

The pedlar gathered up the rest of his bags in a desperate swoop and then pursued Tim, but the bags impeded him. Tim taunted, dancing away from him, zigzagging, running around him, deriding the man's inability to catch him.

The scene was a mime, no sound from either of them. Then the pedlar lunged and Tim tripped backwards. When he was on the sand the other man fell on him and they were grappling for possession of the bag Tim had picked up. The pedlar cast it aside, out of Tim's reach. He was kneeling on Tim, pinning him beneath his weight and striking him about the head with the flat of his hand. The sound of the blows echoed.

Rain's fingers gripped Tim's wallet. She moved forward again, not wanting to become involved but not daring to leave Tim in this predicament. As she drew nearer harsh voices rose, the pedlar hissing his anger, Tim furious. Suddenly the man stood up and gathered all his bags. Tim did not rise. He pulled himself to a half-sitting position, twisted away from Rain, and hurled abuse. The pedlar marched into the blackness, untouched by Tim's words.

But Rain Morgan pressed back into the shadows, horrified. In Tim's rage she recognized his voice as she had heard it on board the *Jonquil* the night Sabine Jourdain was killed.

17

Oliver sprawled on the couch. Rain was tense, perched on the edge of a hard chair. 'It's not a mistake, Oliver. It was definitely Tim's voice on the yacht that night.'

'Yet you didn't recognize him until you heard him speaking French to the pedlar.'

'*Shouting* in French. It was the same, threatening somebody in a rage. If you'd heard those two scenes you'd be convinced, too.'

Oliver yawned. 'But Barbara Coleman lured you all the way to Nice today to insist Joseph killed Sabine Jourdain.'

'Yes.'

'And you'd already decided the Josephs knew something about the murder.'

'Yes.'

Another yawn. 'This morning you discovered they hadn't been with Peter Leary as they'd told us. Of course, we don't know that they gave the police the same alibi, do we?'

'All I know for certain is that Sabine Jourdain had a

row with a man on board the *Jonquil* before she was taken dead from the water, and that man was Tarquin Poulteney-Crosse.'

Oliver sat up. 'Shall I make some coffee?' He didn't wait for her answer. She knew she would not be able to sleep with so much tantalizing information spinning in her mind. While Oliver was out of the room she abandoned her chair for the couch, kicked off her shoes and curled up.

When she had handed Tim his wallet, she said nothing about the pedlar. Tim was lying on the sand, looking in the direction the man had gone. He could not know she had been on the beach long enough to see what had happened. His voice, as he thanked her, was low, his manner subdued. Just for a second she could have believed she was mistaken about him.

Oliver brought her coffee. 'I don't think you should tell Foucard about Tim, even if you're sure yourself that he was with Sabine Jourdain. Foucard hasn't believed your story of the row, has he?'

'He hasn't believed much of what I've told him, but is that a good reason not to tell him I've recognized the man? If Joseph wanted Sabine Jourdain dead, as Barbara Coleman says, then he probably got someone else to do it. And the man who was on the boat with her must be suspect.'

'It's up to Foucard and his superiors to decide who the suspects are . . .'

'If I tell him about Tim at least he'll have a sensible line of enquiry.'

There was a lengthy pause while she wondered how far she was justified in interfering. Merely showing an interest was often enough to move events in one direction rather than another. If Tim were guilty and told her so, he would not be the first person who had admitted a crime to a journalist.

If he later denied it to the police, that would not be unusual, either. What was it she had said to him about the missing family silver? *'I'm not about to make a citizen's arrest.'* A journalist would rarely turn you in whatever you claimed you had done. People boasted to journalists, it might not be at all difficult to get Tim to say exactly what had happened on the *Jonquil* the night Sabine Jourdain was killed.

Oliver broke into her thoughts. 'You're not seriously thinking of telling Foucard?'

'No, but I'm thinking of asking Tim for the truth.'

In the morning they decided Oliver was to lure Tim to the flat with offers of breakfast and a shower. Rain, meanwhile, would pack and telephone Holly Chase with a diary item about Tim.

Over breakfast Rain would steer the conversation around to asking Tim what he was arguing about with Sabine Jourdain. It would be the perfect private situation in which Tim might be ready to explain himself, and Oliver would be there to witness any confession he might make.

Rain packed half her things and then picked up the telephone. Holly's number was unobtainable. Sighing, Rain remembered the story of the gas board digging up the cable at Spinney Green. She went back to the packing.

Sun streaked the room, beckoning her to the balcony. She leaned against the rail. It was going to be a clear day, perhaps the hottest of the year so far. Windows had been flung open in the close-packed buildings for fresh air to reach the stuffiest corner. In a nearby building a woman darted on to her balcony and closed shutters, anticipating the heat.

Rain caught herself smiling Oliver's wistful smile, thinking his irresponsible thoughts. It would be fantastic to stay here. Maybe in the old town itself where the centuries had come and gone and left no trace. Maybe on Cap d'Antibes among the pines and the roses. Perhaps she could fade away in a faded villa like the Villa Fièsole where the Durance coterie had faded to nothing. Or perhaps she could be like Merlyn Joseph and find herself a rich man who would install her in a yacht.

A key in the door, and Oliver was letting himself and Tim into the flat. Rain reflected that, even for Antibes, she would draw the line at sleeping on the beach.

She laid the table, sun falling across it, and each item she placed—cups, sugar bowl, plates, a basket of fruit, croissants—added their shadows to the room. She found herself rearranging things slightly, to perfect the pattern of shadows.

Tim and Oliver were on the balcony, their voices coming to her across the warm stillness. She heard Tim asking how much longer Oliver and Rain would be there, and Oliver fudging the answer. 'I don't want to go back at all. I think you've made the right choice; sun and sand and . . .'

Coffee was made and she called them, setting down the pot to complete her shadow picture. Oliver gave the table a puzzled look. He began to straighten things. Shadows overlapped each other, forms became indistinct. He said, with a laugh: 'What on earth have you done?'

She saw it as he saw it, a crazy thing which made no sense. As he shuffled things into proper places, the shadows made none. She gave an embarrassed smile. 'It was a piece of domestic art, a still life with shadows. You've spoiled it.'

Oliver pretended to apologize for her. 'She's not always as odd as this.' He invited Tim to help himself, and Tim stretched out a hand and carried away a croissant so that the arrangement she had constructed lost its pinnacle.

'Do you paint?' Tim asked Rain. The knife he slid towards her and into the butter had a menacingly long shadow blade. Rain watched the shadow.

The telephone rang. Rain was nearest. They heard her say in a bright voice: 'Good morning, James. Yes, I'm still here. I don't know exactly, not much longer. By the way, I've found what I was looking for. Do you remember me asking if you'd heard of . . . That's right.'

There was a gap while Cobalt was talking and all they heard was Rain's murmur of interest. Finally she said: 'I'll call you before we fly out if I have anything for you.' She rang off.

Tim and Oliver had finished eating. Their conversation halted as she rejoined them. She was afraid of running out of time before she got to the point. She said to Tim: 'We were talking about art, I think. How well did you know Sabine Jourdain?'

'How did you know I knew her?' He was guarded.

'I heard something.'

'I didn't know her well. We met a few times. She was almost a distant relation, did you know that, too?'

Holly Chase had said so. She nodded. 'You looked her up?'

Tim's fingers moved through his hair. He shoved his chair back from the table. 'I know this is going to sound a bit silly, but in a way it was because of her that I came here.'

'Not silly, intriguing.'

Encouraged, he said: 'Well, you remember what we were saying last night, about Scott Fitzgerald . . .'

'Yes,' said Rain firmly as she tore a piece off a croissant. She did not want any more of Scott Fitzgerald if she could help it.

'Well, it all came together in my mind, you know the way things do sometimes? I'd been studying Fitzgerald, reading, seeing the film and the television series and thinking all along what a wonderful life he'd led in the South of France . . .'

'Yes,' said Rain even more firmly.

'At the same time, in the back of my mind, there was the thought that, actually, I had a distant connection who was doing just the same thing.'

Rain could not think what it was Fitzgerald had done that Sabine Jourdain later copied, but regardless of that she spurred him on: 'Yes.'

Tim said: 'Then one day, there it was. Just like that. The realization that I'd been hankering all along to come here, and be part of it.'

'I see,' said Oliver, who did not, but thought it time he said something.

Rain ripped another piece of croissant. 'But Sabine Jourdain—and Fitzgerald, for that matter—weren't ever sleeping on the beach. As far as I know, that is.' She thought it best to defer to Tim's superior knowledge.

Tim laughed, as she had expected. 'No, I haven't read anything to suggest that. But I didn't know *I* was going to sleep there, either.'

'You hadn't realized it was the freest way of life and so forth?' Oliver again showed he was attending.

'What's free?' asked Tim, and for a horrible moment Rain and Oliver feared they had struck his philosophical vein and 'what is life?' could not be far behind. But they were being pessimistic.

'Nothing's free, as far as I can see,' said Tim. 'You can't just rent a villa or a flat overlooking the Med and install yourself for a peppercorn rent like people used to. The beach is all I can afford.' He gave Oliver a sidelong glance. 'Because, whatever you think, I did not steal the family silver.'

Oliver raised his hands in a gesture of surrender. Rain said: 'Where did you intend to stay?'

'I hoped Sabine would find space for me. When I got here I discovered she didn't live in the town any longer. The famous Durance coterie had come to an end and all that was left was Sabine painting in the hills and another old woman living in a neglected villa in Antibes.'

Rain asked whether he had been to Sabine Jourdain's home. He said: 'She didn't want anyone to go there. The woman at the villa, Barbara Coleman, wouldn't tell me where it was and so I went to Durance and he was equally determined about it. Even when I said I was family— well, yes, I know it wasn't true but it seemed near enough the truth to use to persuade them—neither of them would give her away.'

Rain noticed that he had not provided an answer to her question. She let him get away with it. She said: 'Did you meet her in Antibes?'

'At the villa. Barbara Coleman mentioned Sabine was going to visit her so I went, too.'

'Was it a good meeting?' She was seeing it from Sabine Jourdain's point of view: a young foreigner pursuing her and intending to latch on to her.

He shrugged. 'Actually, I didn't think I made much impression on her. She seemed a bit preoccupied. And then I thought maybe I'd been expecting too much. I'd looked forward to it for ages, there'd been a build-up but it was quite different for her.'

While Rain finished her breakfast, Tim told her how he had decided to see her again and how he found out from Barbara Coleman when the next visit to the villa would be. Both women had been surprised when he turned up a second time.

Oliver asked: 'What did you talk about?' It was a fair question, given the circumstances of Tim's visits.

'Oh, you know,' said Tim vaguely. Rain covered a smile as he went on. 'Scott Fitzgerald, Durance, that sort of thing.'

Rain saw his eyes go to the clock. She said: 'You got to know Benedict Joseph as well, did you?'

Tim frowned. 'Benedict Joseph?' Rain waited, unsure whether this was an act. Tim's face cleared. 'Oh, you mean the American. The dealer? No, I don't know him.'

Rain said: 'But you've been on his yacht, haven't you?'

Rain saw him weighing up how to respond. She went on: 'We've both been there. Once we were there at the same time. On the night Sabine Jourdain died.'

Tim squirmed, reminding Rain of a schoolboy caught doing something naughty. She let him suffer a bit longer, then said: 'You and Sabine had a row, I heard it. What was it about?'

Tim flared, as when he had denied stealing the silver. 'I didn't kill her. You're not to say I killed her.'

'I haven't said that, but I'd like to know why you quarrelled.'

Tim inspected Oliver and saw the same accusation. He said: 'This is why you invited me here, isn't it? So you could test your theory that I killed the old woman.'

Rain said: 'I want to know what you were quarrelling about. It wasn't a mild disagreement, it was . . .'

Tim swivelled away from her. 'All right, *all right!* We had a row, but telling the police we had a row isn't going to bring her back to life and it isn't going to find out who killed her, because I didn't.'

Rain kept silent. He spoke again: 'Why should I kill her? What possible reason could there be? I hardly knew the woman.'

Oliver said: 'You knew her well enough to be on that boat with her.'

'I wanted to talk to her. I saw her walking through the harbour and I followed. She went on board. I hung around deciding what to do and then some people came off the boat. They got into a big car and drove away. Benedict Joseph and his wife—I know now that's who they must have been. I thought I'd go on board and talk to Sabine. She told me to go away and stop pestering her.'

His face grew bitter, he was thin-lipped. He said: 'She got very angry. I got angry, too. You know how it is: one minute you're talking, the next there's a blazing row. I went. I left her standing there.'

Outside a dog barked. A new pattern of shadow lay across the table. A motorbike screamed along the coast road. Tim stood up. He said: 'I won't stay for a shower, I'll go for a swim instead.' He tossed back his hair and glared down at Rain.

She sensed him wanting to release a far greater fury than he dared. She believed he sometimes dared. To defuse the moment she said, conversationally: 'You'll go straight back to the beach, will you?'

He said: 'You've no reason to suspect me of killing Sabine.'

She stroked back her errant curl. Her voice was very soft. 'Except that I heard you threaten to.'

18

That was not one of your greatest successes,' Oliver West said to Rain Morgan as the door slammed and Tarquin Poulteney-Crosse ran downstairs.

She poured coffee, saying: 'He didn't pretend I was wrong about him being on the yacht that evening.'

Oliver spooned sugar. 'They couldn't, surely, have been arguing about him repeatedly popping up and wanting to talk to her. There must have something else.'

'Yes, I'm sure of that. She probably did tell him to go away and stop following her around, but that wouldn't be a reason for him screaming he'd kill her.'

She looked at the clock. It was time to ring Holly Chase at the office with a brief story about the faintly ducal connection roughing it on the beach.

'Hi!' said Holly. 'How's the suntan?'

'I've been far too busy to look for one of those,' Rain said. 'I tried you at home earlier—hasn't anyone mended your cable yet?'

'Oh, sure. Normal service was resumed yesterday

morning. Then the water board came and dug the cable up.' Peals of laughter.

Rain gave Holly a couple of paragraphs. Holly sounded disappointed. 'Is that all?'

'No, but it's all that's fit to print.' She left Holly to wonder about that, and rang off.

Oliver said: 'What did Cobalt want?'

'Someone's tipped him off that Sabine Jourdain was painting Durance's pictures. He wanted to know whether that was as wild as it seemed.'

'Fancy him asking you. Why didn't he keep it to himself?'

'I was the quickest way of checking it. He wouldn't want to waste his time chasing that story if I'd already done it, and I can get a story into print more quickly than the British magazines he supplies. Even so . . .'

Oliver nodded. 'Even so, you didn't help him. You didn't confirm it.'

'I need to know a bit more. With Tim here I couldn't ask him.' She began to dial a Nice number. While it rang she said: 'There was something else, too. He's found Barbara Coleman.'

Oliver rolled his eyes. He was weary of Barbara Coleman and her elusive behaviour. After a minute or two Rain replaced the receiver. 'No answer. He must have gone out.'

'Good,' said Oliver. 'Then we can finish packing and go to the airport. If you want to phone Cobalt you can do it easily enough from London.'

'You wanted a day in Nice. I can offer you half a day and then we can take the later flight.' Then: 'Better still, let's dash off to Nice now and have one more night here.'

He was willing to be persuaded. 'But supposing Cobalt isn't at his flat?'

'I know where I can find him around lunchtime.'

Minutes later they were on their way in high good humour, Oliver thumbing a guidebook and choosing the things he wanted to see.

'If you can find Cobalt quickly and finish with him equally quickly, then you'll be able to come along,' he offered.

'I'll probably have to pump him, he refused to be explicit on the phone so I don't think he's keen to tell me everything. If you want to do all the things on your list you'll have to do some alone.'

Oliver made a disgruntled sound. However quick she was he always thought her work took too long and prevented them doing the more pleasurable things he had in mind. But he was not going to quibble about it this time.

The excellent weather had brought out more sunseekers and it was harder than before to find a parking space in Nice. In the end Rain had to leave the car some way from the rue de Rivoli. Oliver was not displeased. The walk meant he would be able to claim in future that he had promenaded on the Promenade des Anglais.

Cobalt was not home. Rain and Oliver went back down the badly lit stairs. Out of doors it was too bright to see, the sun brilliant in contrast to the interior. A woman with a toy poodle grumbled as Oliver trod on it. They left her complaining volubly about foreigners, the dog yapping his agreement.

Rain's memory guided her to the café where she had sat with Cobalt. He was there, straight red hair pale in sunlight, blue eyes masked by dark glasses. He was in shirtsleeves, his jacket crumpled on a chair beside him. On the table was a nearly empty glass. The waiter watched it, ready for his cue to bring another drink.

'I came instead of phoning,' Rain explained and introduced Oliver. The waiter swooped. Rain ordered a *citronnade*. She said: 'I couldn't talk when you called, James, because Tarquin Poulteney-Crosse—better known as Tim—was with us. But I'd love to hear what you know about Sabine Jourdain and where Barbara Coleman is.' The sun was so strong, it cast the colour of her mauve blouse on to her skin.

Cobalt's mouth curved in his mischievous smile although she could only see her reflection in his lenses. 'In exchange I'd love to hear what you know about Sabine Jourdain painting for Durance. You didn't sound amazed on the phone, therefore I'm led to believe you knew.'

'I don't know nearly enough. Enough to put together a good story but not enough to rush into print with it.'

Cobalt nodded, indicating this was what he had suspected. He said: 'Are we going to work together on this?'

She hesitated. She did not know how good his contacts were, whether he had sufficient grasp of the art world to interpret the information he might uncover. She trusted him to look after the *Post*'s interests before he sold the story to any other outlets, but she did not know whether she could trust him with the story.

Oliver filled the gap. 'If you two are working together you've only got today to do it. We're flying home tomorrow.'

Rain demurred. 'That's the latest plan,' she said to Cobalt. 'I'd stayed to look for the aristocratic drop-out. Now he's found, but if there's a hope of getting to the truth about Sabine Jourdain in the next day or two I could linger.'

Out of the corner of her eye she saw Oliver move irritably. Then he beckoned the waiter and ordered more drinks. Cobalt said to her: 'I should think the *Post* could afford to pay to keep you here a few more days.'

'It's costing next to nothing,' she said, and explained where they were staying.

Oliver said: 'We call it Operation Shoestring.'

Cobalt gave a short laugh which became a nagging cough. When he recovered he had decided to stop fencing. 'There's a man I know—his name is Georges—who has a job at the Hotel Negresco. He phones me from time to time when he has heard something he thinks will be of use to me. It's generally rubbish, but every so often there's a story, so I always listen to him.'

Cobalt took a sip from his glass, then resumed: 'Yesterday he rang with a yarn about some trouble at the hotel. Apparently one of the reception clerks, a man called Edouard, turned up at work with a black eye and other signs of having been in a good fight. Edouard was sent back home, they couldn't have him at work looking like that.'

He turned away to greet a man slouching by. Then: 'Georges said Edouard told his colleagues he'd been attacked in the street the night before by some youths he didn't know. A plausible story, but then Edouard spoiled it by resisting going home.'

Oliver said: 'Perhaps he wasn't going to get paid if he didn't work.'

'That wasn't the reason. He was afraid to go home. He passed the day skulking around cafés, and when Georges met him by chance later on he confessed he'd been beaten up in his flat because he'd agreed to do a favour for someone and it had gone wrong. Edouard said he'd been obliged to keep an elderly English woman there for a few days, but she'd been slipping out.'

'Barbara Coleman!' Rain was alarmed at this proof of what the woman had told her.

'I went to the flat and found Barbara Coleman.'

'Was she all right?' Rain asked.

'She hadn't been harmed, but she said Edouard was attacked while she was there and it had been done as a warning to her. She didn't see the men who did it. She believes she must stay out of sight or something similar will happen to her.'

Rain groaned. 'I met her. I let her go back to that flat.'

Oliver came to her defence. 'Yes, but you didn't entirely believe her story, did you?'

She said: 'Don't you think that makes it worse?'

Cobalt coughed again. They waited. He told them what Barbara Coleman had said about Sabine Jourdain and Durance. It was the same as she had told Rain.

'You mustn't go to her, Rain,' said Oliver. 'Unless you can be certain she'll come away with you, you mustn't go. Somebody could be hurt.'

'She won't leave,' said Cobalt. 'Don't you think I tried to make her come with me? She refused. She was sure it would get Edouard and his wife into trouble, and she kept saying it was only for another day or two.'

Rain said: 'I think that means until I leave for London.'

'There you are,' said Oliver, triumphant. 'The sooner we go the better for everyone.'

There was an uncomfortable pause during which he wondered what had caused it. Eventually Rain said: 'Barbara Coleman has been threatened, Edouard has been beaten up and Sabine Jourdain has been murdered— and all because no one is to know she was the painter and not Durance.'

Cobalt's freckled forehead creased. 'Is there so much money in it that people would go to those lengths? I don't know much about art but it seems so . . . *extreme*.'

It was an echo of Rain's own words to Barbara Coleman but she said: 'The art world can be extreme, and Durance hasn't declined as many old artists decline. There's always been a market.'

Cobalt fingered his empty glass. 'Would anyone actually kill to keep those prices high?'

'I'm sure someone already has,' Rain said, and thought of Tim and Joseph and wondered how they were linked in murder.

Cobalt said: 'There was nothing in the papers about Sabine Jourdain's death being connected with the paintings. My police contacts say it's thought she was the victim of a random attack by a thief.'

Rain told him she had heard nothing to suggest the police were suspicious about the provenance of the paintings. She mentioned Foucard's visits. Between them Rain and Oliver told Cobalt almost all they knew about the night of the murder and about the paintings.

Oliver asked Cobalt whether Barbara Coleman had not told him she suspected Joseph of murder. Rain had decided to keep that to herself a while longer. Cobalt said: 'She didn't give me a name, but she said her friend was killed by "the Americans". I couldn't get her to say more. I'd told her I worked for the *Post* and she said she'd already told Rain all about it.'

He fumbled in his jacket pocket, took out a notebook and wrote a few lines on a page which he tore out and gave to Rain. 'That's where she is, if you change your mind about calling on her.'

A man stopped to speak to Cobalt. He broke into the discussion for so long that Rain grew impatient. She hoped that when he left she and Cobalt could decide how to divide the work on the story. There were several strands to pursue. The one which was uppermost in her mind was Maurin.

Barbara Coleman had said Maurin was responsible for keeping her hidden, and therefore the men who attacked Edouard could have been acting for him. The deduction sickened Rain. What Cobalt reported confirmed the man had a dangerous side. Rain could not leave the Maurin strand to Cobalt. She must tackle him herself, although there was someone else she wanted to see first.

To her annoyance Oliver and Cobalt appeared settled for an afternoon's drinking. Neither of them showed any inclination to do other than sit outside the café in the sunshine, and Oliver had shifted the conversation far away from the Durances and murder.

'If you stay here much longer you won't have time for all that sightseeing,' she warned Oliver. But it was a waste of breath.

'You carry on,' he said. 'We'll be here for a while yet.'

She could see that. She asked, a shade tartly, where she might expect to meet them again. Cobalt was heading for a renewal of the morning's hangover, Oliver would expect to head for Antibes with her later. Oliver attempted some arrangements. Cobalt suggested they meet up at his flat in the early evening. Rain accepted that. When she left them she walked to the Hotel Negresco.

She saw her man straight away. One of the clerks wore dark glasses and she could guess why. She caught his attention, asked whether he was Edouard and lived at the address Cobalt had given her.

'It's all right,' she said, hoping it was. She told him her name, what she wanted.

He shook his head. 'No, I didn't recognize the men who came to my flat.'

'Do you know who sent them?'

He made an empty gesture. She said: 'I understand Philippe Maurin arranged for Barbara Coleman to stay at your flat. Don't you think he could have sent them?'

'Perhaps he did, perhaps not.'

'What reason did Maurin give for asking you to take in Barbara Coleman?'

Edouard shook his head, he began to back away. Rain raised her voice a fraction. He did not want her to do that, to draw the attention of his colleagues. She said:

'He must have given you a reason.'

The clerk came closer, his voice lower than before. 'It was a favour, a private arrangement. I was asked to be discreet. I knew what that meant. I would be paid well but I had to keep my mouth shut.'

'Did you know him before this?'

'Slightly. My wife used to work at his house. Look, I'm trying to do what he said. It was supposed to be for just a day, or maybe two, but it has already been a week . . .'

'. . . and you kept your mouth shut but you were beaten up and threatened with worse. Why shield people who've treated you like that?'

His colleagues were watching, pretending not to. 'Look,' he said, 'I'm trying to protect my wife and myself. I'm not interested in protecting anybody else. I wish I'd never taken Maurin's money, but all I can do now is keep quiet and wait for it to end.'

'If you've got the money and it was for a favour lasting a day or two, then why don't you just tell him the arrangement is ended and let Barbara Coleman leave?'

He smiled at her naivety. 'I've got *half*, I get paid the rest when it's over. That's one answer. The other is that I don't wish any harm to come to Miss Coleman and she may be safer where she is until they say she's free to go.'

'They? I thought we were talking about one man, Philippe Maurin?'

'Surely he isn't doing this on his own? Why is he hiding the old woman? He told me before she came that she was asking for somewhere secret to stay for a short time. Now I know that's a lie, and she only stays because she's afraid for me and my wife. My wife is sure Maurin's not the type of man to be violent and that the men who came weren't sent by him.'

'By *whom*, then?'

Another empty gesture with his hands. Rain said: 'Can you describe the men?' But all she got were what Foucard would have called stereotype Frenchmen, and Denis was not there to laugh.

Rain took a sheet of paper from the reception desk and wrote on it her name and phone number in Antibes. 'I'm staying here, at least until tomorrow. If you remember anything you can tell me, please ring.'

He folded the paper and tucked it into his pocket. Some tourists were booking in, she could not detain Edouard longer. She stood in the foyer for a few minutes, jotting into her notebook the things he had told her. Then she went out into the heat.

She had taken a very few steps when she heard someone running up behind her. She tingled with apprehension but when she looked back it was Edouard.

'There is this for you,' he said, thrusting out an envelope. 'I am sorry, I didn't remember it while we were talking.'

He hurried back to the hotel, trying to rush but also to keep up the appearance of quiet dignity his employers would expect of him.

The envelope was typed with Rain's initial and surname. On the sheet of paper inside she read the baldest message. 'Chagall. 4.00. B.C.'

She was so pleased to learn that Barbara Coleman was eager to talk to her again, and that she had been given the perfect reason for spending part of her day revelling in Chagall's colour, that she smiled as she cut inland towards Maurin's gallery.

19

Through the window of the gallery in the ruc de France Rain Morgan saw Maurin had company. An expensive-looking man in a black coat with a velvet collar was appraising a painting. Maurin was absorbed in his client and did not see Rain enter.

It was a full half minute before he turned his head to see who his next potential customer might be. He did not show disappointment that it was a mere journalist and one who was more interested in a dead artist whose work he had never handled.

He inclined his head gracefully. She returned the greeting with a sweet smile. She hoped it would throw Maurin off guard, persuade him she had come for a little of his flirtatious conversation at the least, a few more questions about Durance and Sabine Jourdain at the most. He would not be prepared when she asked him why he had sent two men to beat up a pathetic hotel clerk and frighten a vulnerable old woman.

He was not. He came as near to gaping as he would allow himself. His rich client had barely left the salon before Rain lobbed him her questions and waited for his painful answers. He floundered, recovered and said: 'Rain, you have misunderstood something. You must let me explain.'

She folded her arms, leaned against a table. 'By all means, please do.' She tried not to sound triumphant. She had tripped him and she enjoyed the feeling, but she must not be triumphant. She had been taken in by the man, accepting him as charming company when they first met, playing along with his flattering nonsense. If Oliver had not come to France with her the playing might have gone further. It embarrassed her to remember the way Maurin had attracted her but she must not let that embarrassment colour the way she acted now.

He smiled his disarming smile. She declined to be disarmed. He said: 'Barbara Coleman is what you English call a chatterbox. If she is not prevented from chattering she could cause herself much trouble.'

'You mean her chattering could cause someone else much trouble and he doesn't want to risk that.'

He gave the perfect Gallic shrug. She almost wished Oliver were there to see how it should be done. He said: 'I am trying to explain. You came here once before asking questions and perhaps I did not give you the best answers.'

She was confident that was true. She said: 'I was asking you then about the changes—the developments, as you called them—in Durance's work. Now I believe Durance didn't paint those pictures. Perhaps he did some of the work on them, but I don't believe he did everything sold under his name.'

He was indignant. 'You are accusing me of selling fakes?'

'Not that. Not exactly. But I think Sabine Jourdain did most of the work on the paintings and I think you knew it.'

Maurin made an elaborate gesture, flinging a hand to

his brow. Rain was reminded of amateur opera companies, of Madeleine Corley. She said: 'If there's another explanation I'd love to hear it.'

Maurin looked at his slim gold wrist watch. 'Perhaps we should go somewhere and talk quietly and sensibly about this.'

She knew it would not be sensible to go anywhere quiet with him. She said: 'Where do you suggest?' hoping the answer would be somewhere public and safe. He said they should go upstairs to the room above the gallery, and she could think of no way of refusing. He locked the front door and up they went.

The first floor was cool, the light low. When he threw open shutters to let in air and light, pictures sprang at her from the walls. Maurin brought an already opened bottle of wine. It was chilled, enticing. She drank sparingly. He said: 'Now, let me try to explain.' And tried.

He said that Sabine Jourdain had always worked on the paintings with her *maître* and that over the years the amount she did varied. The ideas were always Durance's, he always initiated the paintings and when his hands permitted he carried out the work, but as he had become increasingly crippled the execution had been left more and more to his protégée.

He treated Rain to another of his smiles. 'I do not need to explain to you that this is often how artists work. You will already know that Henry Moore does not himself chip away at his piece of stone . . .'

It was a seductive argument. Rain made an effort and said it was a specious one. 'Sabine Jourdain decided to call a halt to this arrangement, didn't she? She intended to bring the matter into the open.'

Maurin almost laughed. 'You may believe that if you wish. I certainly cannot stop you and she is not here to ask.'

'She was murdered before she could talk about it.'

He said: 'Sabine Jourdain had years to talk about it if she wished to do so. No, Sabine Jourdain fell among thieves while she was walking through the harbour. She was there because you had not kept your appointment with her and so she had to make her own way home in the dark.'

He had scored a point and she knew he knew it. He had always known how to handle her: the right flattering remark, the careful timing of the smiles. Before she could think how to respond without sounding defensive he was saying: 'You are angry with yourself, remorseful because if you had not been late this thing would never have happened. I understand that. If it were me I should want to . . .' He made a gesture indicating helplessness. 'But it is not fair that your remorse should be turned in the direction of seeking someone else to blame.'

She felt her skin burn, it was intolerable to have to listen to this. A telephone rang. Maurin stood, elegant near the window, and listened to his caller. His words gave no clue what the call was about. He rang off.

Then he said to Rain: 'You could say I have been trying to help Barbara Coleman, helping her to keep out of trouble. Soon she will be back at home and all this will be forgotten.'

Rain's discomfort gave way to anger. '"*All this will be forgotten!*" Aren't *you* forgetting something? That her friend is dead?'

'Certainly I cannot forget that. You have indicated to me yourself that since she is dead there will be no more Durances for me to sell. None of the same calibre, I mean. Durance himself may manage something once in a while, but there is no one who can help him achieve those masterpieces in the way that Jourdain did. No one else was of the same mind as he. He was able to feed his ideas through her as other artists use a brush or a pencil.'

'She was a tool. She was used by him. Is it any wonder she was ready to say so and make an end of it?'

Maurin said with energy: 'You can prove nothing. You may believe what you choose but I ask you to accept that you are wrong on that point. Sabine Jourdain would never have betrayed Marius Durance.'

'How can you be so sure?' She was interested in his change of tone. It was as sharp as Tim's had been when Oliver accused him of stealing.

'Rain, you must know how I could know. I was as close to those two as anyone.'

'Except Barbara Coleman, perhaps.'

He agreed with a bow of the head. 'That brings us back to Miss Coleman. You will want to know when she can go home.'

'First I would like to know why it was necessary to send two men to the flat to attack the hotel clerk.'

He assumed an expression of utmost sincerity. She fought against believing in it. 'I have heard nothing of this until you came into my gallery a quarter of an hour ago and accused me. Why should I be organizing the beating up of hotel clerks? Or the intimidation of old ladies? Do you really think I am a man to do such things?'

She could not choose an answer. At that moment it was easier to be persuaded of his innocence, his scathing rejection of violence. But she knew other things about him. She said: 'Edouard was beaten up on someone's orders. He is walking about Nice with dark glasses and bruises. Barbara Coleman is at his flat and not allowed home . . .'

'I have told you, she is there for her protection. Perhaps I made a miscalculation. Perhaps that was not the ideal place to lodge her. At the time I had to find somewhere quickly and Edouard agreed to it. I have told you, Rain, I was trying to put her somewhere safe and secret for her own safety. She is a painter, she is a friend of Sabine Jourdain and of Durance. I have known Barbara Coleman for years. Why is it odd that I should try to help her when she is in difficulties?'

Put like that it was plausible, Rain returned to an earlier approach. 'You haven't said whom you are protecting her from.'

He parried with a familiar answer. 'From herself, of course.'

The conversation had come full circle. Rain wanted to persist but she had an appointment to keep. Maurin would be at the gallery any other time she wanted him. Barbara Coleman might not be at the museum again.

Reluctantly Rain left and drove to Cimiez and the museum. On the way she thought about Maurin. He had not told her all he knew, she was sure of that, but he had confirmed her deduction about the provenance of the Durance paintings—although he had stressed she could prove nothing.

She thought about Barbara Coleman and her ill-treatment at Maurin's hands. She had been physically hurt when she was dragged from the villa and she had been held captive ever since. How did this balance against Maurin's tenderness with Durance? And if it was true that Sabine Jourdain would never have betrayed Durance, why was she killed? Was it possible the police version (which Cobalt had heard and Maurin had repeated) was correct and the killing was a random attack by a thief on a passer-by?

Rain could try and get some answers from Barbara Coleman when they held their whispered conversation before Chagall's windows, but she must make up her own mind about Maurin's character. She could put him into the scale alongside Joseph and Tarquin Poulteney-Crosse whom she believed culpable of murder, or she could give him the benefit of the doubt.

Guiltily, she knew she wanted to exonerate him, and that her reasons were unworthy. If he were not attractive, if he had not attracted *her*, she might be less eager to acquit him. She tried to picture him looking like a French version of Cobalt, for whom she felt no physical attraction at all, and then she tried to calculate whether, in that guise, he was not a more likely murderer.

She reached the Chagall Museum before she had her answer. The museum was more crowded than on her previous visit, alive with the subdued noise of a lot of people trying to make no sound. She went to the suffused blue light of the room with the stained glass windows.

Rain took the seat she had sat in before, in the deepest shadow the room afforded. But this time it would be different, this time she was not going to obey any silly rules. She was going to insist on driving the woman away from Nice, because Barbara Coleman must be taken out of the clutches of Maurin and anybody else who interfered with her liberty.

Rain had no clear idea what to do with her, apart from taking her to the Villa Fièsole, and she was already seeing the warped logic of Edouard's argument: Barbara Coleman might be safer where she was. But on the other hand, she might not. There was a reasonable case to be made out for keeping her away from Nice. Rain wondered whether she had the cheek to install her in the Antibes flat borrowed from her newspaper colleague.

People came and went as she sat thinking about this. They made shadowy forms that lowered themselves into seats, sat transfixed for a while and then rose and glided away. Four o'clock had passed, Barbara Coleman had not arrived.

Patiently Rain concentrated on the windows, instead of being alert to every sound. And then there was a commotion: raucous voices, the tramping of many feet, and a deep German voice addressing a party of tourists.

The noise was some way off, it rose and fell as the guide led his troop through the rooms of paintings. Eventually they must reach the windows. Rain comforted herself that however disruptive they were, they would not be in there long because they were dealing with everything else with extraordinary speed. She let the light and colour soothe her.

Even when the German guide ushered his party into the room for his top-of-the-voice lecture, the spell was unbroken. Following his instruction, his party hastened to the windows. There were twenty of them, creating a hubbub, looking for the prosaic detail of construction rather than letting themselves be beguiled by the beauty of the creation.

And as their noise surged, discordant as the first squall of wind on a calm day, Rain Morgan sensed a figure in the row behind her. Before she could turn she felt something about her throat. Chagall's blue intensity faded to darkness. She lost consciousness.

20

She was lying on a hard surface. There was the pain of light in her eyes and far off voices whose words were incomprehensible. She did not know where she was or what had happened.

She shut her eyes and breathed painfully. People were all around her but she felt distant. Someone was pulling at her clothes, a hand shook her shoulder, and then a thumb rolled back her eyelid. She did not understand why they should be doing this and her failure to understand reminded her of something. She snatched at the memory but it was too obscure. All she had was the image of a woman lying on the ground and people desperate to help her. The woman had not responded. She had lain unmoving in the midst of their activity.

The light hurt Rain's eyes. She dragged her head away. There was an angry moan as she did so and a pain in her chest, which made her wonder whether the moan had not been her own. The thumb left her eye and the lid snapped shut against the light.

The voices changed key. She heard the fear in them subside. She wanted to be left alone just as she was, wherever she was, but the people would not leave her alone. They were speaking words she could not grasp but now they were speaking them to her rather than to each other and their tone was sympathetic, cajoling.

Through them there cut another, familiar, voice. She opened her eyes again and saw, hazily at first, Oliver.

'She's all right,' he was saying, 'But don't crowd her, she needs air.'

No one took any notice of him. He stroked her face. 'You *are* all right, aren't you?' He needed her confirmation.

She managed the slightest nod. She tried to frame a question. Oliver said: 'Don't worry about it yet. I'll tell you what happened once we get out of here. Do you think you can sit up? It might encourage some of them to lose interest and go away.'

She grunted and let him help her sit. Someone had fetched a glass of water, the worldwide response to apparent catastrophe. Oliver held the glass as she drank. There were murmurs of approval from the onlookers.

Her mind cleared rapidly. She felt her strength returning, but there was pain in her eyes, chest and throat.

She knew now why the voices had been unintelligible: they were speaking in French. Her mind was still too lazy to concentrate on what they were saying. She recognized a couple of the museum staff but the rest who stared were strangers. She clung to Oliver's hand. 'I think I can stand now.'

He helped her up. Her legs were weak but she could walk. He said: 'We'll go out to the car, if you think you can walk that far.'

'I'm fine.' She sounded far from it.

She smiled a faint smile for the people who hung around waiting for more drama. Oliver said: 'You don't have to say anything. I haven't told them you speak

French and they've discovered I don't.'

As they started to move off a woman touched Oliver's arm and handed him Rain's shoulder bag. Faces followed them as they went slowly towards the museum exit and out into the sunlight.

It was exceedingly hot inside the car. They sat there with the door open to let the temperature drop before driving off. Oliver looked around. There was no one else about. 'Now,' he said, 'tell me what the hell happened in there.'

She shook her head, wished she had not because it hurt. 'I can't remember.'

'I can tell you this much: someone tried to garotte you and almost succeeded.'

There was silence while she absorbed that. She received random bits of memory, tried them in different patterns, hoping to make sense. She said: 'I remember looking at the windows, and German tourists coming in and then . . .' But she did not know what came next.

Oliver said: 'I hope you *are* all right. There was a man who spoke a bit of English and he said they were going to send for a doctor, but I told them you suffered from fits and you'd be all right.'

'You told them *what!*' Even for one of Oliver's expedient fictions it was extreme.

'I had to say something. It was all a bit of a shock.'

She put a hand to her aching throat. 'Yes,' she said with irony.

'If it had been anything else then a doctor would have been a sensible idea, but once somebody stops strangling you, you recover, don't you?'

'I don't know. I've never been throttled before.'

'Well, you do. Once the air passages are freed you must recover.'

'How did you know someone had been strangling me

if everyone else in there was willing to believe I'd had a fit?'

Oliver dangled a piece of cord in front of her. There was a small loop at one end. 'Because when I found you I took this from around your throat.'

She shuddered and turned away. He said: 'You're not going to be sick, are you?'

'I haven't got the energy.' Then: 'Could you put that thing away? I'd rather not think about it yet.'

'Sorry. I thought it might surprise your memory.'

'Oh, it surprised me, but I haven't seen it before.'

He changed direction. 'Why were you at the gallery?'

'Perhaps I wanted to see the windows again. You know I did, I was entranced by them the other day. But how did you find me here?'

'That,' said Oliver, 'is a curious tale. I was sightseeing after leaving Cobalt at the café. He said he was going to go back to his flat. Do you remember we all said we'd meet there?'

'Yes. It's not time yet, is it?'

'Not yet. Well, I was wandering around looking for a rococo palace . . .'

'The Palais Lascari.'

'That's the one. I didn't find it, but instead I found Maurin. He came rushing out of an alleyway just ahead of me but he didn't see me. He was making for a taxi, which might well have been waiting for him. He wrenched open the door and gave some instructions to the driver. All I understood was one word: Chagall.'

'You came out of curiosity?'

'I'd wanted to see it of course, but I also wondered why he was so desperate to get here. It's not as though he's a tourist with only a few hours. Maurin can visit the museum any time he likes.'

'Did you see him when you got here?' She wanted to

183

hear Oliver say no, for it all to be a mistake.

'No,' he said. 'But Maurin had gone roaring off in a taxi and I'd had to find the bus stop and so I didn't seriously expect to. Instead, I found your car outside. I went straight to the stained glass windows thinking I'd be sure to find you there. I'd hardly gone into the room when there was a cry as a woman found you slumped in a seat.'

'Didn't she see the cord around my neck?'

'Apparently not. She couldn't lift you so she stepped back for me to do it. I saw the cord and took it off and put it in my pocket. It was just a reflex—I knew it had to come off and I didn't want them all fussing about it. Some of the men carried you out into the light in the gallery.'

Rain said she found it very hard to believe Maurin responsible. Oliver said: 'He's involved in the deception over the Durances and he's abducted Barbara Coleman to keep her quiet about it. Perhaps he's found out how much you know.'

'I told him myself.'

'Well, there you are. He's protecting the secret of the Durances. He tried to kill you and that makes it look very much as though he's the person who killed Sabine Jourdain.'

People were coming from the museum, some looking with open curiosity at Rain and Oliver. Oliver said: 'We have a small problem. It's not much after what you've just been through, but I'd hate to end up in a French jail and, as I forgot my licence, I'm not insured to move this car.'

She smiled. However big the disasters, the small problems always turned up, too. 'I'll manage.'

'We could get a bus or a taxi into Nice...'

But she was thinking about something else. 'Oliver,

how did you get into this car? You didn't take the keys from my bag, did you?'

'The car was unlocked, you must have left it unlocked.'

She demurred. It would be breaking the habit of a lifetime. She opened her bag and sifted the contents, trying to discover whether it had been searched. Her notebook was there, the piece of paper Cobalt had given her with Barbara Coleman's Nice address was there, everything she could recall was there except the keys.

Checking her skirt pockets, she came up with the car keys. She found something else, too: an envelope with her name on it. Another piece of memory slotted into position. 'This is why I came here this afternoon.'

He read out: '"Chagall. 4.00. B.C." Where did this come from?'

She gave a rueful smile. 'When I was given it I believed it came from Barbara Coleman. Now it's clear it didn't.'

She told him about her easy acceptance that there was a repeated message from Barbara Coleman. 'I was so keen to meet her again I didn't challenge this at all. I didn't wonder why she'd taken to using a typewriter when her last messages to me were handwritten, and I didn't ask myself how Edouard could have talked to me all that time without mentioning there was an envelope for me.'

'You think he tapped this out as soon as you left the desk and then ran after you with it?'

'Yes. He must have read her note to me the other day, because this is just a truncated version of it. *Of course* he was the messenger who took the note to the hotel. Who likelier? She's living in his flat and he's working at the hotel. She must have told him I kept the appointment.'

'I thought he was supposed to be incarcerating her, not arranging her social life.'

Rain agreed it was very puzzling. Oliver went on: 'He

doesn't need to be a linguist to concoct this. It's a bilingual message, isn't it?'

Rain started the car. She said: 'We ought to go straight to meet Cobalt but there are other things I want first.'

'Such as?'

'A steadying drink, and to know who tried to kill me.'

'The first,' said Oliver, 'should be easy.'

With uncharacteristic slowness Rain drove into Nice. She kept away from the rue de Rivoli and they went into a café near the port.

Rain fingered her throat. 'There's sure to be some bruising, isn't there?'

'We'll get you a scarf.' He looked at her with concern, seeing how strained she was. It would not do to ask her to drive back to Antibes that evening. She needed rest and time to get over the shock.

Rain said: 'I don't want to tell Cobalt about this. Does that sound absurd?'

'No. If you'd prefer, we don't even have to see him. We could phone and say we've changed our plans. Rain, let's book into a hotel in Nice for tonight.'

He saw her relief. 'I don't relish the drive, but we could get back by train.'

'And then we'd have to come here tomorrow to deal with the car. It's not worth the effort. We'll just find a hotel and have a quiet meal somewhere and then you can get to bed early. You'll be much fitter by the morning.'

But she was shaking her head. 'No, I want to see Cobalt as we arranged. After that we can go to a hotel and so on, but I think I should see him.'

'But why?'

'Because . . .' She could not explain. It was only partly that she disliked breaking arrangements, more that she wanted to let Cobalt see she was alive and well. 'If he hears rumours about what happened at the museum I want him to know that nothing terrible happened after all.'

'We'll see him and not mention anything about it.'

'Yes. I don't think we need say we went there, do you?'

'What if he asks where we were?'

She altered her plan. 'Why don't you say you went to the Chagall museum? I can mention that I spoke to Maurin at his gallery.'

There was something wrong about her scheme but she could not clarify what it was. She tried, saying: 'On the other hand, perhaps he ought to be told. Warned, if you like.'

'Warned? You think the same thing could happen to him if he pursues the story?'

'Yes.' But that was not quite what she meant. Deep down she did not believe Cobalt needed to be warned about things. She was still trying to cope with the matter when Oliver said they ought to leave if they were to meet him as planned.

On the way they stopped for Rain to buy a silk scarf which complemented her blouse. No one would have guessed she was wearing it for any other reason. Once more they mounted the dark steps of the building in the rue de Rivoli and once more the lift was motionless and the stairway light failed at the most inconvenient moments.

Cobalt showed them into his sitting room. Rain recognized the stale smell, and her glance went to the half-open shutters. She wanted to throw them wide and let in as much air as possible, as Cobalt had done on her earlier visit. But the room was not well lit and she thought it wiser to live in the shadows as she did not want to explain why she looked ill.

'Find yourselves somewhere to sit,' said Cobalt with

a wave towards the clutter that obscured most of the furniture. 'What'll you have to drink? Wine?'

'Thanks,' Oliver called after him as Cobalt headed for the kitchen. Rain gave Oliver a warning look. She could not face a repetition of the morning session. Oliver assumed an expression of extreme penitence.

Rain looked at the litter of newspapers, discarded clothes, sheets of paper covered with Cobalt's messy typing. The Great Novel was still on the table, but had made no progress since she last saw it. Involuntarily she found herself going out on to the balcony for air, rather than clearing a space to sit. She gripped the rail and looked down the street.

'A sea view?' asked Oliver, joking.

'Actually there is. Come and be convinced.'

He followed her out and stared where she pointed. In the background there was the sound of Cobalt's doorbell but there was too much noise from the street below for them to hear any more. After a few minutes a young woman came out of the street door below them and walked away. Possibly Cobalt's caller had gone. Rain went back into the sitting room expecting to see Cobalt there.

The room was empty. She wandered around it for a minute until she realized it was odd there were no sounds from him. She called his name. 'James?' But he did not answer.

Oliver came in from the balcony. 'Where's he got to?'

They went into the passage. There were four other doors off it. Rain looked into the kitchen. A bottle of wine stood open, half-used, on the table, three glasses beside it. She put her head into the next room, an untidy and empty bathroom which looked as though the washbasin had not been cleaned for months. Oliver and Rain

188

exchanged troubled glances. He pushed open the bedroom door.

An empty bottle stood beside the bed. A pair of trousers flopped from a chair. The bed was unmade. Face down on the floor beside it, his light hair darkening with blood, lay Cobalt.

21

Oliver dragged Cobalt on to his back. Cobalt groaned and mumbled and made it clear he was alive if far from well. Rain felt her legs weaken and sank on to the edge of the bed.

'This is terrible,' she said. Her voice was faint.

Rather more robustly Cobalt asked: 'What hit me?' It was a question Rain would have doubted if she had not been there to hear it.

Oliver picked up the empty bottle. 'This, I should think.' He peered at the end of it, wondering about bloodstains.

Cobalt sat up, swore and rubbed his head. He inspected the blood that came off on his hand and swore again.

Oliver said: 'Who hit you, James?'

Cobalt was struggling to his feet, muttering. It sounded more like anger than injury. He lurched out of the room. From the bathroom they heard running water. When he reappeared his hair was soaked, he had taken off his shirt and was carrying a large square of sticking plaster. He held this out to Rain. 'Let's see what your nursing is like. Can you find the hole and plug it with this?'

'I might if I could reach. Sit down.'

They were back in the sitting room. He cast around for a chair, shoved some papers aside with a foot and perched on the edge of an armchair. Rain dabbed at the blood with a wad of paper handkerchiefs. She was relieved the cut was small and not very deep although it was bleeding steadily. She did her best with the sticking plaster. 'You ought to get this looked at by a doctor if it doesn't stop bleeding soon.'

'It'll be all right.'

'But what happened?' She was almost angry that he was taking it so calmly.

He actually laughed at her. She stood there, the blood-soaked tissues in her hand, and he laughed at her. Irritated, she swept away, flushed the tissues down the lavatory and returned to hear Oliver pursuing her question.

Cobalt got up from his chair as though nothing had happened to put him off his stroke. 'Let's have that wine, shall we?'

'But, James . . .'

He met her in the doorway. She was effectively barring his way. He smiled that exasperating smile again. 'You know how it is, Rain. Occupational hazard.'

Gently he pushed her aside and went to fetch the wine. When he carried the tray back he had already poured his own glass and drunk half of it. He topped it up, then gestured to Oliver and said: 'Help yourselves.'

Oliver poured glasses for himself and Rain. Cobalt was ready for a refill. Rain caught Oliver's eye. She said to Cobalt: 'How's the head?'

'The wound is fine. It hardly penetrated the hangover.' He laughed loudly.

Oliver said: 'Look, you don't want to treat a thing like

this too lightly. You were knocked out cold, and a head wound coupled with alcohol can be serious.'

'Yes,' said Cobalt and took another gulp. 'Oh yes, I've covered inquests in my time, too.' He adopted a stilted voice as though he were giving evidence. 'The deceased was a well-nourished man in his mid-forties. There was some evidence of organic degeneration caused by over-use of alcohol. The fatal injury was a blow to the head, not a very heavy blow but the deceased had taken a substantial amount of alcohol in the hours before he suffered the injury, and the effect of alcohol is to increase the flow of blood to the brain so that, et cetera, et cetera, et cetera. Therefore I give the cause of death as cerebral haemorrhage.'

He shot Rain a mischievous smile. 'How am I doing? Have I passed the memory test? Would you like me to totter along a white line? Would I be fit to cover World War Three for the *Daily Post* if it broke out right now?'

'Oh yes,' she conceded. 'All of that, but you're drunk and you seem to have forgotten who came here just now and hit you.'

He reached for the bottle but Oliver got there first and pretended to be reading the label. He said: 'Who was it, James?'

'I'll give you a description. It was a short dark Frenchman. I didn't see any more because there's no light in my passage and the light on the stairs was out. And no, before either of you start making up theories, I didn't take him into the bedroom. I don't know how I got in there. So that ruins your idea that I was hit with the bottle standing beside the bed. He couldn't have rushed passed me into the bedroom, seized the bottle as a convenient weapon—he couldn't have known it was there, anyway—and then dashed back out to hit me before dragging me . . . do you see what I'm saying?'

Oliver felt he was being ridiculed and tried not to look offended. 'All right, so it wasn't the bottle by the bed. What was it, then?'

Cobalt shook his head, which might have meant he didn't know or might have been admonishment for Oliver who was still holding the bottle of wine. Cobalt leaned forward and took it from him.

Rain finished her glass. 'If you're sure you're all right, James, we ought to be on our way.' They had not told him they were not going back to Antibes and she saw no point in trying to talk to him about Maurin or Sabine Jourdain or Barbara Coleman while he was in this state.

'I'm sure.' He tipped the bottle up so that the last of the liquid flowed into his glass. They stood to leave and as an afterthought Cobalt got up, too, and saw them to the door.

Rain wanted to say she would phone in the morning, or later that evening perhaps, to check that he was all right, but she guessed he would reject her concern. The door closed between them.

Rain and Oliver began down the stairs. The place felt more sinister than it had ever done before. When the light went out, Rain had the suspicion they were not alone on the stairs, that someone was watching them, perhaps they actually passed close to a figure pressed into the shadows. She found herself listening for breathing and when there was a shout from below her heart pounded, foolishly, because it was only the whoop of a homecoming child racing his brother into the building.

Rain and Oliver crossed the rue de Rivoli and looked up at Cobalt's flat. Rain said: 'I don't know whether to admire him or despise him. Fancy being able to dismiss an incident like that!'

Oliver said he guessed it was partly because Cobalt had led the sort of life where being thumped over the head with a bottle was not a unique experience.

'What's the other part?'

'Sheer relief. He was relieved to have got off so lightly. When he opened the door and saw who'd come for him he didn't expect to be waking up at all. A drop of blood and a headache would be sheer relief after that.'

Rain asked whether he had told Oliver much about his Fleet Street days, and Oliver could name some of the papers Cobalt had worked for. 'I'd like to know a bit more,' Rain said.

'When we get home.'

'Yes, of course.'

They booked into a hotel and Oliver suggested they eat at one of the restaurants in the old town. It was quite close. Rain rallied although she would have been happy to stay where she was, lying on the bed. She wanted above all else to sleep and blot out the terrifying events of the day.

She adjusted the scarf to cover the bruises forming on her neck. It was best, she decided, not to dwell on the thought that this evening was one she was not meant to see. If there were to be nightmares, she could not control that; but she would not waste her waking time frightening herself with a terror which was past.

Many of the buildings in the old town were six storeys high and the lanes so narrow that all but pedestrians were banned. Built for defence and coolness in a hot climate, the old town was a compact and charming maze for the modern tourist.

The restaurant was popular, with a good atmosphere. At other times they might have drawn the evening out. Instead they left early and began the walk to the hotel. And then they spotted the Tunisian pedlar.

He came out of a restaurant, his bags bobbing on his arm as usual, and spoke to two men in a darkened doorway. As Rain and Oliver approached the three shrank back, but when Rain looked round she saw the pedlar peering after her.

She clung to Oliver's arm. 'He's watching us.'

'So what? We were watching him. I expect he's trying to think where he saw us before.'

A few yards on they turned a corner and when she next looked back Rain saw the Tunisian again. He was gaining on them. She whispered: 'I'm sure he's following us. Let's hurry.'

But hurrying did no good. Whenever she looked round the tall, robed figure was getting closer. Oliver said he felt foolish running away and it would be best to slow and let the man pass. Rain could not bring herself to put this to the test.

Oliver said: 'We'll go into a bar until he's gone.'

The bar was crowded but they found a table in the centre, amidst noisy tourists. Rain sat facing the door, and did not relax until she had seen the pedlar walk by. She sighed. 'Thank goodness, he's gone.'

Oliver patted her hand. 'Of course he has, he wasn't really interested in us. Why should he be?' When the waiter came he ordered coffee.

'I've no idea, but no idea either why he hit Tim two nights ago. I've no idea why a lot of things have happened.'

Oliver squeezed her hand. He thought she was overwrought and the best way of dealing with that was a good night's sleep. He hoped it would not be too long before she was brave enough to leave the bar. When the coffee came he started to talk about a detail at the restaurant they had just left. Suddenly he stiffened.

Rain spun round and saw what he had seen. The pedlar was behind her. The bar had an entrance from another street and he had come in that way, threading between the tables, offering his goods, but with most of his attention on her. She did not wait to see what he would do when he reached her. With a gasp she was on her feet and pushing her way to the door. Oliver dropped some cash on the table and rushed after her.

He caught her up outside and snatched at her arm. 'Rain!'

'He's coming!' she said frantically.

'No, he's not. He's going around the tables with his bags, like he always does.'

'Then why not the other bars? Why the one we went into?'

'You're being hysterical. Why should he?' His question trailed away as the pedlar burst out of the bar, saw them and ran forward.

Now Oliver was running, pulling Rain along. Somewhere behind him the huge figure loped. Oliver cast the occasional glance back. The intensity on the man's face was all the persuasion he needed to increase his speed. Oliver was convinced the man was closing the gap, he refused to think what might happen when he caught up with them. The slap, slap, slap of the pedlar's sandals grew louder.

A group of Dutch tourists swarmed out of a restaurant behind Rain and Oliver and the pedlar lost ground. 'Quick!' Rain said, unnecessarily. 'Down here.'

They took an alley which doubled back the way they had come and then they branched off it. They slowed to give themselves a respite but realized in the succeeding moment that they had run into a dead end. There were no bars to slip into, nothing but shuttered shops and a blank wall six storeys high. There was no choice but to backtrack. As they regained the other alley, they saw the pedlar pounding towards them. They ran away, although this was taking them further into the old town when they had hoped to escape from it.

Again the gap between them was closing, again they used the cover of straggling tourists to disguise the direction they took. They had a choice of alleys. Rain said, exasperated, that each route led to the same point and that meant back to the Tunisian.

'Then how the hell do we get out of this?' Oliver demanded.

She knew he was feeling ridiculous to be running away and cross not to have achieved it. She made a helpless gesture. And then a dreadful noise began. Oliver leapt. 'What's that?'

It was a cacophony of metallic sounds, a rattling, rumbling, roaring, high-pitched noise and it was growing even louder. Oliver said: 'It must be a vehicle. I thought none were allowed in here.'

Rain hushed him. She was working out where the sound was coming from. 'This way.'

Oliver was close behind as she ran towards the pedlar, then cut off to the side. Trundling along the lane they entered was a line of galvanized garbage trucks, empty and snaking on their rounds to collect the day's debris. Rain raced down the lane to meet it, thrust herself into a doorway to let the head of the column pass, and drew Oliver in beside her.

She clambered over the side of the last truck and crouched down out of sight. Oliver followed, his face a mixture of disgust, relief and amusement. They were rattled and bounced as the tail of the column swung about, but they were safe. In the end, they were safe. When the trucks paused while negotiating a particularly tricky turn, and Rain recognized where they were and that it was a good place to be, they climbed out and took a short route out of the old town and back to the hotel.

By the time they reached their room they were laughing uncontrollably.

'I thought you were exaggerating,' Oliver admitted, 'until I saw the menace in that fellow's eyes.'

'I remember the moment when you decided to believe me. It was when you began running faster than I was.' She stretched out on the bed.

'Why didn't you tell me you were going to jump into a refuse truck?'

'Because you might have stopped me. I knew if I got in you'd come too. There wasn't time to argue about it.'

Oliver looked with distaste at his clothes. 'Well, I'm never doing it again, just remember that, will you?'

'You won't have to. And don't make a fuss, you were lucky the trucks were empty. Even if they'd been half full it would have been our only escape route.'

Oliver looked hard at her to see whether she could possibly be serious, but she had closed her eyes. He was still wondering when he realized she had fallen asleep.

He sat quietly, thinking the thoughts he could not while she was awake. He was reliving the harrowing moment when he discovered her unconscious, her neck in a ligature. It seemed impossible that it had happened, but from his pocket he unwound the cord and let it dangle from his hand.

It was such a simple thing, but once the straight end was threaded through the loop to make a noose it became a murderous weapon. The cord was the sort anybody might have. What would it normally be used for? Hanging a picture, he thought. It would be ideal for that.

Rain stirred. He wound the cord tightly and buried it in the bottom of his trouser pocket. He did not feel he ought to throw it away but it must be kept from her sight. He went to her, gently persuaded her to wake sufficiently to undress and get under the covers. He helped her out of her things and put them on hangers so they would be less creased by morning.

Drawing the sheet up over her shoulders he saw how the bruising on her neck was developing. He caught himself repeatedly checking that the door to the room was locked, the key in the lock so that another could not be inserted from outside. He even checked the window.

But he did not feel silly about being so careful. Sabine Jourdain had been shot, Barbara Coleman had been abducted, someone had tried to strangle Rain, the reception clerk and Cobalt had been beaten up, and Rain and he had been chased through a maze by a man with a ferocious determination on his face. He lay awake for a long time looking for possible connections between the incidents and listening to Rain breathing.

22

They woke very early next day, sent down for coffee and sat talking in their room. Rain appeared quite recovered, apart from the deepening bruises on her neck. She sat in front of the mirror and wound the scarf to conceal them.

'That,' said Oliver, 'was the work of a bungling amateur.'

She shot him an alarmed look. 'Well, don't let's criticize him, it could have been fatal.'

'I've been thinking about it. A professional would have done the job properly. You wouldn't have had a chance.'

'Perhaps he was interrupted. He could have panicked and run off. People were wandering in and out of that room the whole time, he might have been seen.'

'No one suggested it when you were found. The man who spoke English didn't relay that to me. No, I don't think your attacker was seen. I think he was an amateur who either thought he'd succeeded or else was so nervous about what he was doing that he left knowing there hadn't been time to kill you.'

Rain felt sick as she listened to him. Oliver said: 'A

real professional would probably have used a finer cord. He'd have to pull it very tight and hold it there for about three minutes to make sure. He could quite easily accomplish it in a public place of that sort because everyone's attention is drawn away from the area where you were sitting. When one turns from gazing at those windows, it isn't very easy to see.'

'What sort of string is it?'

'Picture cord, I think.'

'Have you still got it?'

'Yes, but . . .'

'It's all right. I don't mind seeing it now.' She was not convinced that was true.

He brought it out of his trouser pocket, held the straight end and let it uncoil in front of her until the loop swung down. She swallowed hard, then stretched out her hand and took it. She said: 'Would it have been strong enough?'

'The man who used it must have thought so.'

She fingered the cord, was reminded of the horrifying moment when she felt a constriction around her throat and the colours of the room receded. She made an effort to sound relaxed. 'It's new, isn't it? The ends are cleanly cut, they haven't frayed and they haven't got dirty. It looks as though somebody cut a length of it and set out to kill me with it.'

'I doubt whether it would be much use as evidence if you went to the police. Their forensic tests could probably prove it had been around your neck and in my pocket, but it's been badly mistreated as a piece of evidence.'

She smiled. 'It would probably indicate to the police that you did it. No, I don't see any purpose in reporting this. All I want to do is collect our stuff from the flat and head for the airport.' She returned the cord.

Oliver coiled it slowly in the palm of his hand. He said: 'Maurin asked the taxi driver to take him to the museum yesterday. He'd have picture cord, wouldn't he?'

Rain refilled their cups. 'He would, but so would countless other people in Nice. If Maurin wanted to kill me, surely he wouldn't attempt it in a public place where he might be recognized.' She was shocked how easy it was becoming to imagine the people around her guilty of murder: Joseph, Tim, and now Maurin.

Oliver said: 'If Joseph got Tim—or anyone else—to kill Sabine Jourdain, Maurin probably knows it. He's involved in the deception about the Durances and he admits abducting Barbara Coleman. For all we know he could be involved in the murder. Once he knew you'd found out about the paintings, he might have thought you'd go on to discover the truth about the murder. He could have a very good reason to kill you.'

She shook her head. 'I don't really think Maurin had anything to do with it, not that nightmare in the Chagall museum and not the murder.'

They left soon after, driving around the bay on a deserted road. Holidaymakers were dawdling over hotel breakfasts and asking themselves whether today would bring a repeat of yesterday's sunshine. Local people were busy among the shops and markets inland or thinking about starting their working day. No one at all was on the beach.

Rain sped along the wide empty road between the blue sea and the high mountains where ochre patches were precarious villages. Far ahead the outline of a fort signalled Antibes, beyond it the Cap ran out to sea. She had no regrets about going home. She would complete the packing, telephone her office to say she was on her way, ring Cobalt and ask him to look after the murder case and the inquiry into the provenance of the Durances. But when she got to the flat she found it ransacked.

She suspected something had happened because the door to the flat was open and light fell across the landing. Oliver had gone to a shop and she was on her own. She stood with her hand on the door jamb and surveyed the wreckage. All the internal doors were open and she could make out the tumbled travel bags she had left half-packed and which now spilled their contents across the room. The cupboards and drawers in the kitchen were emptied on to the floor. Cushions in the sitting room were flung about, minus their covers.

There was a step behind her and she whirled round to meet the knowing look of a woman from another flat. 'I am so sorry,' the woman began without a trace of sorrow in her eyes. Rain heard her out. There had been a noise in the night. This morning they had noticed the door open, seen the mess. Oh yes, they had called the police. It would be best if Rain called them also.

Oliver bounded upstairs, and slowed when he saw the figures on the landing. 'Oh no! Not *now*.'

The woman repeated that she was sorry. She still did not look it. Rain thanked her, ushered Oliver into the flat and shut the door. She rang the police.

'I suppose we shouldn't touch anything until they get here,' said Oliver.

'I hope they hurry, there's a lot of clearing up to do before we can leave.'

'What's been stolen?'

'Everything seems to be here. I think it was a search rather than a robbery.'

'What on earth could anyone be searching for?'

'Something small, which might have been hidden almost anywhere. Look at the way the pots of herbs have been tipped out. And why else should the cushion covers have been ripped off? Or the kitchen clock taken off the wall?'

They sat on the balcony in the sun, depressed at both the break-in and the delay it would cause. Rain said she would make some coffee, surely the police couldn't object to that much interference with whatever evidence the mess offered them? She opened the fridge and Oliver heard her give an exclamation.

'What's wrong?'

'I hadn't expected all the containers in here to be emptied out, too!' She slammed the door on the mess. He opened it, unwilling to believe in so detailed a search. There was a deep plastic salad tray and the milk and orange juice had been tipped from their cartons into it. Everything which had been kept hygienically wrapped was ripped open and thrown into the tray.

Oliver said: 'This is crazy. Whoever would do a thing like that? What are we supposed to be keeping in there?'

Rain had no explanation. She picked up an emptied canister from the kitchen floor. 'Unless you want to scoop it off the floor, there's no coffee.'

Oliver plucked a bottle of white wine from the rack in the fridge door. 'Presumably our visitor didn't have to pour this out to see there was nothing else in the bottle. This is all we have to drink.' He rummaged for a knife to cut the seal.

They had settled on the balcony again when the doorbell rang. To their surprise the police who stood there were Foucard and Denis. Rain thought a burglary beneath the notice of men with an unsolved murder on their hands. She did not say so. Foucard did.

'You see, we have to take an interest in everything which hinges on the strange case of Sabine Jourdain.' He took a glass from a shelf in an opened cupboard and advanced on the bottle of wine. Denis hung back, unsure whether he dared emulate his superior. He did not.

Oliver took pity, offered a glass which Denis had no problem accepting. 'It's truly all we have,' said Oliver. 'Take a look in the fridge.'

The men looked blankly at him. Rain saw they were still to go on pretending Foucard and Denis understood no English. She chose not to let them know she had proof this was a deception. She translated Oliver's remark. Denis whisked open the fridge and sucked on his teeth. Foucard said: 'They were very thorough, your friends, but did they find what they were looking for?'

Rain said: 'Hardly friends, Monsieur Foucard. And I've no idea what they came for or what they took.'

'This flat belongs to your colleague in London, I believe? Tell me about this colleague.'

Rain said he was a very ordinary middle-aged journalist, a staid sort of man who wrote about local government matters. Foucard said: 'You make it sound as though he is the most boring man in the world.'

'I had never thought of him like that before.'

It was a short hop for Foucard to suggest that as her colleague was such a dull man it was unlikely the flat had been searched for something belonging to him, more likely that the hunt was for something belonging to Rain or Oliver.

Rain laughed. 'I'm interesting enough to have my flat broken into, am I?'

Foucard made a little gesture with his head. 'But of course. You are interesting to me because of the events of the night of Sabine Jourdain's murder. Have you remembered more, perhaps, about that night? Or are you still going to tell me that you were alone, alone all evening except for a half hour in a café?'

Rain turned away impatiently. 'I've told you all I can about that.'

'All you can? Or all you care to?'

She stood looking towards the balcony and beyond it the sea. He was right, she did know more. She knew who the man on the boat with Sabine Jourdain was. But she had not known when Foucard last spoke to her and he could not know she had found out. She decided not to shift her position. Telling him would mean more questions and delay her departure. Tim would almost certainly deny having been on board and there was already no one to corroborate her story about the disturbance in the lounge. Foucard would reject her fresh information as he had rejected the old.

There was a curious silence. She looked round. Foucard's eyes were bright, a strange expression in them. Then she felt something on her arm and discovered her scarf had come undone. As she had turned from him it had slipped down. Casually she lifted it to her neck and retied it.

She picked her way over the scattered things and went on to the balcony. Foucard followed. He said softly as he looked up at a gull wheeling above coral roofs: 'Perhaps you would care to tell me instead where you have been since yesterday morning, and what has happened to you?'

'Is that interesting, too?'

'If you do not wish people to become interested, you must tie your scarf more securely. I have seen such bruising before.' He waited for her. The gull screamed. He said: 'Tell me, Miss Morgan, who attempted to kill you and why should anyone have done so?'

Rain gripped the iron rail of the balcony. It seemed a long time since she had stood there watching the boats and noticing how brief lack of caution led to trouble. She had never heard Foucard speak so soothingly, so encouragingly. His abrasiveness, the challenge he always

206

presented her, was gone. It would be very simple to tell him everything and leave him to unscramble the truth contained in the confusion. But she brought herself up sharply. It would not be simple at all, because nothing she had told him so far had been trusted.

She ignored the lure. 'We went to Nice and stayed overnight at a hotel. Oliver wanted to do some sightseeing and we felt too tired to drive back afterwards.' She named the hotel and the restaurant where they had eaten. Foucard concealed his disappointment.

Rain asked whether there was any progress in the murder inquiry. It was difficult not to achieve the overtones of saying: 'Haven't you solved that yet?' She decided she had failed because he grew hard again, talking about lack of cooperation. He said: 'But this case will be solved, all of us on the investigating team feel certain of that. We shall have our answer. We have certain leads and each one will be painstakingly pursued.'

From inside they heard Denis and Oliver. Oliver was trying to find out, in very slow English, when they could tidy up the flat and leave Antibes. He still had hopes of the lunchtime flight. Rain translated. Foucard said: 'One of our officers will come and look for fingerprints later today. You may clear up after that.'

Foucard spoke rapidly to Denis and they made movements to leave. Foucard said to Rain: 'I shall see you again, Miss Morgan. Providing, of course, that you take care to stay alive.'

23

Rain and Oliver heard Foucard and Denis rattle downstairs and then cobblestones rang beneath their feet. Sun struck across the room, bounced fiercely up from the shiny surfaces of containers littering the floor and tossed shadows from the drawers and furniture which had been hurled about. A gull floated down to the balcony rail, his shadow an enormous presence beating about the room.

A car engine throbbed, people called greetings, there was the creak of shutters opening in one flat and the sound of a radio in another. Oliver took Rain's hand. 'Come on, let's get out of here. We can't stand around waiting for the fingerprints man, he could be hours.'

'I'll leave the key with the neighbour we spoke to. She looks the type who'd enjoy letting the police in.'

The woman confirmed she would be pleased to help and this time looked as though she meant what she said. Rain and Oliver went out into the sun. Oliver suggested a bar, then the beach. Rain said: 'My conscience dictates that I drive down the Cap and interview Peter Leary. Would you like to come and take some photographs?'

'No, but I will. I don't think you should go alone.'

The flowers climbing the walls of the villa bobbed in a gentle breeze, inside the house a man was singing. He broke off at the ring of the doorbell. Peter Leary welcomed Rain with a warm smile. She explained who Oliver was, and the smile was switched to him.

'Coffee?' asked Leary, showing them into a cool kitchen. 'I refuse to think about alcohol before lunchtime. The day slips away too easily, I have to be rather disciplined.' The pan of water was boiled, he poured a spoonful through a filter over a ceramic coffee pot on an old fashioned stove. 'I'm here for the light, not the cheap alcohol.' The coffee grounds were moistened, compacted. He filled the filter.

Then he said: 'If it sounds as though I've said that before, you're right. I have to remind myself. There are too many distractions here, too many excuses for looking and thinking and seeing people and delaying painting.'

'How long have you been here?'

'I came out in November and took this place for six months. It's what I've always promised myself and thought I'd never manage.' He refilled the filter. 'Unfortunately my wife couldn't come because she teaches, but I expect that has curtailed my sightseeing and increased my output.'

Rain asked whether it had been an especially productive period. He said the studio was full of things to show her. 'I'm rather pleased with some of that stuff.'

Rain asked: 'Did Benedict Joseph like it?'

'Ben loved it. He's talking about an exhibition in New York.' He laughed. 'I must remember to be cautiously optimistic about that, there's nothing definite.'

Rain understood his caution. Leary belonged to that second string of artists, very good but never thrust into the public consciousness. Every few years he was rediscovered by an enthusiastic critic or gallery owner, although the success never gelled.

It happened to lots of people in all walks of life, and always looked like a pity. She questioned whether what they lacked was not ruthless ambition. If Joseph gave him an exhibition it could make a huge difference to Leary's reputation, yet she wondered how likely it was that Joseph would help him. They had started off friends but Joseph's first wife had left him for Leary.

Oliver, thinking along the same lines, asked: 'Has Joseph previously taken your work?'

'In the early days he was keen, but . . .'

Rain and Oliver thought they understood the 'but.' Leary went on: ' . . . he branched out, he got more choice. We lost touch.'

'Did you know he was going to be here?' Oliver asked with what Rain feared sounded like suspicion.

Leary topped up the filter. 'No, I'd no idea he comes to Antibes or in what style he lives when he's here.'

Oliver said that chartering the *Jonquil* was style indeed. 'Have you been on board?'

There was an embarrassed smile as Leary said: 'Oh no, I heard he was there so I walked through the harbour and took a look at it. I was astonished.'

'The interior is even more astonishing,' Rain promised him and mentioned the opulent chinoiserie.

Leary poured coffee into wide china cups and they sat around the rough wooden kitchen table and drank. He said: 'It was rather curious the way things happened. I wanted to meet Marius Durance—I've always especially admired his work and it seemed crazy to be so close and not come face to face with him. One day, when I felt bold enough I presented myself at his studio. It was locked but he has a flat on the ground floor of the same building. Have you been there?'

Rain said she had been into the studio but not the flat. Leary said: 'My French is only adequate and he doesn't speak English but we managed a conversation about the things that matter to us. I was very disappointed he didn't have anything of his to show me. Maybe it was locked away in the studio or maybe it was true he had nothing there. I'm afraid I usually have stuff unsold, I find it hard to imagine a studio without a few finished paintings lying around.'

Oliver asked: 'Did you meet him again?'

'Yes, I went to the flat a few times. He appeared to enjoy talking to me and invited me to call in whenever I was passing. I took some work to show him and he was very generous about it.'

'Did you always find him in the flat?' Oliver asked.

'Yes. If he was home at all he was in the flat. Then one day a couple of months ago he returned, just as I was leaving assuming I'd missed him. He said he'd been to see Ben who was living on the *Jonquil*. I told him I knew Ben and when I left Durance I went down to the harbour. I don't know whether I ever meant to call on Ben or not—it's been such a long time—but I was interested to see the boat. Durance had said it was big, but that was an understatement.'

Rain asked: 'How did you and Ben meet up again?'

'Durance told him I was living here. I didn't know that until Ben phoned this week and asked whether he could come over.'

Rain could see things from his perspective. Leary had been diffident about approaching Joseph although it might have advanced his career, but Durance appeared to have done it for him. Joseph had subsequently been to the villa on the Cap and talked about a show in New York. But her own perspective was different: Durance had told Joseph that Leary was living nearby but Joseph had done nothing about contacting his old friend until he needed an alibi for the night of the murder.

They went through to the studio. Leary's new paintings were vibrant studies making full play of the Mediterranean light. He deserved a much higher reputation and Rain wished she could trust Joseph to help him acquire one.

Leary talked about his work with eloquence and intelligence. Oliver photographed him. The paper would run a worthwhile feature. If Leary got nothing else, Rain would see to it that he got that. For herself, she wished she could have bought one of the paintings, she knew she had the ideal space for it on one of the walls of her long white sitting room in Kington Square.

They ate lunch in a shady restaurant and then Leary went back to his flower-hung villa. Rain and Oliver called at the flat but the fingerprints man had still not been. Oliver wanted to go to the beach. His friends were already there. Someone handed him a can of beer and Rain knew he intended to stay some time. She decided to be touristy and go and buy souvenirs.

But as she walked from the archway which linked the beach and the harbour, she saw Merlyn and Benedict Joseph driving away. On impulse she hung back until they had gone. Then she darted to the *Jonquil* . . .

There were no sounds aboard as she crossed the gangway. Ahead of her the doors to the lounge were open. She went straight in. The room was immaculate. Rain called out, asking if anyone was about. She heard only the slap of water against the harbour wall, the occasional cry of a gull. Then the door at the far end of the room opened and the steward, Ross, was with her.

'Mr and Mrs Joseph are not here,' he said in a formal tone. 'Would you like to leave a message for them?'

'I haven't come to see them. I've come to talk to you.'

He wore the slightest frown. 'How can I help you?'

'You can tell me where you and the rest of the crew were on the evening Sabine Jourdain was killed. And you can tell me who tidied up this room.'

'I don't understand.' Implacable.

'It's very easy to understand. Unless I get answers to my questions then you and the rest of the crew will find yourselves explaining to the police instead. Which would you prefer?'

He was too well schooled to betray emotion. 'The police have already asked us about this. I told them we knew nothing.'

'Quite. You lied to them. They won't like that.'

There was a pause while she feared the ploy had failed. Then he said: 'What do you propose to do with this information?'

'Nothing. Your neglect of duty is a matter between you and your employer. I'm not interested in that. I simply need to know where you all were.' She heard herself sounding very pompous but Ross didn't bridle. He was probably used to being spoken to by pompous individuals.

He said in a quiet voice: 'You'll give me your word that what I tell you will not get back to the Josephs? If they were to report it to the company the whole crew could lose their jobs.'

'Exactly. And if the police question the crew thoroughly then the company is certain to be informed, one way or another.'

Ross stepped forward and spoke even more softly. 'Very well. I'll trust you not to tell the Josephs, but why should you want to know?'

'Because it will help information about more important matters drop into place. Now, where were you?'

'On the *Mésalliance*. There was a party and some of

us were invited. The people who'd chartered her had flown to Paris for the weekend and her crew had a party. There were a lot of people there, from a number of boats.'

'Did the entire crew of the *Jonquil* go to this party?'

'No. A few were off duty that evening. Some who were working intended to slip away for an hour or so. But Mr and Mrs Joseph went out during the evening and, in the end, everyone on duty went to the party. The plan was to go in relays and not to leave the *Jonquil* unattended, but there was a muddle. I suddenly realized that unless one of the off duty staff had returned very early, there could be no one on board.'

'What about Sabine Jourdain? She was waiting here for me, wasn't she? She was expecting some supper. Surely you didn't all disappear and leave her alone?'

'You were late and so she ate. She said she always ate early and perhaps you wouldn't be able to come after all, so she'd eat.'

'Even so, you left her here alone afterwards.'

'When I went ashore she was in the study speaking to someone. I don't know who it was.'

'Did you think it was me?'

He frowned again. 'No, I knew it wasn't you.' Then his face brightened. 'Yes, of course. The reason I knew it wasn't you was that I could hear a man's voice. I went up to the door, meaning to look in on her before going, but there seemed to be an argument going on and I decided not to interrupt.'

'Who was the first of the crew to return?'

'I was. When I realized the boat could be unattended I ran straight back here.'

'And what did you find?'

'The lights were off. I went straight to the shade deck and checked the study and bar but there was no sign of the old woman or anybody else. Then I came down here, switched the light on and saw the room in disarray.'

Rain wanted him to be careful not to gloss. 'Don't tell me you tidied it all by yourself.'

'I wasn't going to. I did what I could. I cleared the pieces of smashed vase and flowers, I used towels to dry the water from the carpet, I rearranged the furniture. Then one of the others came and he helped me rehang the curtain and move the damaged screen.'

'What did you do with the screen?'

'We swapped it. There are six identical screens on board so that different room arrangements can be made. Only two are in use and the others are in a cabin used as a store. We exchanged the broken vase for a similar one from a guest cabin that isn't in use at present and we swapped the screen.'

'But the damage will be discovered eventually.'

'It could be years. When somebody decides to redo the rooms and wants all the screens they'll find out but probably not until then.'

'Show me the screen,' Rain said abruptly. He looked taken aback. She said: 'I want to see the damage.'

'All right.'

They moved along passages and down to the cabin deck. Rain could hear sounds of activity as the crew went about their business. The boat was just as it should have been on the night of the murder and had not been. Ross fetched the key to the storeroom. When he returned she asked: 'Do you know where the Josephs went that evening?'

'No.' He slid the key into the lock and pushed open the door. Rain saw the spare furnishings as he had described. Four heavy screens, one behind the other, were held in a recess behind a locking bar. The front screen was unmarked, but she had anticipated that. The one she insisted on inspecting was at the back.

Ross unlocked the bar and let it swing down. Then he began to shift the first screen and leaned it against an adjoining stretch of wall. When he got to the fourth screen he stood it up for her to inspect.

The fracture in the panel was hideous. Rain imagined the force with which the bronze bird must have been thrown. Seeing the screen confirmed for her everything she remembered about that evening, and proved Ross's story. She nodded. 'Thank you for showing me.'

As he folded the screen she stepped forward to look closely at the adjacent panel. She did not want Ross to know what had caught her eye. She asked him to hold the screen just where it was and she went round the back of it, out of his sight. Then she knelt down and ran her finger over a bullet hole.

$\int$he met Oliver on her way to the rue du Bateau. He was returning from the beach, face flushed by the sun. 'Have you bought all your souvenirs?' he asked.

'Not so much as a stick of rock.' She told him where she had been, what she had seen.

'Are you sure it was a bullet hole?'

'As certain as I can be.'

'But you had to squat down to look at it. Why should someone have fired so low?'

'I don't know.'

'What became of this putative bullet when it passed through the screen?'

'I checked, on the pretext of comparing the reverse sides of the screens. Behind the one in the lounge there's a hole through the wooden panelling.'

Oliver said: 'There's nothing to say the shot that damaged the screen and wall was fired on the night of the murder, is there?'

'No, and if it was the shot that killed Sabine Jourdain there'd have been blood in the lounge. I can't imagine

Ross tidying away signs of murder. I didn't find blood and I don't believe he did.'

'The police think she was killed by a stranger while walking through the harbour, and dumped in the water. But if they were to examine that bullet hole and find it was caused by the same sort of gun that killed her...'

'I can't suggest they do that.' She told him about her promise to Ross.

'That's all very well, but we're talking about murder.'

'I know, but we're not talking about positive proof. You said yourself, that hole could have been made at any time. If it was definitely linked to her death I might have to break a promise—which I'd hate doing because the repercussions for the crew could be very serious— but it's too vague to go to Foucard and run risks with other people's livelihoods.'

They reached the flat. The fingerprints man had still not been. Rain telephoned the police and spoke to an officer who was unconcerned whether she cleared up or not. He had no idea when the fingerprints expert might be free to call.

Oliver hung the clock back on the kitchen wall. 'What's the right time?'

She told him. The afternoon was wearing away. Oliver corrected the clock and set it in motion. He looked round. She was standing quite still, fingering the ends of her scarf.

'Rain?'

'Sorry. I was thinking about our intruder. What he was looking for was something very small if he was prepared to tip out tiny containers. I can only think of two things small enough and valuable enough: precious stones or drugs.'

'Unless he wanted to sniff the nutmeg he was out of luck.' Oliver put his arm around her. 'Look, let's forget

218

it. There's no damage done, there's no theft. Let's just shove everything back into the cupboards, clean the floor and go. We could be on the last flight.'

The telephone rang. Oliver passed the receiver to Rain. Cobalt went straight to the point. 'I've heard a funny story and I'm ringing to ask you if there's any truth in it. Has someone tried to harm you?'

'Where did you get that story from?'

'Just a contact. As I said before, people tell me things all the time. They're often rubbish, sometimes they're true, but I always have to listen.'

'Of course.' She wondered how much he had drunk to be explaining the trials of the journalist to her. She said: 'I want to know who gave you that information.'

'It wouldn't be fair to say. You know how a contact can be lost.' He broke off and she heard him coughing.

She said: 'Tell me what the story is and I'll tell you whether your contact is any good.'

'He says you were tricked into going to the Chagall museum on the pretext that Barbara Coleman would be there again. Instead, someone was sent to kill you. I gather he failed.'

'By a whisker. I have the bruises to prove it.'

Cobalt swore. 'I'd hoped it was an exaggeration. You mean they really tried to . . .'

'Yes. Oliver says it was an amateur job, but I promise you it was a good try.' She waited. Cobalt said nothing. She said: 'Come on, James. Let's hear his name.'

He ignored that. 'When did this happen?'

'Yesterday afternoon. Please, his name.'

'Before you came to my place?'

'Yes.'

He swore again. She said: 'Let me guess. Your contact also knew you were attacked yesterday. He knows so much about these things that he must be involved in some way, but he lets you have bits and pieces of information because you pay him.'

'He'd heard someone hit me, but that doesn't mean he was involved.'

'Did he refresh your memory about your attacker?' She hoped she did not sound too sarcastic, she did not want him to ring off.

'All right, I knew all along who came to the flat and thumped me. But I've no reason to tell you.'

'That's true, but neither have you got a reason to shield the person who tried to kill me.' He did not respond. She went on: 'I'll make another guess and you can tell me whether I'm right or way off target. You believe we were attacked for the same reason and probably by the same person. It's all to do with Barbara Coleman and the provenance of the Durances, isn't it? You were being frightened off because you'd started asking questions, but I was to be killed because I'd found some answers.'

Cobalt said irritably: 'I haven't been aiming to get you killed and I haven't discussed with anyone what you've found out.'

'But am I way off target?'

'Not way off. The contact is Georges, the man I mentioned earlier, who told me Edouard had been beaten up. Yes, I pay him for information. And yes, he knew I'd been hit.'

'Who hit you?'

Cobalt groaned, weary of her persistence. 'A smalltime crook who got caught in the crossfire when I was working on a story a couple of years ago. He ended up behind bars and made threats when he got out. Until yesterday it was all talk. When I saw him in the doorway I thought he'd come to settle that score. Today, when I heard what happened to you, I realized it wasn't that. I already knew he and his brother were responsible for beating up Edouard.'

'There's something I don't understand. Edouard invented that fake message about the museum but why did he send your crook up there after me? I can appreciate Edouard would rather have me wasting my time at the museum instead of going round to his flat and trying to persuade Barbara Coleman to leave, but sending someone to kill me was rather an over-reaction.'

'Rain, Edouard didn't send anyone to kill you. He just reported that you were asking questions, and explained how he'd dealt with it. He probably thought he'd been rather smart but today he discovered you were supposed to be dead.'

As they spoke the sky clouded, the brilliantly lit room darkened. A chill wind came through the open doors to the balcony. Rain shivered. There was going to be a storm.

She heard Cobalt's voice down the line. 'Rain? Are you still there?'

Her voice was faint. He did not hear her the first time, she had to repeat what she said. 'I think I was with Maurin when Edouard rang him.'

Oliver closed the balcony doors. Through the glass they could see the sea streaked with shades of grey. The mountains that had given the scene its depth and colour were now vague grey shapes, like the background of a Japanese print.

Rain ended the phone call. 'You were right,' she said to Oliver. 'Everything points to Maurin.'

She was appalled at being forced to accept this. Sabine Jourdain had been killed because of what she was prepared to say, Barbara Coleman had been kept out of the way because of what she knew and Rain was to be killed before she could publish the story. No wonder Maurin told her she could believe what she liked as she could prove nothing. He knew by then that he would kill her, because when his telephone rang Edouard said she would be at the museum. It presented a far better opportunity for an unsolved murder than killing her on his own premises.

Oliver was happy to be vindicated. 'Well, I never liked him. I always said so.'

He was slapping about with a dustpan and brush, getting up the worst of the spilled coffee and other foods. Rain was assembling the vacuum cleaner ready to finish the job. It was an unsuitably domestic scene for two people labelling someone a murderer. The conversation ended when the vacuum cleaner started up. While Rain used it Oliver did a few more chores in preparation for leaving the flat, finishing by packing their bags.

The sky was gun-metal but the deluge had not come when they set out for a café. They tried to talk of other things than murder and violence but there were too many reminders. Rain worried how long she would bear the bruises, whether it would still be cold enough in London for her to wear high-necked sweaters when she got back.

The *fromagiers* and sellers of glistening fish and plump fruits and vegetables had cleared their stalls from the market hours ago and left the place to scavenging pigeons. Now the pigeons were leaving, confused by the premature darkness into believing night had fallen. Lights were on in the shops and houses as Rain and Oliver approached the Bar de la Marine.

Oliver wanted to go there because it had a sheltered terrace where they could sit outside, but it was too full of memories: it was the place where Rain had sat on her own while Sabine Jourdain was fighting for her life on board the *Jonquil*, where Tim had left behind his wallet, where Rain had first seen the pedlar.

She felt exhausted and defeated. The Great Idea had become a major disaster, she had been lucky to escape with her life. Some words of Foucard's churned in her mind: *'I shall see you again, Miss Morgan. Providing, of course, that you take care to stay alive.'*

Oliver reached across and squeezed her hand. It was odd to have to think of him as someone who had saved her life. He was so much better at getting her into scrapes. But he had been there at the right time, he had acted swiftly and effectively and she was alive.

He said: 'Would you like another drink, or shall we go and get some souvenirs? We've got time before the last flight.'

'I'll take the drink, please. I'm not sure I need reminding of this trip.'

He signalled to the waitress, then said: 'If you change your mind we might be able to get something at the airport.'

She shook her head. 'I don't want anything. That piece of cord will be quite sufficient to bring every detail flooding back.'

ind flurried through the streets. Pigeons found sheltered ledges, dogs that were normally unconcerned snarled as their owners tugged them on leashes. People were edgy, too.

'This looks like the end of the world,' said Oliver who had ordered a beer. Rain never knew how it was that a man who spoke no word of a foreign language could master the intricacies of ordering a favourite type of beer in any country on earth.

Plane trees tossed in the wind. Petals from somebody's pot plant dusted across the street. Arms reached out of high windows to haul in washing. Oliver's beach friends straggled into the café, grumbling at the abrupt change of weather.

They chattered like starlings denied a roost, but the red-haired girl sat silent, as though her mind was far away. She took no interest in Rain but this time she did not care about Oliver either, or anyone else. The others talked around her and across her, as she sat looking down at her glass. She was not bothering to drink.

Another woman asked where Tim was. Tim, she was

told, had turned back as they neared the café, saying he would come later. His friends Jock and Tony were there. Altogether the beach group occupied three tables close to Rain and Oliver.

One of the men, bearded, with roughly patched jeans and a loud laugh, leaned on the back of Rain's chair, his head close to hers, and talked to Oliver as though she were not there. After a spell of this, during which he gave no hint of moving, Rain decided to escape. She rose, the chair tipped with the man's weight. She told Oliver she had changed her mind about the souvenirs.

'Shall I see you back here?' he asked.

'No, come to the flat.' That was a more reliable plan if they meant to catch the next flight.

The man slid into her chair, still talking, apparently unaware she had ever been there. She walked towards the lanes of shops, the wind fluttering the ends of her scarf. She supposed it made her look jaunty, yet she felt anything but that. She tried to remember why a gathering storm upset people. There were sensible, scientific explanations about the effect of the changes in air pressure. The result was a feeling of anxiety. Faces around her were shut in, people failed to concentrate on what they were doing and there would be more driving accidents. Every task, every decision was an unusual effort.

Children were bickering, mothers scolded. Rain passed them, looking in shop windows where she had previously admired goods. The colours which had appealed were now crude, robbed of the sunlight.

She felt cross with herself for her inability to choose. Pressed against a window, she bullied herself to reach a decision. Wind rattled an awning above her head. The shopkeeper locked his door against her.

She moved away, uncertain where to go, then ran down an alleyway and across the Place Nationale. Waiters were folding sunshades, removing tables and chairs. A handful of figures scurried away, otherwise the square was empty. There were no shadows.

Around a corner, next to the shop where the key had been cut, she reached a gallery with an exhibition of ceramics. A black-haired woman with a long, sad face was inside. She made a show of welcoming Rain, her words lost in the shrieks of two girls as their skirts blew high.

'You would like something special? For a present, perhaps?'

'Yes,' said Rain. It was going to be a present for herself, a comfort after the bad things she had endured. She would take home something special and beautiful so that she would not remember the Côte d'Azur only for the bad things. The gallery was showing the work of several good craftsmen potters, some local and some not. Against the plain walls and fittings, the form, glaze and colour of the pottery were shown to advantage.

Rain narrowed her choice to three pieces. There was a tiny bowl, wafer-thin and coloured with flowing shapes in grey and ochre. She held it, enjoying its matt texture and its feather weight. There was a shallow bowl with handles that looked like twisted ropes and a clever glaze which was sometimes green, sometimes silver. And there was a vase, a sensuous white form.

The woman put the three pieces on a table for Rain to compare more easily. Rain lifted each and saw how the dark blobs of their shadows stretched to magnified shapes as she held and turned them. She pictured a corner of her flat, a table lamp illuminating the soft sheen of the vase, side-lighting sending a wavy shadow along a white wall.

She bought the vase. She knew Oliver would say what was the use of a vase whose line would be ruined if you stuck flowers in it. She knew she had better not tell him how much it had cost. She did not care. She had her beautiful souvenir.

As she had said the pot was a present she did not stop the woman gift-wrapping it in lavish style. A few minutes later she was hurrying through the sombre squares and lanes.

Oliver, she decided, would have to wait until London before he saw the pot. It would be a shame to undo the wrapping before they travelled. She tucked the parcel under her arm and ran.

She climbed the dark, stepped alley from the market place to the rue du Bateau and emerged opposite her car parked on the cobbles. Oliver had not loaded their things into it, but she still hoped he was in the flat rather than the café. She looked up, but there were no clues.

It struck her how tatty many of the buildings appeared now the lack of sun had robbed them of their charm. She opened the street door with just the slightest qualm, remembering the night Foucard and Denis had stepped out of its darkness.

As she mounted the stairs she heard a radio playing in one flat, a woman's voice in another. Then she was twisting the handle and discovering Oliver was not home. He was easily waylaid by anyone who asked him to stay and drink.

She went inside, the door clicked behind her. It was not until she was in the sitting room, leaning forward to put her precious parcel on a table, that she realized with a flash of panic that she was not alone.

She stopped instantly, the pot in her outstretched hands. She did not waste time thinking it could be

Oliver whose quiet movement she had sensed in the bedroom. If it were Oliver he would have called out to her, come to meet her as soon as he heard the key in the lock.

Gradually she straightened, gathered the parcel to her as though her instinct to protect it somehow protected her too. Her eyes were wide, fixed on the partly open door of the bedroom. There was no sound, but the fear along her spine insisted that someone was there.

Foucard had once gone to that door, thrown it wide, given the room an all-embracing glance, satisfied his curiosity. She entirely lacked the courage to approach it. Without even realizing it, she had begun to back away.

It was foolish to cling to the pot, she knew that, but was unable to persuade herself to part with it. She ought to put it down. She could put it beside the wooden table lamp on the cupboard by the door. Or she could set it down on a shelf alongside an empty flower jug. She ought to put it down, anywhere, and take up a weapon. But what? To reach the things most useful to defend herself she would have to go near the bedroom and she was still, uncontrollably, backing off.

She had no doubt her entry had been heard, that the soft sound she had only just noticed was of someone ducking out of sight. It was no comfort to think he might be as frightened as she was.

She prayed for Oliver to come crashing into the flat and take control. But she had been lucky once, it was too much to hope for another equally timely arrival. She must get to the door and run away.

Yet in the time it would take her to reach the café, tell Oliver and return with him, the flat would be empty and she would never know who her intruder was. There were no signs of a search this time. Whoever had come last night had been determined to find something but must have left without doing so. It was more probable he had returned than that someone else had come.

Rain felt the cool surface of a cupboard behind her. She was only feet away from escape. Moving backwards, she negotiated her way silently to the door. She had a plan. She insisted on knowing who her intruder was, and so she would wait down by the car to see who emerged from the building.

She moved a few more inches and made another plan. If she went out into the rue du Bateau her suspicions might latch on to an innocent person coming from one of the other flats. She would wait on the landing instead.

The door handle was against her back. She turned round so she could twist it and run. Her hand was slippery with sweat and the handle slid from her grasp. It shot back to its resting position.

The sound startled her. She snatched at the handle and as she did so the parcel slipped. She grabbed it, then wrenched the handle. The door opened six inches and she saw a sliver of dark landing, stairs coiling away to the street.

Behind her she felt the vibration of feet. Escape was blocked as a hand reached over her shoulder and slammed the door. Then her shoulder was in a fierce grip and she was spun into the room. She held the precious pot safely to her as she thudded against the wall of the sitting room.

And as she hit the wall, the breath knocked out of her, she saw the intruder for the first time.

Tarquin Poulteney-Crosse stood facing her, his colour high, his hands clenched. He was breathing noisily, a hand clawed through his hair.

Rain made an effort to control herself, control the

situation. She found her coldest voice: 'Tim, what do you think you are doing?'

The headmistressy tone should have reduced him to an ill-behaved schoolboy. He did not react. She said: 'Why are you in here?'

His hands were restless, clenching and unclenching. He did not move away, nor take his eyes off her.

He said between gasps: 'I was looking for something.'

'Drugs?'

'If you know, why ask?'

She removed one hand from her parcel. The movement was a mistake. He tensed again. She leaned back against the wall and said wearily: 'If you think I'm going to attack you, forget it. You're bigger than me, you're stronger than me and you've just proved you're more violent than me. Why don't we sit down?'

She did not think it wise to add she had suffered so many traumatic incidents in a few days that this was a minor one, nor that her knees had turned to water and refused to hold her up any longer.

He said nothing and she went, with smooth, unflustered movements, to the couch and dropped on to the yielding cushions and prayed for Oliver to come and quickly. Sabine Jourdain had faced Tim in a rage and Sabine Jourdain was dead.

He was still standing there, behind her now, and she was acutely aware of the significance of that. The person who had nearly strangled her had come at her from behind. She was desperate to turn and watch him, to find out what he was doing, defend herself if need be.

But she dared not turn and admit her fear. Her game was to pretend a confidence she did not feel. She must not let a nervous glance betray her. If she did, he would feel obliged to tell her nothing. While she claimed to have the upper hand he might well explain much.

'Well now,' she said, astonished by the calmness of her voice. 'Let's talk about drugs and why you thought you might find some here.'

She heard him stir, move towards her. Her scalp prickled but she forced herself to keep still, maintain the charade that she was not afraid. He came nearer. She thought fleetingly of the weapon he might have picked up to strike her over the head as she sat at his mercy. Several things could have come to his hand. The flower jug? The lamp with the heavy wooden base? Or did he carry a length of picture cord in his pocket?

She had released the parcel containing the pot. It lay on the couch. Her hands rested beside her, poised to spring to her protection, but the lightly curled fingers tightened until the nails forced into her flesh.

He came nearer still. Her nerve snapped and she turned, rising as she did so, her hands coming up in defence. It was a momentary gesture, missed by Tim as he brushed past the end of the couch on her other side and went to an armchair.

'The drugs,' Rain demanded in a voice which revealed nothing but composure.

'I thought you'd got hold of some.'

'Why did you think that?'

'Because of Rosie.'

'Who's Rosie?'

'You know Rosie—that ginger-haired girl that Oliver was . . .'

'I know the girl you mean.' She made sense of Rosie's odd behaviour. 'Rosie takes drugs, does she?'

'Not only Rosie, a lot of people.' He was including himself.

'Quite. But why did that lead you to imagine you could find drugs here?'

'I thought Oliver was getting them for Rosie.'

She tried not to look amazed. 'Go on.'

'Rosie didn't have any money and the man who supplies the stuff wouldn't let her have any more. Then Rosie met Oliver and suddenly she had what she wanted.'

Rain suspected this was rather flimsy evidence on which to accuse Oliver of trafficking in drugs. She decided to be tactful rather than derisive, which might have roused Tim again. 'If you wanted drugs and you thought Oliver had some, why didn't you ask him instead of breaking in here?'

He gave her a withering look. 'And have you writing in the newspaper that I was a drug addict? Papers always get it wrong. There are addicts and there are people who just use the stuff occasionally.'

'I see.' She recognized the argument: addicts were other people until it was too late. She said: 'It was you who broke in here last night, was it?'

'I came to tell you something, but no one was here so I got in and took a look.'

'And before you left, did you take a look at the mess you'd created?' She could not resist the sarcasm.

'I was in a hurry.'

'You were thorough, I'll grant you that. You left no corner undisturbed, no pot untipped.' It was difficult to believe this, her work and Oliver's had been equally thorough.

'I told you, I was in a hurry.'

'You had been meticulous, why did you come back today?'

'Because you'd been to Nice. The man who sells the stuff here gets his supplies in Nice. I thought you might have brought something back with you. I saw you and Oliver in the café when we all came up from the beach. It was an opportunity to try again.'

Rain brushed hair from her forehead. It was damp. 'Perhaps I'm being obtuse, but why should our visit to Nice suggest we were shopping for drugs? And how did you know we'd been to Nice?'

He shifted uneasily in his chair. Then: 'You were seen in Nice, by somebody who knows the drugs scene.'

'Who?'

But it was too much to hope. Tim had no intention of telling her that. She tried another line. 'All right. What was it you came to tell me yesterday?'

'I've got some information about Sabine Jourdain. I thought you might pay me for it. It's a very good story.'

'You'll have to tell me before I can judge that. What's it about?'

'Supposing I tell you and you refuse to pay?'

'That's a risk you'll have to take. You're in a buyer's market.' She had no doubt it would be worthless but, like Cobalt, she always had to listen.

'I could give it to another paper instead, couldn't I?'

'Naturally, but you'd still have to say what the story was before you were offered anything for it.'

He got up, impatient, and walked about flexing his fingers. He repeated: 'It's a very good story.'

'Give me a clue.'

He was growing agitated. She said: 'Is it to do with the murder?'

'No. You're not to think I killed her. I didn't do it,' he said furiously.

'Well, if it's not about her death, what is it about?' She wished he would stop pacing about. He paced and said nothing. She tried to guess what he might have found out about Sabine Jourdain that did not hinge on her death. She hoped that if he said he had discovered she met Scott Fitzgerald she would be able to treat the

233

suggestion with the seriousness Tim would think it deserved.

But he said: 'It's about Durance's paintings. She was doing them for him.' He looked triumphant, as if to say: 'There, don't you think *that's* a good story?'

Rain said: 'Tim, it's a good story but it's not worth anything to me because I already know about it.' She felt sorry when she saw his triumph wrecked. He sighed and flung himself down on the chair. He had not merely failed to interest her in a story, he had found the only thing he had to sell was worthless and he urgently needed money.

Rain said: 'I found out during the last few days. How did you?'

He was not looking at her. He was leaning forward, the sweep of his fair hair obscuring his face. 'I went to the old house where she lived and I saw the paintings. I knew immediately what they were, she couldn't very well deny it.'

'When was this?'

He sat up, pushed his hair back. 'Soon after I came here. I wanted to find out where she lived. I worked it out, from things Barbara Coleman told me, and I hitched a lift in a car going up the valley and walked the last mile or two. There was a crazy woman in a cottage. She ran out and tried to send me away but I pretended Sabine was expecting me, so she took me to the studio. She was really odd, she showed me the way but she kept saying she wouldn't come in because she wasn't allowed to set foot in there.'

Rain could picture the scene well enough. Madame Alègre would make an impression on anyone. 'Did you ever tell anybody else about this?'

'No, I promised Sabine I wouldn't. But now she's dead, that's the end of the promise, isn't it?'

'You didn't even say anything to Barbara Coleman?'

'No. If I had she'd have told Sabine and then Sabine wouldn't have . . .' His sentence trailed into silence.

'Wouldn't have what?'

'Sabine and I had an arrangement.'

'Blackmail?'

'I suppose you'd call it that but I didn't look at it that way. She wanted the secret kept, I wanted money.'

'How many times did you ask her for money?'

'She gave it to me three times, then she got difficult.'

'Is this why you were following her around? Why you went on board the *Jonquil* that evening?'

'Yes. She'd paid up before so I couldn't see why she was refusing to do it again. That's what we had the row about.'

'What exactly happened on the *Jonquil* that evening?'

'I saw her go on board. I thought she might not be there long and when she left I could stop her and try to persuade her. That American and his wife left the boat and drove away, later some of the crew came ashore too. I walked about the harbour, making up my mind what to do. Then I thought I might as well go and look for Sabine.'

'Did you see anyone else on board?'

'No crew, no one. There weren't many lights on, either, and I began to think she'd left. Then I heard her voice in a room. She came out, saw me in the passage and hurried me into the lounge. She told me to stop pestering her. She said there would be no more money. I was really annoyed but she kept refusing. She said I'd been given all I'd get and I said it wasn't enough.'

'Not enough for what?'

'To pay off the man who supplies the drugs. You see, it starts off very cheap. You're amazed how little it costs to get the stuff and then suddenly the price shoots right up.'

'Once you're hooked.' All that amazed her was that he had not expected that.

'You heard me losing my temper and yelling at her. I was threatening to give the game away about the Durances...'

'I didn't hear anything about pictures, I only heard you threatening to kill her.'

'I don't remember what I said, but I'm sure I never meant to do that. I might have *said* it.'

'You definitely did. And didn't you throw that bronze bird at her?'

'I'm a rotten shot. It missed her by miles and hit one of those screens.'

'She must have been terrified, an old woman like that...'

'If you'd seen her you wouldn't say that. She came at me with a stool in her hand—who do you think was terrified then? She wasn't young but she was very strong. Anyway, I was the one who ran. The last I saw of her she was standing in the lounge aiming a stool at me. I slammed the doors on her and ran. She was very much alive then.'

Rain said: 'Was that the last time you saw that room?'

'No. When I ran away I was going to the beach, but as I got near it I recognized someone I was avoiding. I turned back to the harbour to wait for him to go away. By then I felt really bad about what had happened. I wanted to see Sabine was all right and say I was sorry. I went on board very quietly this time because I thought if she wasn't on her own I could retreat. I couldn't find her but I had the feeling I wasn't alone. Do you know that creepy feeling when you're sure someone's there but you can't see or hear anything?'

'Yes,' said Rain, who had come to know it well.

'Well, I'd been on the boat a few minutes when I heard someone pounding along the gangway and going ashore, so I knew I'd been right.'

'Did you see who it was?'

'No, I stayed hidden and gave them time to get away. After that I waited at the harbour until it was safe to go back to the beach without seeing the person I was dodging.'

Rain said: 'You're being very discreet, Tim, but the person you were avoiding was that pedlar, wasn't it?'

He looked surprised. 'How did you know?'

'I've noticed you're not on very good terms with him. Why don't you admit he's peddling rather more than leather bags?'

'Somebody's already told you,' he accused.

She denied it but did not tell him she had seen him fighting with the pedlar or that the man had chased her and Oliver in Nice. She said: 'Why did you tell him Oliver and I were involved in drugs?'

'I wanted him to leave me alone. I didn't care what I said to him. What does it matter? You're going home soon, but he doesn't know that. Rosie's got the stuff again and she didn't get it from him, so I told him Oliver had supplied her. He stopped bothering me, I'd given him something more important to worry about. I know he believed me because when I told him you went to Nice yesterday to buy more, he said he'd seen you there. I wonder he didn't warn you off!'

'You let him believe Oliver and I were moving into his territory?' She wanted to say that not only was that ridiculous but it was dangerous, she wanted to tell him about the frightening minutes in the maze of old Nice. But she knew it would be a waste of breath. He was careless of his own safety and showed wanton disregard for everyone else.

Down below the street door banged and footsteps tramped upstairs. Oliver knocked on the door of the flat. Rain let him in. Before she could speak he said: 'Sorry, I've lost the key you gave me.'

He started to say a cheerful hello to Tim when he became aware of the tension. Rain said: 'Tim's our intruder. Last night's mess and a more tidy visit this afternoon when he came to see whether we'd stocked up with illegal drugs on our trip to Nice.'

Oliver heard the rest with amusement, a reaction which disappointed Rain but calmed Tim. Rain knew Oliver was picturing himself back in the wine bar in Chelsea telling everyone how he'd been mistaken for a drug dealer and nearly done to death in a Mediterranean backstreet by an underworld rival. In the future it would earn a lot of laughs, but Rain did not think it deserved any yet.

Oliver put his head into the bedroom. 'Oh, I see,' he said. 'You've only tipped out our travel bags this time.'

Tim said, in a matter of fact way: 'I checked everything else yesterday, but those weren't packed then.'

'Well, be a good chap and pack them again, will you?' said Oliver.

Tim was startled but saw that the determination in Oliver's eye belied his friendly tone. Meekly, Tim repacked the bags as Oliver stood over him.

When it was done, Tim drew a key from his pocket. 'This dropped out of your pocket on the beach.'

Oliver took it. 'So this is how you got in here without damaging the door.'

Tim stood there like a schoolboy waiting to be dismissed from the headmaster's study. 'I might as well go,' he suggested.

'Certainly,' said Oliver. 'And be careful never to come back.'

Tim hesitated. 'I don't suppose you could . . .'

'No!' said Rain and Oliver together.

Tim said: 'It would have been easier if I *had* stolen the family silver, wouldn't it?'

'Perhaps you could find someone else to pay you for your story,' suggested Oliver as he ushered Tim out on to the stairs. He imagined Tim, with his very good French, having no difficulty in getting local journalists to listen to him.

At the time it sounded like an innocent idea.

26

On his way out of the building Tim passed Cobalt running upstairs. Cobalt was accompanied by a slim, white-haired woman who moved just as briskly.

'This is Barbara Coleman,' Cobalt said when Rain opened the door.

Rain looked from one face to the other, uncertain how to respond. Cobalt's face was grim but Barbara Coleman wore a sweet smile.

'I just knew we'd meet properly, my dear, after all that nonsense in the Chagall museum. Very cloak and dagger, wasn't I? But I was so confused, I do hope you understand . . .'

Cobalt interrupted her. 'Rain, after I rang you this morning I made a few more enquiries and then went and told Barbara she was to come with me.'

'He was quite decided about it, rather bossy actually . . .' said Barbara Coleman.

Rain looked at Oliver. He read her mind and drew the woman away, leading her down the room to a comfortable chair. Rain heard her flow of talk about the journey from Nice break off as she noticed the view from the window, an oppressive sky, a turbulent sea. 'Such a shame about the weather, and you haven't long to enjoy our Mediterranean climes, have you, my dear?'

Oliver could be heard beginning a suitable reply before the woman babbled on about something else. Rain asked Cobalt: 'What were your enquiries about?'

'Not the Durance paintings. I wasn't ever convinced we were attacked because of that business. I intercepted Edouard on his way to work at the hotel and got the truth out of him. His wife's a drug addict.' He grimaced. 'No doubt Barbara was too delicate to mention that to you.'

'Not a word of it. Presumably Maurin knew when he asked the couple to take her in.'

'He knew all right. The wife used to work as a domestic at his house. She had to give it up when she became too sick. He knew they needed any extra money they could get and would let Barbara stay in their spare room without asking questions.'

'Did Edouard lie to me and to your contact at the hotel—Georges, wasn't it?—because he was covering up his wife's condition?'

'He admits it now. The brothers who beat him up are involved in the drugs racket. I knew that much because drugs featured in the court case which sent one of them to prison a couple of years ago. There never was any threat from them to Barbara—they didn't know she was at the flat because she was in her room when they burst in. But Edouard lied to her about the reason for the attack.'

'That was terrible. It made her feel she had to stay there or else he'd be in worse trouble.'

Cobalt said: 'He didn't mind her staying longer because it meant he was to be paid more. It suited him to have her believe she had an obligation to stay.'

'How does Maurin come into this?'

Cobalt shrugged. 'Edouard thinks Maurin knew nothing about the brothers going to the flat until someone told him.'

'That was probably me.'

'He says he phoned Maurin after you'd been to the hotel because he wanted to report that you were asking questions about Barbara. He told Maurin he'd pretended she wanted to meet you at the museum. Half an hour later Maurin rang back and demanded to know if there was any truth in a story that he'd been hurt and Barbara threatened. Edouard admitted he'd been attacked but denied it was anything to do with Barbara being there.'

Rain asked whether Edouard had told Maurin about her first appointment at the museum. Cobalt said: 'He says not. He found out himself because he read the note Barbara asked him to deliver to you. It sounds as though Maurin was paying him to keep Barbara there and she was paying him to run errands—deliver the note to you and the photograph to *Nice Matin*—and to turn a blind eye when she went out.'

'All for the usual reason—he needed the money.'

Cobalt said wryly: 'Yes, and he only told me about it because I paid him.'

Down the room Barbara Coleman was still chattering, Oliver putting in the occasional word. Rain whispered: 'Does she always . . .'

'She hasn't stopped since I collected her. I was seriously thinking of taking her back.'

'Has she said anything useful? Did she mention the Durances?'

'She talked mostly about Sabine Jourdain. She's still convinced Joseph killed her and she means to go to the police and say so.'

They stopped speaking as Barbara Coleman came up to them. 'Now, my dear,' she said to Cobalt, 'you promised to take me home. I'd rather like that. Do you think we could go to the villa now?'

'Certainly, Barbara,' said Cobalt. 'Why don't we all go over there and see you home?'

He looked enquiringly at Rain who nodded. Oliver wore a look of weary resignation as he followed them. They all went in Cobalt's car. He and Rain intended to talk about the murder case once they had left Barbara Coleman there. Until then it would be virtually impossible to discuss anything. Rain was reminded of Maurin's remark. *'She is what the English call a chatterbox, I believe.'* She was.

Cobalt joined the coast road and they roared along the ramparts of the ancient town. The excitable Miss Coleman countermanded Rain's directions with inaccurate and unhelpful ones. Eventually they pulled into the lane behind the house.

The door in the high wall was open and they went into the garden. The bright tangle of plants had become a funereal monochrome, and there was a dullness where there had previously been a dazzling glimpse of the Mediterranean.

Barbara Coleman was saying something about the former beauty of the garden and its decline, but wondering aloud whether it was fair to say decline because what was happening was that the garden was returning to nature, and further wondering whether it was really and truly nature because some of the plants were not native to the region and did not entirely belong there, and then wondering whether that was not a strange remark to come from one who had made Provence her home for so long that she felt quite a part of the landscape.

They approached the steps and Rain fastidiously

avoided touching the rail as she descended. Barbara Coleman had no such inhibitions. Her blood was there, but she had apparently forgotten about it. Cobalt, who did not know, gripped the rail.

They stood outside the back door while Barbara Coleman sorted through her handbag. 'I'm sure I had the key. In spite of the abruptness of my departure, I'm convinced I had the key. It's always kept in here, you see, unless it's in the lock, but if I'm out of doors you can be sure it's in my bag.'

Her fluffy white head was bent over the bag. The bag gaped black, her hand was a grey shape jabbing into it. Rain and Cobalt exchanged looks. Oliver grunted and strode about the paved veranda impatiently. They would all be relieved when the key was found, when the storm broke.

'When we get inside . . .' Cobalt began to Rain and Oliver in a whisper.

Barbara Coleman interrupted with a cry of joy. She had found her key.

They filed indoors. The old woman went along a short passage, passed a scullery and continued on a few yards. She gave an exclamation and hurried forward. 'Oh look, the light is on in here.' She thrust open a door to a small sitting room.

'What can this mean?' she asked, eyes wide, appealing to them all. They crowded behind her in the doorway. Cobalt had resumed his grim expression. Rain was thinking that Barbara Coleman was not only a chatterbox but inclined to be dramatic, too. Oliver, looking bored, brought up the rear.

Barbara Coleman gave an exaggerated shudder. 'Do you suppose there is someone already here?'

Oliver said: 'No, that's been burning ever since you went away. We saw it on the night Sabine . . .'

Everyone except Barbara Coleman wished he had not mentioned it. She said: 'Since the night Sabine was murdered? Really? That's most interesting, don't you think?'

Rain said: 'You must have left it on.'

'Oh, but I'm sure I wouldn't have done any such thing. I hardly ever come into this room, and I am most particular. Whenever I go out of a room I am certain to switch off the light. After all, why should one leave it on?'

She came out of the room, leaving the light on. Oliver leaned forward and switched it off. They all followed Barbara Coleman down the passage. Rain was close behind her. She sensed Cobalt and Oliver fall back, and heard Cobalt say: 'I'm going to take a look around. I'd like you to come with me.'

Rain bridled. That meant she was to be left with Barbara Coleman and Barbara Coleman was tiresome company. They came to a kitchen with a spacious drawing room beyond at the front of the house.

'Here we are,' said Barbara Coleman, padding into the centre of the room. 'The best room for company, do they still do that in England?'

Oliver stared at her in bewilderment. Cobalt looked thoroughly annoyed. Rain took in the old expensive furniture, the floor length windows which, beyond their bolted shutters, would have coastal views. She also noted the depth of dust over everything. She said: 'This is very grand, Barbara, but shouldn't we just go to the rooms that you use?'

The woman looked perturbed then said: 'Oh, they aren't very impressive. But come, if you must.' She went into the hall, down a narrow passage and into a large room with long, shuttered windows and again, Rain guessed, a sea view. Barbara Coleman hurried to the windows and began to fold back shutters.

Oliver took over and the room sprang into focus. There was an easy chair and a television set, but the room was dominated by a table covered in paints and an easel with a partly finished painting on it. All over the place there were her completed paintings. They hung on walls, they leaned against each other in piles by the walls, they were stacked in corners.

'In the day,' said Barbara Coleman, 'I can see as far as the Esterel . . . Oh, I'm forgetting, this is the day, isn't it? It's just that it's so dark. I'm not accustomed to that. Usually, you see, we have wonderful light. That's what artists crave, wonderful light! We have it here. All the time. But not today, alas, not today . . .'

'Yesterday was wonderful,' Rain said soothingly, hearing the rising panic in the woman's voice.

'Yesterday? Oh yes, that was very good. Wonderful, you might say.'

Cobalt said: 'You work in here, do you, Barbara? Spend most of your time here?'

The fluffy white head bobbed in agreement. 'Oh yes . . .'

He said: 'Well, we'll just check the rest of the house before we leave you.'

Rain understood he meant that he and Oliver would go, but Barbara Coleman said: 'Oh yes. Yes, of course. That's most kind.' She went for the doorway, her speed catching them unprepared. Rain remembered her story about dashing away from Maurin, racing from the car and into the garden. It had seemed a little exaggerated that an elderly woman could move so rapidly and catch a younger man off guard. Now she did not doubt it.

She wondered whether Barbara Coleman painted as fast, whether that accounted for all the unsold work around the room. But she knew there was no need to believe that. Barbara Coleman did not sell much work and that was all there was to it.

Rain hung back and looked at some of the paintings on the wall near the door. They were small and neat and many were flower studies. The scale of the work varied but they were generally scenes from nature, the type of thing popularly believed to be the easiest to sell but not necessarily the easiest to paint. Barbara Coleman was proficient but being a fulltime artist required more than that and Rain judged that she had no more to give.

She tried to picture how the woman had fitted into the Durance coterie. She was not a good artist and she was wearing company, but she must have some redeeming qualities, although Madeleine Corley and her companions at Tourettes sur Loup had not hinted at any.

'Rain? Come on.' Oliver was impatient. She hurried out.

'Sorry, I was looking at her paintings.'

He made a thumbs down sign. Cobalt and the white-haired woman were halfway up a flight of stairs. Rain and Oliver ran to catch them up. Barbara Coleman's bedroom was another high and handsome room, cluttered with paintings. The bed was untidy, as though she had merely pulled up the covers. A nightdress was thrown over a chair and on the bedside table were an assortment of pill bottles. She went to the table, closed her hand around a bottle and slid it into her skirt pocket.

'There you are,' she said, and flung her arms wide. 'Now I've shown you even my sleeping quarters. Everything is just as it was left.'

They trooped downstairs after her. She was offering them cups of tea and it was churlish to refuse. Cobalt touched Rain's arm. 'Oliver and I are going to look around. Will you keep the old girl talking?' He did not notice how silly his request was.

'What are you looking *for*?'

Cobalt checked the woman wasn't watching, then mouthed: 'Drugs.'

'*Here?*'

Barbara Coleman heard her and looked up. 'What's the matter, my dear?'

Rain reassured her, the woman turned back to her tea caddy. She was telling a story about buying it in Sunningdale before she first came to France, because there was a rumour that one could not buy decent tea the other side of the English Channel.

Rain whispered to Cobalt: 'Why here?'

He gave her his maddening smile and when he replied he aped Barbara Coleman's speech. 'The perfect place, don't you think, my dear?'

'*Whose* drugs?'

Cobalt shook his head, refusing to answer any more questions. He tapped Oliver's arm and signalled him to follow. With a heavy heart Rain watched Barbara Coleman, who was still reminiscing about the shopkeeper who had sold her the caddy, set out four cups and saucers and round up four teaspoons from a drawer. Shortly Rain was going to have to explain to her that two of her guests had sneaked off.

'There!' said Barbara Coleman and turned round. 'Now all we must wait for is the kettle. I won't look. A watched pot, you know.' Her smile drooped. 'Where are James and Oliver?'

'They'll be back, I shouldn't think they've gone far.'

'But, my dear, *where* have they gone?'

Rain was no more vague than she had reason to be. 'I think they're just taking a look around.'

The woman's sweet smile reappeared. 'Oh, aren't they kind? So very kind. James has been kindness itself all day. And now Oliver, too. They say unpleasant things about young people today, but I find them so helpful.

Isn't it good of them spending all this time to be sure I shall be quite safe here?'

Rain made appropriate noises. No more was required. With barely a prompt, Barbara Coleman talked on. She had forgotten about her tea caddy and the friendly shopkeeper in Sunningdale and she had soon forgotten about the kindness of young people and was reminiscing about the days when she was not alone at the villa but shared it with seven others.

She said: 'There was Marius Durance, naturally, and Sabine, of course and . . . but you wouldn't know of the others. They've moved on. Some of the dear girls took a studio together in Tourettes sur Loup, I believe it's quite a fashionable place for artists these days.'

She took a quick peep at the kettle, then went on: 'Some of our group even went to America, that's supposed to be the important place to be. Did you know that? The Americans say it's the centre of the art world, but quite *where* in America I wouldn't understand. If I went there I shouldn't know which bit to aim for. Suppose one went to Boston and found one ought to be in Chicago? Or one picked Washington when the better place was Los Angeles? With France one always knew. It was either Paris or it was the Côte d'Azur. One couldn't get it wrong.'

Rain supposed not. She thought she knew what it would be like to find yourself in Boston when you ought to be in Chicago. It would be like finding yourself in the kitchen with Barbara Coleman when you would rather be with Oliver and James Cobalt searching for drugs.

The kettle boiled and tea was made. There was a little discussion about the length of time a perfectly made cup of tea ought to be brewed and a little anguish because there was no milk to offer the guests. Then a wizened lemon was discovered and so lemon tea saved the day.

'Are you still convinced Joseph killed Sabine Jourdain?' Rain asked as she watched the tea poured.

Barbara Coleman stopped pouring and fixed her with a very severe look. 'Totally.' For several minutes she had nothing more to say.

Then Rain said: 'Are you going to tell the police that?'

'Yes, I've quite made up my mind. One cannot keep that sort of information to oneself.'

'When will you tell them?'

'Tomorrow. It's rather late today, don't you think? You're not going to try and talk me out of it, I hope.'

Rain had not been thinking of doing that. She had been worrying what might happen to Barbara Coleman if she continued to make known her opinion that Joseph was a murderer. From somewhere in the house she heard a sound and to cover it spoke again. 'How do you think Joseph did it?'

'She was pushed into the harbour and left to drown, wasn't she? She could never swim. Not like the rest of us. We all used to go swimming from the beach here but Sabine was never a swimmer. I expect Joseph knew that and took advantage of it.'

'Who told you she drowned?'

Barbara Coleman took a sip of scalding tea. 'It was in the paper that she'd been taken from the harbour. I knew she couldn't swim so it was obvious she drowned.'

There was a distant thud. Rain spoke louder. 'Are you suggesting Joseph pushed her into the water as she walked through the harbour?'

'It would be easy enough, wouldn't it, my dear? Even if she saw him she wouldn't expect anything evil to happen. It would all be over before she could call out. And even if she had cried out, who takes any notice of anyone shouting, even screaming? You know what happens— people hear but they don't want to become involved in case it's all a game and they are made to feel foolish.'

She sipped again then said: 'James and Oliver are missing their tea. Perhaps we ought to fetch them.'

'I'll go.' Rain did not want the woman upset by finding them behaving oddly. She did not know what sort of oddness to imagine, but they had been a long time and there had been peculiar noises.

Rain went to the main hall. She cocked her head to try and make out sounds but there were none. Upstairs, she thought. She was almost sure the earlier sounds had come from upstairs.

At the foot of the stairs she paused. It was black above. Most of the shutters were still closed and she would have welcomed light. She had never liked being in the dark, especially being in unfamiliar places in the dark. Surely Oliver and Cobalt would have put the stair lights on if they had gone upstairs? Or had they been afraid to do so in case it drew attention to what they were up to?

She could not find the light switch and stood, her hand on the newel post, deciding whether to go up in the dark. Then there was a noise from the rear of the house, the scrape of a door being opened. They had been on the ground floor all along.

Rain sped towards the sound. When she saw them she was going to tell them about the tea and in the same breath demand to know what they had found and why Cobalt had anticipated finding anything in the Villa Fièsole.

But as she rounded a corner the questions dried on her lips. She was face to face with Benedict and Merlyn Joseph.

27

For a split second Joseph looked as agitated as he had been on the *Jonquil* the day after the murder. Then the great smile came. 'Rain!'

Merlyn, behind his shoulder, said nothing. None of them knew how to go on. Then Joseph said: 'This is a strange place for us to meet.'

They were all standing in the near dark. Rain felt her palms damp with nervousness. Joseph said: 'Were you looking for something?' Despite the smile his voice was weaker than usual.

Rain was worried for Barbara Coleman. It shocked Rain to realize the Josephs might already have heard of her accusations. If Maurin had told them she had gone home, the woman's wagging tongue might already have put her in danger.

Rain gathered her wits and said she had come to see the villa, the last place the Durance coterie had settled before disbanding. She hoped he would go away before meeting Barbara Coleman, before discovering what Oliver and Cobalt were doing.

Merlyn said, irritably: 'Well, come on, Ben, we can't

stand in this passage for ever.'

'No.' He took a step forward. Rain had to choose whether to let him pass or lead him into the house and try to steer him away from the kitchen. At that moment she heard rapid footsteps. Barbara Coleman came into the passage.

'Rain?' she called. 'Now *you've* vanished. What *is* going on?'

Rain went to meet her. She heard the Josephs' astonishment and their feet close after her.

'Who's that?' the old woman asked, peering into the gloom. Rain wished somebody would switch the lights on. There must be lights. Why wouldn't anybody find a switch?

Merlyn did. Suddenly there was the flare of electric light above them. Barbara Coleman made a little jump backwards, a shaking hand went to her lips but not fast enough to cut off her cry of fear. Rain took her arm.

Barbara Coleman was trembling. The Josephs did not appear much happier. Merlyn recovered first. 'You've come home, Barbara?' She made it sound as though this were something illegal.

The old woman attempted to regain some dignity. Up went her chin. 'It was time I came,' she said. 'This is my home.'

'Well, yes . . . ,' began Joseph.

Merlyn said: 'That depends, doesn't it? We own this place.'

Barbara said: 'Durance would never forgive you if you turned me out. This is the only home I have.'

Rain appealed to them: 'Is there any question of her having to leave?'

'That's up to you, isn't it, Barbara?' Joseph said, as though there were a secret bargain struck between them.

The woman was defiant. She drew her arm away,

saying to Rain: 'We should finish our tea, don't you think, my dear?'

She walked off. Rain and Joseph faced each other a moment longer until Rain, too, went to the kitchen. She was afraid the Josephs would follow and find the extra cups and ask who else was in the house. She had no doubt it would be a very bad idea for them to go in search of Oliver and Cobalt.

Barbara Coleman raised her cup and took a sip. Rain wished for her sake that the cup had not rattled in the saucer. She lifted her own cup, her eyes on the doorway through which the Josephs might come. She could hear them whispering in the passage. Barbara Coleman gave a snort of disgust. She said something under her breath, something Rain could not catch. Rain asked her what it was.

'*Americans!*' repeated Barbara Coleman with utter disdain.

Just then the Americans arrived in the doorway. Joseph had resumed his smile, Merlyn was less threatening. 'We've poured you some tea,' Rain lied. They came in but did not look at the cups.

'Why have you come?' Barbara Coleman demanded. 'I am here because I live here, but why are you here?'

'Now look here, Barbara,' said Joseph in a rather sharp tone. His hand went forward as he spoke. Rain believed he was reaching towards one of the cups on the table, but Barbara Coleman stood across the table from him and she recoiled.

'Don't come near me!'

'Barbara, what do you think I'm going to do to you?' He looked perplexed.

Merlyn said: 'She's a fool, Ben. I don't know why you let her stay.'

Her words were partly lost in Barbara Coleman's wild

cry. 'I know what you did, you can't stop me saying so.'
Her control had snapped.

Her arm swooped and the cup of tea was dashed in
Joseph's face. He yelped. Merlyn darted at Barbara Coleman rather than help her husband dab at his scalded
face and stained shirt.

'You mad creature!' she shouted.

Rain dragged Barbara Coleman away, with an urgency
that took them both off balance. Merlyn seethed, but
the old woman was beyond her reach. To strike her now
she would have to attack Rain first.

There was a hubbub. Barbara Coleman was making
incoherent accusations, Merlyn was shouting about the
state of the woman's mind, Joseph was swearing about
being in terrible pain.

When she could make herself heard Rain begged the
Josephs: 'Surely it would be best if you could do what
you came for and leave?'

Barbara Coleman squirmed from her grasp. 'You killed
Sabine,' she shrieked at Joseph.

There was a horrified silence. Merlyn was quickest to
break it. 'How dare you say such a wicked thing.'

'You knew about it, Merlyn,' said Barbara Coleman,
nodding her fluffy head in confirmation, 'and he did it.'

Rain said: 'Barbara, please, don't say any more.' She
touched her but the woman jerked away.

Joseph said: 'No, don't stop her, Rain. I want to hear
what she's got to say.'

Rain said: 'But . . .'

He snarled at the old woman. 'Come on, let's see how
you justify that accusation. You can't go around calling
people murderers, you know.'

'I know what you did and I know how it was done.
You were both in it. You two and Philippe Maurin

pretended to be her friends, but look what happened to her.'

Rain renewed her grip on the woman. She wanted to put an arm around her and steer her away. Barbara Coleman struggled against her, shouted: 'Leave me alone, Rain. Even you can't bear to hear the truth. That's been the trouble all along, hasn't it? That's what went wrong with the Durance coterie, no one could tolerate the truth. They all wanted flattery and nonsense and if they did anything that wasn't right they expected people to cover up for them. It's not loyalty, that kind of covering up. People make a virtue of loyalty but it's not always a good thing. Look what loyalty did for Sabine! She was killed because of it . . .'

She ended with a high-pitched wail as Merlyn reached her and shook her. The white hair flopped back and forth and the wispy figure crumpled. Merlyn was savage, saying through gritted teeth that she was never, never, never to repeat such evil nonsense.

Barbara Coleman, battling to free herself, shouted: 'You killed her. The two of you killed her. It was murder.'

The last word contorted to a scream as Merlyn let her go with a thrust that sent her rocking unbalanced in Rain's direction. Rain caught her in both arms, held her tight, and knew it was only her grasp which kept the woman upright.

The Josephs were squabbling about whether Merlyn should have done what she had just done, whether Barbara Coleman had not truly deserved it. Rain was trying to soothe the old woman. But through it all Barbara Coleman kept up a hysterical chant of 'Murder! Murder! Murder!'

Rain murmured to her an unconvincing: 'It's all right.'

Joseph retorted: 'It's not all right if she's going around saying that.'

Rain glared at him over Barbara Coleman's head. '*Somebody* killed her friend.'

He said: 'And I suppose she's been trying to convince you it was me.'

Rain met his gaze. She felt again the fear she had known when she walked into him in the dark passage. He said sarcastically: 'Oh, that's just fine. She's convinced you, has she?'

Merlyn said: 'What possible reason could Ben have for wanting Sabine dead?'

Rain said: 'If Sabine Jourdain planned to reveal how much of Durance's work she'd been doing for him, a lot of people would have preferred she didn't.'

Beneath Rain's chin Barbara Coleman's white head quivered and a broken voice chanted: 'Murder! Murder! Murder!'

'Yes,' said Rain. 'Sabine Jourdain was murdered and it looks as though it was to prevent her from talking.'

Merlyn handed her husband a tea towel and he scrubbed at his shirt with it. Joseph said to Rain: 'Do you really believe I killed her?'

Rain noticed he had not argued about Sabine Jourdain's role in painting the Durances. 'No,' she said, 'actually I don't think you did.'

Merlyn said: 'Who, then?' Joseph flashed her a look which she ignored.

Rain thought of Maurin and his clients like the Contessa Mantero. She rejected Cobalt's story about Edouard and the drug dealers. In her mind the murder and the attack at the Chagall museum were inextricably bound up with the secret of the Durances. She said: 'Someone else who would stand to lose as much as you would if the truth came out.'

For an instant the Josephs' eyes met. Rain saw in that glance all the confirmation she needed that the Josephs were covering up for their friend.

28

The skies had opened. The town was awash, the sea like hammered pewter. Indoors electric light flickered. For a few seconds the lights at the Villa Fièsole failed entirely, and in those few seconds there was the sound of the back door being opened and footsteps in the passage.

Maurin appeared in the kitchen doorway. Rain felt her protective grip on Barbara Coleman tighten, but the woman was relieved to see him. She did not know about the incident at the Chagall museum, she knew nothing but her conviction that Joseph was a murderer.

'Philippe!' Her cry was one of welcome.

Maurin was puzzled she was not alone. 'I guessed you'd be here, Barbara. I thought we should have a little talk.'

'Yes, we can talk, Philippe, but I'm not going back to Nice. It was an unpleasant flat and the woman was ill. I'm going to stay here, this is my home.'

He raised his hands in acquiescence. 'Very well, you are here and you may as well stay.'

Merlyn said: 'We can't have her going around saying

what she has just been saying. She thinks Ben killed Sabine.'

'I know it,' Barbara Coleman shouted, but Rain hushed her.

'You tell her, Philippe,' Joseph said. 'She won't even listen to us deny it.'

Rain saw the guarded looks between Maurin and the Josephs. She thought it probably suited Maurin to have Barbara Coleman believe Joseph guilty. Joseph would be going back to the United States soon and would be beyond her gossip, but if Maurin convinced her of Joseph's innocence, then how long would it be before she realized that he, too, had a strong financial motive for wanting the truth about the Durances kept secret?

Maurin said: 'I am surprised you brought Barbara home, Ben, if you are worried about what she might say.'

'We didn't,' said Joseph.

'We couldn't have, you didn't even tell us where we could find her,' said Merlyn.

Maurin looked at Rain and raised an eyebrow. 'So? It was you, was it?'

She could have sworn his eyes lingered on the scarf about her neck. She saw no reason to give him any information he did not already have.

Joseph said: 'We didn't know they were here. There wasn't a car we recognized in the lane, we were as surprised to find them as you are to find us.'

Maurin made a graceful gesture with one hand. He looked slightly amused as he said: 'I am not owed any explanations, this is your house.'

All the same, Merlyn said: 'We came over to fetch some things we store here.'

Barbara Coleman freed herself from Rain's hold. She was still trembling but wore her defiant look again. 'Phi-

260

lippe, I'm sure they came after me. They knew I would guess they killed Sabine.'

'That's rubbish,' said Joseph. He flung the damp tea towel on to the table.

Barbara Coleman ignored him, she said to Maurin: 'Sabine admitted to me she was painting the pictures for Durance. Later she told me she was frightened of *him*.' She jabbed a finger at Joseph. 'She was afraid of what he might do when she told him she wasn't going to keep up the pretence any longer and everything she did in future was to be sold as her own work.'

'This isn't true!' said Joseph.

'Oh yes, it is. I remember her very words. She said: "I have been used for too long, I must do things for myself now. Durance is an artist, he will understand. But I am afraid of what Benedict Joseph might do."'

Merlyn rushed forward, saying: 'This is crazy. She's making this up. Philippe, you're not going to believe this, are you?'

Maurin shrugged. 'What does it matter what Barbara says? Sabine is not here to confirm or deny their conversation, and neither can she confirm or deny how much of her work went into the Durances. The only person who knows about the paintings is Durance himself and he will dismiss Barbara's story as unfounded speculation.' He looked at Rain. 'No one can offer anything but unfounded speculation.'

Barbara Coleman was livid. 'But it's not unfounded, it's true! She'd been doing more and more of his work for him. There was a conspiracy to stop your buyers knowing, that's all it was.'

'No,' said Maurin. 'Sabine and Durance were not interested in buyers. They were interested in creating beautiful things together. If Sabine had wanted to break away and work on her own she could have done so at any time. She preferred to work with Durance.'

'In the end she wanted to get away, and see what happened. Because of the conspiracy she wasn't allowed to. He killed her!'

Joseph clapped both hands to his greying head. 'If I hear that one more time I shall begin to believe it myself!'

Merlyn said: 'For heaven's sake, Philippe, tell her Ben didn't do any such thing.'

There was a fractional hesitation before Maurin said: 'Will you accept it, Barbara, if I tell you that?'

The white head shook. 'You're quite willing to cover up for him. You're colleagues, friends—why shouldn't you hide the truth of what he did?'

Maurin sounded as though his patience were being strained. He said: 'Barbara, we should have that little talk I mentioned.'

Rain was afraid for her. She said: 'Barbara is very upset. She's had a distressing time. I think she ought to be left alone.'

Maurin took no notice. He said to Barbara Coleman: 'Have you taken your pills?'

She looked sheepish. He said: 'Where are they? I'll fetch them for you, if you like.'

She drew the bottle from her skirt pocket. Maurin said: 'Stay there.' He poured her a glass of water, took it across and stood near while she swallowed a couple of pills. He said to Rain: 'She left them behind when I took her to Nice. I had to buy some more for her to take while she was there. No doubt she forgot those when she came here.'

Barbara Coleman handed back the glass. 'Thank you, Philippe.'

Rain was seeing again the solicitous side of Maurin, the man who could talk kindly to Durance when the man was devastated at the death of his friend. Maurin could bustle Barbara Coleman off to Nice against her will, but he would also go shopping for tablets to replace the forgotten ones.

Maurin said to Rain: 'Barbara will be calmer presently. Then I must talk to her.'

Joseph said: 'Well, just make sure you impress on her that I had nothing to do with any murder and she is not to suggest it.'

Barbara Coleman scowled at him. There was a long, uncomfortable silence. The electric light flickered and dimmed. Then she said: 'I'm going to my room now. I want to sit down.' With one of her fast movements she went into the passage. Joseph and Merlyn went after her.

Rain tried to follow but Maurin blocked her way. 'Rain, there is something I must say to you, too.'

She drew away from him, feeling the cold sap of fear. She was alone with the man she believed had killed once and tried to kill a second time. 'What is it?'

'Barbara must not be permitted to tell these stories.'

'About Joseph killing Sabine?'

'That, of course, but also about the Durances.'

She mocked him with a smile. 'I would expect you to say that. Your problem is that much of what Barbara says is true. Sabine Jourdain *was* doing most of Durance's work, Benedict Joseph *did* have a motive to kill her.'

'Don't overlook that Barbara has a strong motive to dislike Ben. She blames him for the break-up of the coterie. It had been disintegrating for years, mainly because Durance had tired of that sort of pressure. He wanted a more solitary, peaceful life. It no longer amused him to be surrounded by a band of admirers. Admirers can be very exhausting and he is an old man.'

'If Sabine Jourdain could have broken away from him any time she chose, it must be equally true that Durance could have torn himself from those admirers.'

'Perhaps. But Barbara believes Ben was the person who engineered everything. She believes he bought this property from Durance with the sole purpose of turning out the others. The truth is that it is in a dreadful state of disrepair and would have been difficult to sell unless it went to a builder who would demolish it and redevelop the site. Durance was saved a lot of difficulty by selling to Ben and being able to buy a small flat and studio in the town. The move was Durance's plan, Ben only helped. Barbara knows all this, but nothing will deter her from blaming Ben for everything she does not like.'

'Why did she stay on here if she dislikes him so much?'

'She says she has nowhere else to go. She refused to be driven out, as she put it. I'm not sure she doesn't have a funny idea that if she waits long enough people will drift back again, perhaps even Durance. Anyway, Ben let her stay. But if she persists in what she is saying about him now, he will have no choice but to insist she goes. This is what I want to impress on her. In her own interests she must keep quiet.'

Rain said drily: 'I don't think she's easily impressed.'

'Rain, I am perfectly sure Ben did not kill Sabine. And I am certain there can be no proof one way or the other about her work on the Durances.'

She said: 'Barbara Coleman is not the only source for the story that Sabine Jourdain painted the Durances. Someone else I know went to the Villa Souleiado while she was working there and she didn't deny her role.'

Maurin was startled. 'Who was this?'

'I'm sure you'll understand if I don't tell you. She wanted the secret kept and paid him to keep it. He says he didn't speak about it until her death.'

'Again there is no proof, is there? The word of a black-mailer?'

'Yes, all you and the Josephs have to fear are the

prejudiced conclusions of Barbara Coleman and the word of a blackmailer. Oh, I almost forgot. You have to consider me, too, don't you?'

His eyes narrowed. She waited, but he did not speak. She said bitterly: 'You didn't forget me, though, did you? You tried to prevent me publishing what I'd found out.'

She ripped away her scarf and he saw in the uncertain light the marks about her throat.

'*You believe I did that!*'

'Didn't you?'

'No! How can you think it?'

She stood there, in front of him, swinging the scarf in her right hand, accusing him of having failed to strangle her. Maurin floundered, made indignant noises in French, switched to English. '*I know nothing of this.*'

Very calmly she assured him she knew that could not be true.

He blustered that he was a dealer in pictures, not a criminal. He said he had no idea she had been assaulted. He saw from her eyes that she could not, *would* not believe him.

Rain said: 'You were told by Edouard that I had been tricked into going to the museum. Are you going to deny you went there, too?'

'Yes.'

'Perhaps the taxi driver will remember taking you.'

A hand shaded his eyes. He said: 'I thought I had been in time.'

'You timed it rather well, although perhaps you were in too much of a hurry to get away, because I lived to tell the tale.'

'No! No, you have got the wrong tale.' He advanced on her, pleading she should believe what he had to say. She backed off.

She said: 'You knew I'd be there. You took a taxi and

I was discovered with a length of picture cord around my neck...'

'It is still the wrong tale. Listen, I will tell you what happened.'

She swung the scarf, a taunting rhythm as he spoke. He said: 'Edouard phoned me...'

'... while I was in your gallery and had just told you I knew about the Durances.'

'Yes. He called while you were there. He said he had fooled you into going to the museum. No doubt I ought to have told you it was a trick, but he had made the plan to stop you going to his flat. I knew it would keep you out of the way at a time when you might be spreading your theory about the Durances.'

'You mean I could have been discussing it with some of your clients, like the Contessa Mantero?'

'Think what would happen if she were to become doubtful about her collection. Not only would I lose a valued client but her collection might come on to the market, her reasons for selling would become known, Durances all over the world would become suspect and lose their value and dealers would suffer. Rather than let you go to the contessa I thought it wise to let you waste an hour or two at the museum.'

'Why did you follow me?'

'After you left me I telephoned Barbara to see that she was all right. She confirmed what you had told me about Edouard being beaten up and said she was afraid it was all because of her. Of course it was not, but she is intractable once she has an idea.'

'And then?'

'I tried to think who might have been to Edouard's flat. I could guess why he might have had trouble with the sort of people Barbara described: she said she had watched what happened but the men had not spotted her. So I asked around, a word here and there in the sort of places where people hear things. During the afternoon I was given my answer. It was not an astonishing one, in the context of a small-time drugs network. Then, as I was leaving, my informant added what he thought was a rather amusing story. He said the brothers who had hurt Edouard had turned to culture, they had gone that afternoon to the Chagall museum.'

Rain did not think this was enough to suggest the brothers went to look for her and said so.

'On its own, perhaps not, but I'd also been told that day that people believed you and an English journalist who lives here, James Cobalt, were making enquiries about drug trafficking. Put together, it appeared the brothers were going to harm you.'

Rain felt herself wavering. Maurin's story was credible. The only flaw was that he got hold of information so easily, but maybe it was no more easily than Cobalt had done. She decided to let Maurin think she had swallowed his tale. She said: 'They did harm me, and where were you when it happened?'

'I do not know. I took a taxi, as you say. I was a little later than the time Edouard mentioned. I made a quick tour of the museum but recognized no one. So I left, in the same taxi.'

The lights went out. In the darkness he said: 'I know nothing more than I have told you, but I blame myself for what happened. If only I had told you straight away the appointment was a hoax . . .'

The lights reappeared. Rain said: 'Perhaps it would have happened anyway.' She thought of the pedlar who had chased her and Oliver later that same day. 'If the museum hadn't offered an opportunity, they would have looked for another.'

Maurin was eager to agree, diminishing his responsibility. Rain began to replace her scarf, and wished her hands were not clumsy and nervous. She was a long way from believing him. She said: 'You must tell me who these brothers are.'

He faltered. She said: 'Why not? Because I might find them or because I might not be able to? Do they really exist?'

'Certainly they exist! But I shall not tell you their names. If you were to tell the police, or if you were to go after them yourself, there could be difficulties. You have escaped with your life, it is far better that you ask no more questions and go home and forget.'

'Why are you shielding these men?'

'Because they will be in Nice long after you have gone away. If there is trouble for them they will find a way of paying me back for revealing their names. They would eventually find out that I did so.'

'But *you* had no difficulty in finding out who they were? Not everyone is as afraid of them as you're pretending to be.'

'I assure you, Rain, I am not pretending. These people are inconsequential, but they are gadflies. I do not want my family harmed or my gallery burned down, so I shall not say who they are. The man who told me about them is not afraid because he can do more harm to them than they can inflict on him.'

'Oh yes?' She sounded disbelieving.

'Yes, because he is a police officer. Now do you see?'

'You're not going to give me his name, either, no doubt, because he told you something he shouldn't have done and he probably did it because you paid him for it.'

He inclined his head in agreement. He said: 'I have told you all I can about the attack on you. I am sorry it took place but I promise you it would be wisest to go home and forget it.'

'Sabine Jourdain *was* killed—would it be wise to pretend that never happened, either?'

'You have accused me of attacking you, are you also going to suspect me of killing her?' She could not tell whether this was mere sarcasm.

Rain fingered an end of her scarf. Outside there was the noise of water rushing along gutters inadequate to their task. Maurin had challenged her, and she was afraid to meet that challenge.

29

The lights went out. Rain saw Maurin's eyes glittering in the dark, coming closer. She flung herself out of the kitchen and along the passage.

She groped for a door, discovered the handle, rushed into the room. 'Is that you, Rain?' Barbara Coleman's voice, from across the room.

'Yes, it's me.' She fought to sound normal. Barbara Coleman believed herself to be with her friend's killer, Rain was convinced she herself had just left him. Behind her the door moved again. He was in the room with them.

She made out Barbara Coleman's white hair, low down as she sat in an armchair. Merlyn was a dark column near a window, apparently looking out of it although the torrent obscured the view. Joseph was near the easel. Rain wondered what they had spoken about, how long the conversation had lapsed before she joined them.

She waited to see if they would resume, if Maurin would mention anything of their own talk in the kitchen.

He did not, but she did not know whether he was silent about the assault on her because it would upset Barbara Coleman to hear of it, or because he did not want the Josephs to know.

She tried to calculate the effect of telling them all. The old woman might become hysterical again and renew her accusations about Joseph, or she might follow Rain's own reasoning and link Maurin with the attack at the museum and Sabine Jourdain's murder. But how would the Josephs react? Would they be shocked or would they appear to know of it?

Joseph said to Merlyn: 'We'll go just as soon as this weather lets up. We can come back another time.' Merlyn murmured agreement.

Rain crossed to where Barbara Coleman sat, and asked her: 'Are you feeling better now?'

The woman squeezed her arm. 'I'll be fine, my dear. Philippe was quite correct, I hadn't taken my pills and it was one of the days when I did rather need them.'

The lights came back on and then a thud overhead made them all jump. Merlyn whirled round from the window to look at her husband. Joseph made a discreet calming gesture with a hand. Maurin was gazing at the ceiling. Barbara Coleman and Rain swapped conspiratorial glances.

'Is somebody else in the house?' Maurin asked.

Joseph stared at Barbara Coleman, then Rain, waiting for their answers. There were sounds on the stairs. Joseph set off for the door but Rain got there first. Coming down the passage towards her was Cobalt. Oliver was not to be seen.

'Success!' Cobalt called in the most enthusiastic tone she had ever heard from him. He did his imitation of Barbara Coleman's voice again: 'Just as I thought. It's the perfect place, my dear.'

'James, don't say any more . . .'

But Cobalt was calling over his shoulder. 'Come on! Where's the rest of the drugs squad?'

As Oliver's distant voice answered him, Cobalt entered the room and discovered the Josephs and Maurin. His cheery smile vanished. He stood there, the others making a semicircle in the room, and he looked like a criminal before his accusers.

Barbara Coleman gave a histrionic gasp: 'Drugs? Did I hear you say drugs?'

Cobalt's liquid blue eyes went to her. His red hair was flame in the lamplight, but there was no colour in his face.

Joseph demanded of her: 'Who is this? Who have you let into the house?'

She said: 'This is Mr Cobalt.'

Maurin sounded astonished. 'And he is looking for *drugs?*'

Barbara Coleman said: 'You heard what he said, Philippe. It appears he's found them.'

Maurin asked Cobalt: 'What sort of drugs?'

He said, with a shot at casual humour: 'Oh you know, the usual sort which people hide away. Illegal ones.'

Joseph cleared his throat. 'Now look here, Mr . . . er . . .'

'Cobalt.'

'Mr Cobalt. Would you mind explaining yourself? Are you saying you found illegal drugs on this property?'

'That's right.' Cobalt was feeling his way.

Merlyn said: 'Are you sure that's what you've found?'

Cobalt decided humour was still the best policy. 'The box isn't actually labelled "Illegal Drugs" but I'm in no doubt that's what it contains.'

More footsteps in the passage and in came Oliver. Maurin and the Josephs gaped at him, then revised some ideas. Merlyn said: 'You're a friend of Oliver West then, Mr Cobalt? You're not a police officer.'

'Police? Good heavens no,' said Oliver, laughing rather too loudly.

Merlyn was tight-lipped. 'I see.'

'Well, I'm damned if I do,' said Joseph to Cobalt. 'What right have you got to go searching people's houses for drugs or anything else?'

Barbara Coleman began: 'But . . .'

Joseph rounded on her. 'You're supposed to look after this place. It's the only reason you've been allowed to stay on. Well, this is the finish. You can pack your bags and get out. Now. Right away. What's the use of keeping you here if you let anyone who chooses have a free run of the place?'

The woman half rose, clapped hands to her reddened face. Rain touched her shoulder, pressed her back into the chair for fear of a repetition of the scenes in the kitchen.

Merlyn said: 'Ben, that's just a little hasty, we don't know . . .'

'I don't *want* to know any more. I know enough already. She's going around calling me a murderer and she's invited this Cobalt in to turn over the place looking for drugs.' He shook a finger at the crying figure in the chair. 'You're out. Do you understand that?'

Rain hoped Maurin would come to the woman's rescue. Instead he spoke to Cobalt: 'What have you found?'

'Heroin. Quite a lot of it.'

Maurin glanced at the ceiling. 'In the room above this?'

'Yes.'

Barbara Coleman's voice was tremulous. 'That was Durance's studio when he lived here. He would never, never have . . .'

Rain said: 'Assuming it's true that it's heroin . . .'

Oliver interrupted with: 'No one would go to that trouble to hide a box of talcum powder.'

'. . . who could have put it there?' Nobody answered her.

Then Joseph snapped: 'God knows who she's been letting into this house.'

Rain asked where precisely the box had been found. Cobalt said: 'There's a low platform on wheels in the room.'

'That's the throne,' Barbara Coleman explained. 'It's what artists use when they have models to pose. They make an arrangement of things on the throne and then set the pose . . .'

Cobalt ignored her. 'It was below the platform.'

'Just lying there?' enquired Maurin.

'No, beneath the platform there's a short length of floorboard. We raised it and there was the box.'

Maurin said to the Josephs: 'This looks very bad, very bad indeed.'

Joseph snarled back: 'You can't believe I have anything to do with this?'

Merlyn said: 'None of us really know whether it's heroin or not. We must take the box to the police station and ask them to check it out.'

Cobalt said: 'I don't think it should be moved.'

Merlyn said: 'It's not a dead body we're discussing, Mr Cobalt, it's a box of powder. If I take it to the police the matter will be dealt with much sooner than if we leave it where it is and wait for them to call here. You know how long they can keep people hanging around.'

An argument broke out about the wisdom of delivering the box to the police. The Josephs were in favour of taking it, Maurin and Barbara Coleman backed them up. Cobalt, Rain and Oliver were less confident it was the best course. Rain said: 'Wouldn't it be destroying part of the evidence?' She thought there would be no proof it had been beneath the platform.

'Damn their evidence,' said Joseph. 'I just want that stuff out of my house.'

'We can resolve this very easily,' Rain said. 'We can telephone the police and ask them what they want us to do.'

There was a lull in the conversation. They heard water cascading from broken gutters outside and the insistent drip, drip, drip where it had found its way in around a window.

Merlyn stepped forward. 'I'll do it. I'll use the phone in the hall.'

She was almost at the door when Rain said: 'I'll come with you. You'll find it very difficult to explain everything when you don't speak French.'

Merlyn froze, then turned to lean with her back against the door. Rain thought she was trying for a dramatic effect, but she was a poor actress and the result was that she looked petulant.

Before Merlyn could speak her husband said: 'Look, I really don't want the police coming over here. They've already been to the *Jonquil* because of Sabine's death. I have to consider my reputation, you know.'

'So must I,' said Maurin. 'If you want the police here then I ask that you do not contact them until I have left. There is no point in involving me in this regrettable matter.'

Barbara Coleman dragged herself up out of her chair. 'As I'm no longer to live here I would also be pleased not to be troubled by the police.' She marched to the door. Merlyn stepped aside with a supercilious look which the older woman pretended not to see. 'I'm not going to steal your heroin, Merlyn,' she said. 'I'm going to pack.'

They heard her go down the passage, then the disagreement about telephoning the police was renewed. The case for protecting reputations emerged as the strongest.

Rain fought against it. She thought murder and a cache of death-dealing drugs were too serious to be subject to petty considerations like that, but the Josephs and Maurin were not listening.

It was Oliver who noticed Barbara Coleman's exit from the house. He glimpsed the short white-haired figure heading for the back gate but did not say so until much later when Merlyn asked where she had got to.

Maurin was concerned for her. 'Was she carrying her luggage?'

'No, nothing heavy,' said Oliver.

Merlyn demanded to know why he had not reported her departure at the time. He told her it had not been easy to get a word in.

Rain said: 'Where can she have gone?' And Maurin replied that it was easy to guess.

He said: 'I had better see everything is all right.'

'Merlyn and I will come,' said Joseph.

'We do not want a crowd,' objected Maurin.

But Rain felt she ought to go, too. She and Oliver ran through the downpour to Cobalt's car and then had to wait in the inadequate shelter of the wall until he arrived. Cobalt was speaking to Maurin as they came through the garden together. Oliver said: 'I'm uneasy about Cobalt.'

'Why?' She wanted to see whether his doubts reflected her own.

'I think he and Maurin know each other.'

'They appear to know some of the same people.' She

told Oliver about Maurin's explanation for the attack on her.

'Drugs, again,' said Oliver. 'Cobalt is able to get information about criminal activity linked to drugs and so is Maurin. Then Cobalt gets a hint about drugs hidden in the Villa Fièsole and Maurin also turns up here.'

They broke off as Cobalt joined them, unlocked the car. Rain gave him directions. They looked out for Barbara Coleman on the way, but there were taxis about and no one doubted she would have called one. For the last few hundred yards they trundled slowly behind a cab. It pulled up exactly where they intended to and out got a drenched Barbara Coleman who scuttled through the nearest doorway.

Cobalt looked in his rear view mirror and reported that the Josephs' car and Maurin's were not far behind. Oliver asked whether they should go after Barbara Coleman or wait for the others. Rain said: 'I'm not sure why I'm here, except that Barbara is very frightened and might need someone on her side.'

'How very noble,' Oliver said ironically as he opened the car door and stepped down into a puddle.

Rain joined him in the doorway but there was no time to speak before Cobalt splashed through the puddle to them. Barbara Coleman was in the lobby, banging on a door. She was calling, her voice high with frustration.

Another door opened and the caretaker looked out. At that moment Joseph ran into the lobby, reassured her with his affable smile. Her door closed. Rain was sure she was listening on the other side of it.

Joseph asked Barbara Coleman: 'What do you think you were doing, running off like that into the storm? Couldn't you even wait to tell us you were going?'

She shrieked that he was to take his hands off her. He protested that he was attempting to unlock the door. Rain motioned to Oliver that she was going upstairs. She paused halfway up the second flight to hear whether anyone was following, but all she heard was the sound of a door below opening and the voices of Joseph, Maurin and Barbara Coleman going into the flat. She imagined Merlyn watching with her cruel eyes and Oliver being silently attentive and Cobalt quietly playing whatever game he was playing.

Rain ran up the rest of the stairs. The double brown doors were ajar. There were two people in the room, two male figures against the poor light from the window.

Instinctively her hand reached for a light switch. When she found it the scene was stark. Marius Durance had his back to the table where his paints grew dusty. His body was arched as though he had been forced to retreat.

Facing him was Tarquin Poulteney-Crosse. Tim was taller and broader and he leaned towards the old man like a creature caught in the instant of springing on its quarry.

Rain saw them like that for a second, then Tim twisted round and glared at her. Durance recognized her with relief: 'Rain Morgan? You're here in time to forestall my assailant.'

Tim snorted. 'I wasn't going to hit you.'

'Can you be so sure?' Rain asked. 'Perhaps you were going to lose control as you did when you attacked Sabine Jourdain?'

Tim's hand clutched at his fair hair. Rain wished she knew what he was thinking. With Durance it was easy to tell. His hands relaxed, the tension went out of his body. He moved away from the youth. His question was for Rain: 'What had he to do with Sabine?'

'They had a row, on the night she died.'

Durance studied Tim with disgust. Then he said to

Rain: 'He attacked me only with words.'

Tim told her: 'You know why I came here.'

At first she did not, then she remembered Oliver's parting words to Tim in the rue du Bateau and understood how they had been interpreted. She said: 'You came as a blackmailer, to try and extort money to support your drug addiction.'

Tim said: 'I'm not an addict, I told you . . .'

Durance said with quiet disdain: 'He made mad accusations, they were so mad no one would believe him.'

Rain nodded. 'I've heard his story.'

Tim grew restless. 'It's true.' His hands were clenching and unclenching.

Durance roared: 'No, it's mad. You'll never be believed. I won't buy your silence because it's worth nothing. You are worth nothing.'

Tim thrust out an arm and shouted to Rain: 'Here's the evidence if anyone wants it!' Along the wall behind her were ranked paintings. Among them was the one she had seen on the *Jonquil*. She felt it was subtly different now but there was no time to study it. 'You see?' Tim cried. 'These are what I saw at her studio.'

Durance went to him shouting: 'How dare you accuse me . . .'

The doors were pushed wide and Maurin came in with Joseph, then Cobalt and Oliver. Joseph was at his most agitated. Maurin called out: 'Say nothing, Durance. Nothing at all.' He translated for Joseph. Joseph's mouth set in a thin line.

Durance and Maurin spoke rapid French. Tim plunged into the discussion, justifying himself. Joseph said: 'Please, Philippe, what is all this about?'

Maurin explained about Tim's blackmail attempt. Joseph groaned and said: 'At least Barbara Coleman wasn't trying to blackmail anyone.'

Just as her name was spoken her white head bobbed into view. She rushed up to Durance. 'Oh Marius, at last I can tell you how dreadfully sorry I am about poor Sabine dying, and in such a cruel way. You must be heartbroken, you were always so close, I mean even after you were no longer... You always meant so much to each other. No one will miss her as you will.'

Durance assumed a calm dignity, said a polite: 'Thank you, Barbara.' He moved away from her.

But she was not to be put off easily. She followed him up the room, repeating her sympathy and when that did not hold his attention, she began to apologize for her lateness in coming to speak to him about the tragedy. 'Now, you're not to be cross with me, my dear, because I didn't come sooner, the truth is I wanted to come straight away but it wasn't possible. I wasn't even in Antibes, you know, I was in Nice.'

For the first time she interested him. 'In *Nice*, Barbara?'

'Yes, Philippe thought I should be kept out of the way for a few days...'

'Out of whose way?' Durance looked at Maurin.

Maurin gave a slight shake of the head as if to dismiss what the old woman was saying. But she went on: 'It was the day Sabine went to supper on the boat.'

Durance asked: 'The day she died?'

'No, Marius, the day before that. I thought it was rather grand to be going to supper on the boat and I wanted her to tell me all about it later but I never saw her again. The last time I saw her was when Benedict Joseph shoved her into his car outside the Villa Fièsole, and Philippe made me go with him to Nice.'

Durance was astounded. He insisted on hearing her out, at whatever length and with as many digressions as she chose. He would allow no interruptions or corrections from Maurin. Joseph, unable to follow the French, waited in anguish, not knowing what was being said. He saw Maurin grow more wretched as the story was unfurled.

Durance's indignation gave him power, it was as though he actually grew in physical stature. And as that happened Maurin and Joseph were reduced. Once or twice Barbara Coleman sought corroboration of a point from Rain or Cobalt but otherwise not one of the onlookers dared to speak.

When she had done, Durance started a scathing attack on Maurin. 'You're a mere salesman, Maurin, nothing better than that and you'd do well to remember it. How dare you meddle in people's lives? I've told you before that you must not interfere.'

Maurin interjected that he had done it for the best, that he suspected she would spread silly gossip and it was sensible to keep her away from the English journalist. Durance shut him up, saying he had never had reason to doubt the woman's loyalty and inferring that it was more reliable than Maurin's.

When he had finished with Maurin his great dark eyes fixed on Joseph. Durance had poor English and his bitter remarks would have been wasted on Joseph had not Maurin automatically translated the essence.

It might all have ended there if Barbara Coleman had not sought to claim more of Durance's attention and prolong Joseph's embarrassment by rushing on to tell how illegal drugs had been discovered beneath the platform.

What Durance had to say, Joseph never knew exactly because Maurin did not relay any of it but took issue with Durance himself. Durance was adopting the view that if the drugs were found in his former studio his name would be dragged into a scandal. He wanted to know how the damaging package had been disposed of.

Maurin said it had not. Durance struck his forehead with his hand. 'So stupid!' Durance cried. 'It must be moved immediately!'

Maurin, who had been longing for an excuse to escape, said he would go himself to attend to it and made for the door. Oliver whispered to Rain: 'I wonder what he'll do with it? Pop down to the beach and sell it to the pedlar?'

She whispered back: 'Or to your friend, Rosie?' Oliver stopped smiling. In fact, she thought it far more likely Maurin would go home to Nice rather than back to the villa and become 'involved'.

Joseph was trying to get someone to explain to him what the exchanges between Durance and Maurin had been about and where Maurin had gone. Without Maurin, and with no inclination to ask Barbara Coleman, Joseph had isolated himself. Rain left it to Cobalt to help but Cobalt did not.

Barbara Coleman and Durance were talking together, everyone else went downstairs. 'Where's Merlyn?' Oliver asked Rain. Joseph, over-hearing, said she had returned to the *Jonquil*. When they reached the street door they realized his problem. 'It's too far to walk in this weather,' Rain said. 'We'll give you a lift to the boat, won't we, James?'

Cobalt could hardly refuse, but Joseph was adamant he would not accept. He ran out into the wet streets saying he would find a taxi. The others negotiated the puddles to Cobalt's car.

Rain sat beside Cobalt, with Oliver and Tim in the back seat. She did not remember anyone inviting Tim, he had just tagged on to them, but she felt it was safer to take him than leave him near Durance in case he made any further blackmail attempts.

Cobalt drove back to the Villa Fièsole. They were well on the way when he explained: 'Barbara asked me to fetch a bag she's packed. It's in her bedroom but was too heavy for her to carry.'

Rain accepted this but knew his other reason was to check on the box beneath the floorboards. She feared it was a reckless bit of curiosity. Supposing Maurin *had* returned to the villa? Here they were, chasing after him when caution should have kept them away. She and Oliver believed him guilty of murder, she had no idea what Cobalt believed.

When they reached the villa they saw Maurin's car in the lane. 'We're in time,' said Cobalt. He took a camera from his pocket, checked the film, dropped it back into his pocket.

Rain, Oliver and Cobalt all gave Tim rather doubtful looks. It was crossing their minds that it might be safer to leave him in the car, but they had to consider whether they could trust him not to steal it.

'It's up to you,' Rain said to Cobalt.

He shook his head. 'I need to get home again.' Tim went into the garden with them.

The ground was slippery, what had been a path was now a torrent. The veranda behind the house was flooded as drains failed to cope.

They ran into the house with its unlocked back door, along the passage and upstairs. Through the open door of her room they could see Barbara Coleman's packed bag just as she had promised. Further along the landing light came from another room. Oliver hesitated, but Cobalt walked straight in.

They heard his step falter and as they pressed into the doorway after him they came face to face with Philippe Maurin, holding a gun.

30

A sardonic smile spread over Maurin's face. He looked at each of them, his eyes coming to rest on Rain.

Then there was a sharp laugh. Maurin spun the gun in his hand, tossed it on to a stool. 'Four very frightened faces,' he said. 'I wish you could have seen them.'

Cobalt retorted that it was not an amusing thing to do, pointing a gun at people, and he could not see what Maurin found so funny.

Maurin was still laughing. 'You alarmed me, too. How was I to know who was marching up the stairs and in here? I was not expecting any of you.'

Cobalt was not appeased, and Oliver, to prevent further argument, went across to Maurin, saying: 'Let's take the heroin to the police station and . . .' He stopped short. He was standing beside the raised floorboard, looking into the cavity.

'Yes,' said Maurin. 'As you see, the box has gone.'

They all gathered round to inspect the empty space where two of them had previously seen a box. Rain confronted Maurin: 'Did you move that box?'

'No.' He dared her to disbelieve him.

Oliver said: 'Then who . . .'

Rain butted in: 'Did anyone see Merlyn at Durance's studio?'

No one had. She had been last noticed at the wheel of the car when the Josephs arrived there. Maurin said: 'Merlyn was most determined to take charge of the box.'

'So keen,' said Rain, 'that she came back once we were all with Durance.'

'We don't need to look in the police station for her,' Cobalt added. 'She won't have taken the box there.'

'The boat, then?' suggested Oliver.

The boat, it was agreed, was the likeliest place for Merlyn and the box to be. Rain wanted to go there straight away, but Maurin preferred that the floorboard and the platform should be replaced and the arrangement of stool and drapes reconstructed before they left. He was concerned that the room must be left just as Durance would have wished. Oliver and Tim carried out the task while he watched. Maurin picked up the gun and put it in a pocket.

Rain drew Cobalt aside. 'How did you know there would be drugs here?'

'If I say one of my contacts tipped me off, I expect you'll pester me for his name.'

'No, I won't.'

'All right, then: one of my contacts tipped me off.'

He was being especially exasperating. She said: 'But did you suspect the Josephs knew the drugs were here?'

'I wasn't convinced until I saw how anxious Merlyn was to get hold of the box once I'd mentioned it.'

Rain thought about Cobalt and the cache of drugs as they drove to the harbour, with Oliver and Tim once more in the back seat and the windscreen wipers rhythmically at work. The Villa Fièsole was a fairly big house

285

and yet it had not taken him long to find the box. His contact had not merely tipped him off that drugs were on the premises, he had told him where to look. If Tim had not been with them Rain would have questioned Cobalt about that.

Near the harbour entrance Maurin overtook Cobalt, pulled up and got out of his car to speak. 'I do not wish to go to the *Jonquil* with you,' he said. 'If there is anything wrong then I have no need to be involved in it.'

Oliver muttered something unkind about rats and sinking ships but Maurin missed it. Rain said: 'Will you go back to Nice now?' She imagined him next morning parading in his gallery, cossetting his reputation, toadying to his rich clients, dissociating himself from whatever unpleasantness the Josephs faced.

He did not answer, although she knew he had heard her. He went before there were any more questions.

'He doesn't want to be involved *"if"* there's anything wrong!' she said sarcastically once Maurin's car moved off. '*"If"* there is anything wrong Philippe Maurin is definitely involved.'

They drove along the harbour. Rain suggested Cobalt carry on well past the *Jonquil* so that anyone arriving at the boat would not see the car and guess they were there. They walked back in pairs, Oliver and Tim ahead, then Rain and Cobalt.

'Maurin didn't kill Sabine Jourdain,' said Cobalt.

'Oh? And how can you be so sure? He's known the truth about the Durances, he's kidnapped Barbara Coleman, he knew someone hoped to kill me, he probably knew about the Josephs and the drugs . . .'

Cobalt said, with a sideways glance at her: 'What sort of a word is "probably" for a journalist to use?'

'Why are you determined Maurin couldn't have killed Sabine Jourdain?'

Cobalt flicked back his wet hair. 'I don't say he *couldn't* have, just that he didn't. If she was killed to prevent her telling the truth about the paintings, her killer was someone who believed she *would* tell. Maurin didn't.'

Rain concealed: 'He insisted to me that she was too loyal to give anything away.'

'Well, there you are. He thought the danger was Barbara Coleman so he tried to keep her hidden until you'd gone away. That's less shocking than killing.'

'James, you're doing an excellent job for the Maurin defence, but why couldn't he have kidnapped one old woman and killed the other?'

'Because the prosecution would notice that hiding Barbara Coleman made him a prime suspect for the murder of her friend. He's not stupid, he'd know he hadn't a hope of getting away with it.'

She edged around an especially deep puddle before replying: 'Once Barbara Coleman was free to talk, suspicion would point to him. But what might have happened to her if we hadn't found out where she was, if you hadn't brought her back?'

'I don't believe Maurin would have killed her any more than I think he killed Sabine Jourdain.'

Rain asked about the ease with which Cobalt had found the heroin. In return she got his little smile. 'I'd like to claim the credit but you'd find out I lied. One of my magazines in the States has been following up rumours about the Josephs. They have an extremely lavish lifestyle—for instance, do you know what it costs to charter the *Jonquil*?'

She remembered. 'Yes. Your magazine discovered they didn't legitimately earn enough to meet their bills?'

'There were some strands of a drugs story in California but the reporters couldn't link it to smuggling from South America, which was the obvious line of enquiry. So they asked me if it was possible the Josephs were bringing drugs in from France along with their haul of works of art.'

Rain congratulated him on finding the proof. He said bitterly: 'And losing it. I photographed the box in the cavity, but there will be nothing to link the photograph with the Josephs or even with the Villa Fièsole.'

She told him what Maurin said about the reason for the attempt to kill her. Cobalt stopped her. 'I know,' he said. 'In a way that was my fault. Neither of us were attacked because of the Durances but because the local drug dealers knew I was making enquiries about trafficking and they thought you were working with me. I suppose they imagined we were going to expose their uninteresting little rackets, whereas I was only interested in what the Josephs were up to.'

Oliver and Tim were waiting for them at the gangway. 'I'm not sure how we explain our presence,' said Oliver, and let Rain and Cobalt board first.

'I hope,' said Rain over her shoulder, 'we don't meet anyone else with a gun.' The three faces behind her assumed looks of varying panic.

Ross, the steward, appeared, commiserated that they were all soaked through and took them into the lounge. He said the Josephs were not there and Rain let him assume they were on their way and expected to find four very wet friends. Ross offered coffee while they waited.

Rain sat in the turquoise chair with the purple footstool, Oliver was on the settee not far from the replacement Chinese screen, Cobalt fingered the bronze bird, Tim stood in the doorway and watched the downpour slanting over the deck.

Coffee came and when Ross had retreated again, Tim said: 'You'd think there'd be a chase, wouldn't you? They should have rushed back here, started up the engines and dashed out to sea, and we'd have sent a police launch or the local equivalent of the Customs and Excise after them.'

Rain laughed. 'In real life it would take them some time to get this boat ready to go to sea. It uses lots of expensive gallons of fuel to the mile and it probably hasn't got even one of its tanks full so it wouldn't get any distance.'

Tim would not be put off. 'But it would go really fast, wouldn't it?'

'It might cruise at around 12 knots. All in all, the Josephs could make a quicker getaway in a rowing boat.'

Cobalt said: 'In this weather they'd be wiser to stay on land.'

Silence. Just the sound of the wind outside and the angry rush of water against the harbour wall. Oliver closed the door to the deck. Deeper silence. Then he said: 'Perhaps they aren't coming here.'

Rain rang for Ross. She asked whether Joseph or Merlyn had been back earlier. He said not. When he had gone Rain said: 'At least we know why Joseph didn't want a lift back to the boat. He and Merlyn had planned to go somewhere else, and she was taking the box there.'

'They'll have to come back here some time,' said Cobalt. 'I'm going to wait. I want some quotes from them for the magazine story. They'll deny everything, of course.'

He looked quietly confident. The American magazine would pay him very well for his work. Rain wished he had someone to make sure he spent part of the proceeds on smartening up his flat.

Oliver and Tim were talking together, Cobalt was waiting for his prey. Rain felt uneasy. She did not mean to be swayed by Cobalt's defence of Maurin, and yet he had undermined her confidence.

She asked herself whether it was possible that, after all, one or other of the Josephs had killed Sabine Jourdain and whether it happened because she knew of the drugs and not because of the Durances. Rain mulled it over, but in the end thought the theory would not do. Barbara Coleman lived at the villa and she had not known about the cache. If she had, she would have been sure to say so when she was blaming Joseph for the murder. And if Barbara Coleman had not known it appeared unlikely that Sabine Jourdain had. Altogether, the link between the drugs and the murder was weak.

Rain sat there, thinking about Barbara Coleman, a woman who was both brave and pathetic. She must have changed radically since she came to France, a carefree young woman writing home enthusiastic letters about her life in the sun. Rain guessed what had caused such changes: the realization that her talent did not stretch very far; the passing of a way of life which had been so thrilling; impending old age with few friends, little money and no certainty of a roof over her head. She had never had much, and now she had nothing.

And it was thinking of Barbara Coleman, what she had enjoyed and what she had become, that led Rain to a disturbing idea.

31

Rain did not want to explain to the others. The doors to the deck were shut against the weather so she thought she could get ashore unseen. She went into the corridor, up the stairs with the gilded banisters, crossed the cocktail bar and descended the open wooden steps near the gangway.

Lamps glowed through the ports of boats, vehicles had driving lights on. Water swilled over the harbour road but Rain was already so wet she barely noticed as she splashed her way towards the town. Her mind was preoccupied with what might happen at the end of her journey.

A car, moving much too fast, turned a puddle into a wave that flowed up to her ankles. She looked after the car, knowing she had been so absorbed she would never have noticed if the Josephs had been in it. She thought about the Josephs, apparently guilty of an especially heartless and greedy crime, and wondered how they had got drugs into the United States and whether they would ever do so again.

She ran through the stone arch. The Bar de la Marine was full as people took shelter. At Place Massena, she entered the gloomy passage to the rue du Bateau, but she did not go to the flat, she turned right and wound through the lanes instead. As she went she thought about Philippe Maurin.

Maurin had been involved to some degree in everything that had happened. Where he was not active, he at least had guilty knowledge. Her step slowed. At the end of the street in front of her she recognized his car. She had not been wrong. He had come here as she guessed he would. They would meet again, but this time she *would* challenge Sabine Jourdain's killer.

She tapped at the door of Durance's flat. Barbara Coleman opened it. She was strained but managed a smile. 'My dear, you're so wet.' Rain followed her in. The room was disarranged, in the way rooms get disarranged for cleaning. Barbara Coleman found Rain a towel.

Rain said: 'Are you here alone?'

'Yes. I insisted I was going to clean and tidy up. Men can't stand that, can they? They went to the studio.'

'Are you going to stay here or go back to the Villa Fièsole?'

Her face clouded. 'For the moment I shall be here. Then I shall find somewhere new. After the things that dreadful man has done and said I couldn't go back. Do you suppose it was true about him keeping drugs there?'

'I'm afraid it probably was.'

Barbara Coleman shuddered. 'I wonder how long it was going on? I had no idea at all, you see.'

Rain patted her hair with the towel, trying to soak up the water which seeped down her neck and face. 'Has Philippe Maurin spoken to you about finding somewhere else to live?'

'He's being most kind. He came to talk to me about that. He's concerned what will happen to me.' She gave a little laugh, to indicate that this was foolishness on his part and she was not anxious herself. Rain was not tricked.

'Did he make any suggestions?'

'Only that I ought to ask some of my old friends, people like Madeleine Corley, if I could be allowed to join them, but . . . You can imagine how difficult it is to do such a thing. I can't go around my friends begging for a home, can I? And giving a home to an artist isn't the easiest thing. As a breed we take up such a lot of room.'

She came closer to Rain as though she wished to speak without being overheard, although they were alone. 'As a matter of fact, my dear, I have one tiny idea which I will ask Durance about in a while, when I can choose the best moment. You see, there is no one living at the Villa Souleiado now . . . Perhaps he would let me go there.'

Rain said that was a good idea. She felt utterly insincere. Barbara Coleman would detest the solitude, the place would bring back memories of the good times and she would be confronted more than ever with the evidence that the good times had gone. But Rain kept up the pretence until she climbed the stairs to the studio.

Again there were two figures in the room but this time the light was on. Maurin and Durance looked up. They had the paintings leaning up against the trestle table and a chair.

'We are surprised, Rain,' said Maurin. He smiled his most charming smile.

She presumed he meant they had not expected her, but she liked the ambiguity in his English. She was quite sure she had surprised them in the act of carrying out the next stage of the deception concerning the Jourdain-Durance paintings. She joined them near the table.

She said to Maurin: 'I never knew how you and Joseph decided which pictures went to the States and which were sold through your gallery. I suppose you don't have to consider him now.'

His smile faded. 'Ben is a partner in my gallery. The destination of the paintings is a matter for consultation between us. We sell where we believe we can make most money. What are you suggesting?'

'If he goes to jail for trafficking in drugs you won't have to bother about consulting him, will you? Or sharing with him?'

Durance's eyes were flashing. 'What are you saying?'

Maurin translated and Durance looked insulted. Rain went on in English to Maurin: 'You knew the drugs were at the villa. It was you who tipped off James Cobalt. When he started making enquiries into the Josephs' business affairs in France you were obviously one of the first people he'd ask. You wanted to be there when he found the box, your arrival was nothing to do with Barbara Coleman going home.'

Durance intervened again, frustrated at being left out.

Rain challenged Maurin: 'Go on, translate that for him. Tell him the thieves have fallen out.'

'You know nothing of what I did.'

She thought fleetingly of Cobalt and his objection to 'probably'. But the truth was arrived at through probabilities. She said: 'I believe you intended to trap the Josephs with their smuggling. You wondered how they contrived to be so rich from dealing in paintings. There had to be another source of money and you realized what it was, and that they had acquired the Villa Fièsole to use in that business.'

He laughed a mirthless laugh. He said: 'Even if I were to say you are right, you would have no proof. Yes, I guessed about the Josephs. Someone even told me there was a place in Durance's studio at the house where the stuff was left for them. I went there one day and hunted and found the hiding place. Barbara never knew I was there, anyone could go in and out of that house and she would never notice. That is why the Josephs did not mind her staying there. It was safer for them to have one old woman occupying part of the place than to leave it empty and risk a group of drifters moving in. Yes, I knew what the Josephs were doing, but it was not up to me to stop them. How could I?'

Durance demanded to know what they were arguing about. Rain said she would tell him presently, which did little to pacify him, and she went on in English to Maurin: 'Joseph can't operate here without you, can he? Neither of the Josephs speaks the language, they can't discuss things with Durance without your help, and because of the way the paintings were created they couldn't trust anyone else.'

He understood what she was thinking. 'No!' he said vehemently. 'I had nothing to do with them buying drugs. There is a man they meet, an American who has lived here many years, they deal through him. Do not ask me any more, it is dangerous knowledge. But, as Oliver has already challenged their whereabouts on the evening Sabine was killed, I will say this: on that evening the Josephs were at that man's house. A little supper, a little dealing, all very civilized, no doubt. But it does not provide a very useful alibi, does it?'

'Please!' shouted Durance. 'I must know what you're saying.'

'It's nothing to worry you.' Maurin sounded soothing.

'But I *am* worried! What has Sabine to do with what you are saying?'

Maurin laughed again. 'You always worried too much about Sabine. Sabine was completely loyal to you, she'd never have done anything to damage your reputation.'

Durance's voice became a menacing whisper. 'What

do you know of loyalty? You understand nothing but money and making a fine impression before rich people. Without my name you're nothing. You and Joseph are the same, feeding off the reputation and work of others. Do you think I never realized how you were using me? Because I don't care for material things to the degree you do, you chose to believe it didn't matter that you grew rich on my name.'

'Please, don't go on.' Maurin tried but Durance would not be stilled. If Oliver had seen him now he would not think he was a man who was finished, he would see a desperate will to survive and defend himself. Once more, Durance appeared to grow before Rain's eyes as his passion was roused. She saw the spell-binder he used to be and the strength of personality that bound people to him.

He was raving at Maurin, at all the people who had failed to live up to his expectations of them. He began to address Rain. 'This man is of no more use to the world than those artists who came to fawn on me and scrape a little importance for themselves. Where are they now? Once they left my house they became nothing. Take note of that, Maurin. Without me they are *nothing*, they *have* nothing.'

'You're going too far,' Maurin protested. 'You encouraged those people, then when you tired of them you discarded them.'

'No! I've never gone far enough. I've let you play your games, you and Joseph, and I've said it was nothing to me, it was enough that I was a painter. The market place is for people like you, my world is the studio. But there's a price to pay for not going into the market place. The price is having to tolerate people like you and Joseph.'

Maurin defended himself. 'We've always helped you . . .'

'You've always helped yourselves.' Durance's voice was a growl.

Then there was a quietness in the room. Outside, the storm lashed the windows, there was nothing to be seen of the sea or the red roofs. But in the room the Durance paintings created their own world. The Mediterranean colours danced from them and always would, no whim of the weather could destroy their beauty.

Maurin would not face Durance. Durance moved towards the paintings, to the one where the woman stepped from the shadow of the tree into the full light of the sun. Everything Rain had seen at the Maurin gallery and everything the Contessa Mantero had shown her compared unfavourably with this painting. She remembered her conversation with Joseph, not just the discussion about the blues and the greens but the joke about coveting it. *'It's worth killing for,'* she had said.

In the corner of her eye she saw Maurin stir, looking up and gauging whether Durance's rage was abated. Durance was engrossed by the painting. He breathed one word: 'Wonderful!' But his admiration was tinged with bitterness.

Rain's voice was scarcely audible. 'This is why you killed her.'

Maurin's head snapped up. His eyes were wide, his mouth open. But Durance did not look Rain's way. He stared at the painting. Rain saw him in profile—predatory nose, stubborn chin, arrogant eyes. As she watched, the power died in him and a sadness came. He was reduced to a short old man who had once been the great painter Marius Durance.

When he spoke next his voice was uneven. 'There's such confidence in this. It wasn't painted by the pupil of a fine painter, carrying out someone else's wishes. This is what she'd grown into.' A pause which no one dared break. Durance sighed, the long deep sigh of a man who has given up hope. 'This painting bears my name but I had no part in it.'

Maurin recovered himself. He said urgently: 'Marius, there's no need to say any more.'

Durance shook his head. 'If it's so easy for Rain Morgan of the *Daily Post* to get at the truth, it's a secret which can't be kept.'

'No,' said Maurin, growing desperate. 'She's guessing. Please, Marius, I beg you to say nothing . . .'

Durance was still looking at the painted woman stepping from the shadow. 'She told me she wanted to work on her own. Do you know what that meant to me? The end of our relationship. I said to her: "Sabine, we can't be friends if we aren't working together." I thought it would be enough to call on her loyalty, it used always to be enough. And do you know what she did? She laughed at me. She said: "All that has held us together for years is that I've been working for you. It's time I did something for myself."'

Durance appealed to Rain: 'Can you believe a woman I'd taught everything could speak to me like that?'

Rain said nothing, reflecting that the odd thing was that it had taken Sabine Jourdain so long to outgrow her need of that relationship.

Maurin said: 'Marius, I'm pleading with you, for your own sake don't tell her any more.'

Durance ignored him. 'After she moved to the Villa Souleiado Philippe used to bring me the paintings to sign, or I'd go there and do it. But I never saw this one.' He lapsed into silence.

Maurin gave Rain a warning look. She concentrated on Durance instead and said: 'You saw this the first time on the *Jonquil*, didn't you? In the study?'

Durance was surprised. 'You also saw it there?'

'Benedict Joseph showed me, the night we all had supper on board.'

'I suppose you noticed it bore no signature.'

She wished she had done and admitted she had not. 'When I saw it here this afternoon I felt there was a tiny change.'

'The greens have dared to move much nearer to blue than I ever let her go, I put my signature through that blue patch to diminish the effect.'

'When did you do that?'

He did not answer that straight away. He reverted to his story of the break-up of the Durance-Jourdain friendship. Maurin stood by, pained but not interfering, although he occasionally shook his head to deny what Durance was saying.

Durance said: 'Maurin and Joseph believed that as long as Sabine promised never to talk about the extent of her work on the paintings there'd be no trouble. They were worried only about what would happen to the monetary value of the paintings and their business as dealers. They tried to persuade me she was interested only in sculpting in future.'

From below came the noise of the street door. Durance rushed on. 'I wouldn't let her talk to you. I had to be sure she would tell you only about things that happened long ago. Joseph said you couldn't be stopped from coming but he'd arrange matters so you couldn't speak to her. He thought you'd give up and go away, as the woman who was supposed to be writing the book did. The day after we all met you she assured me she'd say nothing damaging and said she'd convinced Merlyn who'd arranged another meeting on the boat. When evening came I was afraid I couldn't trust her, because I didn't know how much you suspected, what clever questions you might have to get at the truth.'

With a heavy heart Rain prompted him. 'You went to the *Jonquil*, too?'

Maurin appeared about to speak, then bit his lip. Durance said: 'I believed that if I were there I could control what she told you.'

'Was she alone when you went on board?'

'I saw no one else. Sabine was in the study and this painting was on the wall.'

His voice rose with indignation. 'She confessed she had not meant to let me see it or sign it and said Joseph had promised to take it to America and sell it under her own name. She said she'd got him to agree that day and it was no use arguing because it was her price for keeping her promise to be silent about her work on the other paintings.'

Maurin gasped, stunned by this news of Joseph's duplicity. Durance said to Rain: 'I can't believe Joseph doesn't understand that selling under her name a painting recognizable as a Durance is equivalent to telling a journalist she had been painting my pictures. As long as she was alive and working my reputation could be destroyed at any time. There would be a scandal, Maurin and Joseph would lose money, so would collectors. But I would lose *everything*.'

Rain asked when he discovered there was someone else on board. He said Sabine rushed out of the study, saying she was not going to wait on the boat any longer. He was following when he heard her speak, so he held back. He took down the painting and planned to leave with it, but then he heard Sabine and a man shouting in the lounge.

'It was fierce. I could not understand what they were shouting, but I heard them throwing things. I didn't go to them, instead I went to the Josephs' bedroom.'

He paused long enough for Rain and Maurin to doubt

that he would resume. Then: 'I knew there was a gun. Merlyn had shown it once, saying they kept it to protect the valuable things they bought. I thought she'd fetched it from the bedroom. I rested the painting by the bed and looked in the drawers. It wasn't difficult to find and it was light and easy to fire, a woman's gun.'

Another pause. Maurin began to speak but Durance prevented him, saying: 'At the time I believed I wanted the gun so I could intervene. What use would it have been if I had gone into the lounge without something like that? Whoever was attacking Sabine was wild, I heard him threatening to kill her. He would have disregarded me, but with a gun in my hand . . .'

Rain said: 'But when you had the gun you didn't stop the fight.'

They waited a very long time for his answer. 'I put the gun in my pocket but I didn't go near the lounge. I took the painting and went through the cocktail bar and down the steps to the other deck and left the boat that way. It's possible I knew subconsciously all along what I was going to do with the gun. Do you think it's possible?'

Rain said she did not know. He said: 'I walked through the harbour. There was a dark place—some boat fitter's equipment was lying around and there was the sailmaker's van as well as parked cars. The pathway was in deep shadow. I leaned the painting against the van and sat on a box and waited. There was nobody around. I stayed there, listening to the fireworks and the noise of a party nearby. I knew she'd come. I can't say how long I waited. A few people came by but I'd swear no one saw me. Then Sabine came.'

Another gap. Again a door slammed down below. He said: 'You can see how simple it was. I walked forward to meet her. We went on a few yards, then I held back to let her go ahead of me where the path was narrowest.

I did it then. Just one shot and I pushed her into the water. Then I took up the painting and carried it back here and I signed it.'

Maurin groaned. He took out a handkerchief and wiped sweat from his face. 'Why do you insist on saying all this?'

Rain said to Maurin, in French now that there was no need to exclude Durance from their conversation: 'You've known all along, haven't you? You and the Josephs have known.'

'Of course,' said Maurin. 'I came here the morning after she died and he told me. We argued about it but in the end he agreed I had to tell the Josephs. And what did you expect us to do? Call the police? Putting him behind bars won't serve any purpose, will it? He isn't likely to do it again.'

'No,' Rain agreed, 'and putting him behind bars would bring to light the reason for the murder. Then the Josephs and you would be ruined, and Durance's reputation lost.'

'We are interdependent as we always were,' Maurin said. 'Ben and I protect Durance's reputation and in doing so we protect our own interests.'

Rain said: 'Despite Barbara Coleman's chattering and despite what I've just been told, you're all safe because there's no proof about the provenance of the paintings.'

'Nor about the identity of the murderer. If there'd been any evidence to link the death to anyone connected with the *Jonquil* the police would have found it by now. I understand they believe she was shot by someone who meant to rob her, the chance victim of a killer she didn't know. That's what the newspapers have suggested.' That was the rarest of murders and Rain expected Maurin knew it, too.

'The gun!' Durance said. 'Did you get rid of it as you promised?'

Maurin said: 'Yes.' He explained to Rain: 'He should have thrown it into the harbour but he brought it back here. I took it from him the next day.'

Durance was satisfied with Maurin's answer, Rain less trusting. She thought of that moment at the Villa Fièsole when Maurin had pointed a gun at them. She wondered whether it was not in his pocket now, how long the interdependence of the three men would last and what might happen when it ended. Maurin had already tried to ruin Joseph by helping Cobalt reveal his drug smuggling. Joseph had planned to sell Sabine Jourdain's work for her and cut out Maurin. Durance was weary of both of them but the price of their silence was as big as the price of Sabine Jourdain's.

Footsteps came upstairs. Barbara Coleman put her head into the room. 'It's all done. The rooms are back to normal, but much tidier and a good deal cleaner.'

No one congratulated her. Rain gave her a distant smile, worried she would get on Durance's nerves. Durance had a vicious tongue and used people cruelly.

Barbara Coleman said: 'I've made a pot of coffee. I think we could all do with a cup. It's such a wretched day, isn't it?'

Rain went out of the room with her. She did not stay for coffee. The storm had blown itself out, there was only steady drizzle. She ran through it, discovering how cold she had grown standing in the studio.

First she called at the flat in the rue du Bateau and made a telephone call. Oliver was not there and she supposed he, Cobalt and Tim had stayed at the *Jonquil*. She went there, guilty at having crept away.

The gangway was slippery beneath her feet. She

clutched the rail to steady herself, reached the deck and went to the closed doors of the lounge. As she had hoped, they opened at her push. But the scene which awaited her was not at all what she expected.

32

Ross was positioning the bronze bird on the floor near a screen. The footstool was overturned, there was other minor disarrangement. Foucard and Denis were watching.

Foucard's lip curled when he saw Rain. Ross reddened. 'It's all come out,' he said in an accusing hiss as she passed him.

'Yes,' said Foucard, 'at last you have a witness to your statements about the disturbance in the room, although we have yet to see whether it will lead us to the killer.'

Rain imagined the route they would take, blaming first the Josephs, then perhaps Tim, then maybe Maurin. She wondered whether they would be misled as she had been by the ramifications of the local drugs trade, and whether they would be helped or hindered by not knowing Sabine Jourdain had painted the Durances.

Denis escorted her to the dining room where Oliver, Cobalt and Tim waited. Oliver demanded: 'Where have you been?'

'I went to Durance's studio. I wanted to see Barbara Coleman and Maurin.'

'You should have said something. We didn't know what had happened to you.' Anger was taking over from relief that she had returned.

'I didn't want anyone to stop me going.'

He looked at her closely. 'Are you all right, Rain?'

'I'm fine.' She did not want to discuss what was upsetting her and asked instead what had happened in her absence.

Oliver said the Josephs had come aboard but close behind were a number of policemen. Cobalt knew one of them and squeezed from him the information that Merlyn had been to the house of an American suspected of dealing in drugs. The house was under surveillance at the time and the police saw Merlyn go in carrying a box. Shortly after, her husband arrived by taxi.

Oliver found it very amusing. 'And then the Josephs came back out and she was still carrying the box and they were both looking furious and arguing. The police followed as they drove away and after a short distance Merlyn got out of the car and dumped the box. She actually threw it away at the side of the road! Well, the police recognized what was in it and when the Josephs got back here they were on their tail.'

'Why did she throw it away? It was worth a fortune.' Rain felt she could not have been attending, she had missed something.

Oliver said patiently: 'It's only worth a fortune when the Josephs can sell it. Our guess is they panicked, tried to get rid of it by selling it back to the supplier, he refused and they panicked some more and threw it away.'

'Where are they now?'

'Where do you think? They're at the police station explaining themselves. Meanwhile Foucard and Denis turned up here and shunted us into the dining room and

306

the police began to take the *Jonquil* apart looking for drugs.'

'Did they find any?'

Cobalt leaned over to answer that. 'I don't know but I've heard they've found a bullet hole in a screen which was hidden away. I suppose they hope it's something to do with the murder although Ross says Merlyn fired off a gun one evening a month or so back. It was an accident and she was drunk. He didn't know what she'd hit.'

Oliver said to Rain: 'When the police trooped on board, Ross thought they'd come to check up again on your story of a fight, and he owned up to lying earlier. He'd no idea they were after drugs this time, instead.'

Cobalt added more details. Rain struggled to look as though her attention was on his tale, as though she admired his facility to make contacts who would loosen their tongues about the most confidential matters. She *did* admire it, but her mind was elsewhere. The enormity of what she had heard at the studio was sinking in.

She thought about Durance: old, lonely, bereft of everything but a reputation which was high now and certain to go on climbing. A doubt raised about the work of the past few years would be insignificant when that output was set against the achievement of the rest of his long life.

Oliver said: 'Was Barbara Coleman all right?'

'Yes,' she said, and told him she had telephoned May Radley to say the woman needed somewhere to live. 'She immediately said she'd let her have part of her house. She has plenty of space and she's very fond of her. She's going to see her about it tomorrow.'

Oliver patted her head. 'Well done, that's your good deed for the day.'

But she was thinking about what she ought to do next. She could understand why the Josephs and Maurin were willing to cover up the murder, but the temptation she faced was more complicated. She had revered the work and name of Marius Durance. Doing what she ought to do would cause a deep disappointment far beyond the man's personal acquaintance, and his crime was a story which, like his work, would live for ever. There were few enough great men, destroying one could not be undertaken lightly.

Tim interrupted her. 'Actually, I've been asking Oliver whether it mightn't be a good idea if . . .' He caught her puzzled look as she tried to get to grips with what he was saying. He began again: 'The point is . . .'

Oliver helped him out. 'He hasn't got a penny and he wants to go home. I said I thought we could buy him a plane ticket.'

She gave a weak smile. Oliver knew he would not be paying any part of Tim's fare. She said: 'I think that's a good idea.'

Tim leaned across to her again. 'Thanks, Rain. I'll pay you back, of course.'

'When you come into your inheritance and sell off the family home?'

'I've changed my mind about that. I don't like admitting it, but this place wasn't at all what I thought it would be.'

For a second she feared she'd stirred up Scott Fitzgerald again, but Tim said, lowering his voice: 'I'll get you the money within minutes of being home.'

'By stealing some of the goods and chattels after all?' Oliver quipped.

Tim kept his voice down and said with malicious glee: 'I've never thought that silver was stolen, you know. They've hidden that teapot and the tureen and they're after the insurance. They used to joke about it, but I knew they'd do it one day.'

Oliver was shocked. 'Do you mean that?'

Tim laughed at his unworldliness. 'Definitely. When they know *I* know they'll hand over the price of my plane ticket without question. You'll see.'

Rain did not know whether to be grateful to him.

Tim subsided into his seat. Rain reverted to thinking about Durance: old, lonely, hands too crippled to paint, trapped by the Josephs and Maurin, trapped by his own pride.

Tim was talking to Oliver. She heard him say: 'Sabine once told me . . .' She missed the rest but she thought about Sabine Jourdain.

Rain had come to France to learn and write about her but she knew very little more now than she had before. Durance had wanted it that way and, for all his fury at Maurin and Joseph, Durance had always contrived to get what he wanted: the young women who had surrounded him; Sabine Jourdain who had left her husband and child to go to him; Joseph and Maurin whom he was happy to work with so long as it pleased him. Maurin had accused him of using people and discarding them, and the worst example was Sabine Jourdain who had lost her life to him.

Even if the story about her doing his paintings did not come into the open, there would be scandal about Joseph's drug smuggling and Durance's name would not escape mention . . .

A steward brought coffee into the dining room. Cobalt fingered the silken bird in the wall panel. Tim stared moodily through a port and reported that the drizzle was dying out. Oliver yawned and paced the room. Rain slumped in a chair. They all wanted to go home.

Rain poured herself coffee. She remembered her first evening on board when she had noticed Durance's hands. She had never been in doubt about his physical frailty, she had come to know much about the unappealing side of his nature long before she saw the way he looked at the painting and knew her hideous suspicion was justified: Sabine Jourdain was not killed because of the greed of either of the art dealers but because of the jealousy of Durance. To give him away, Rain had to convince herself that the paintings stood apart from the man and could not be damaged.

She took her coffee back to her chair. She was tired. She was soaked and cold. She was hungry. Since she had come to France she had been through terrifying experiences, but sitting in the palatial dining room of the *Jonquil* and deciding whether to keep the secret of his guilt or to tell Foucard was no less harrowing.

Oliver came and sat near her. He had found some paper and doodled a cartoon. She saw Merlyn with a glass in her hand and a box labelled 'heroin' under her arm, Joseph and Maurin gagging Barbara Coleman, Sabine Jourdain lying dead. He shaded an amorphous area.

'Where's Durance?' asked Rain.

Before he answered he sketched her in, too. 'That's you, you're involved, too. You represent public acclaim, his besotted women admirers, and so forth.'

'Thanks very much,' she said drily, but understood he was trying to cheer her up.

He said: 'Durance is everywhere and nowhere. If this paper was longer the shading would be his shape. He's just a shadow. Well, he doesn't really exist, does he? Not the legendary figure who was one of your heroes, and not even the painter of some of the best Durances.'

She pulled the paper from his hand and studied it. He always drew her as a fluffy blonde Marilyn Monroe figure and she had never dared ask whether that was really how he saw her. She said: 'We're all in the shadow of the Great Man, are we?'

Oliver took it back. His hand closed on it and crumpled the drawing. 'When were you last so bored?'

Tim came over, caught the word 'bored'. 'We could play the Scott Fitzgerald game, again?' he suggested. 'Let me think . . .'

Before his magpie brain picked out a quotation Rain said: 'Show me a hero and I will write you a tragedy.'

'Very sour,' said Oliver pulling a long face.

'It's not me, it's Fitzgerald.'

Tim disputed that. 'What book?'

'Not a book, from life, but there wasn't much difference.'

Tim's brow puckered. 'I'll think of one in a moment . . .'

'Anything to stop us being bored,' said Oliver ambiguously.

Rain reached her decision. Before Tim had come up with a line, she took her cup back to the table and then headed for the door.

Oliver was watching. 'You're not going to vanish again, are you?'

'No, there's something important I must tell Foucard.'

Not much later they were free to go. Rain and Oliver said goodbye to Cobalt over supper in a restaurant in a narrow street off the Place Nationale. Then they took Tim back to the rue du Bateau to spend his final night in Antibes sleeping on their floor. He had offered to go to the beach but Rain assured him it would be drenched.

She telephoned the *Post* and told Holly Chase and Dick Tavett they were on their way home. Oliver said: 'It's been so long I hardly remember what Tavett looks like.'

'Or Holly?' Rain teased.

In the morning the sun was back, dazzling Rain and

Oliver as they stood on the balcony. Tim was taking a shower. Oliver said: 'I wonder whether they'll find the gun Maurin had was the one that killed Sabine Jourdain?'

'Maurin has probably thrown it into the sea by now. I doubt they'll ever find any proof Durance did it. They might discover the bullet hole in the screen was caused by the sort of gun that killed her but . . . Durance won't choose to tell the police all he told me.'

Tim joined them, carrying Oliver's copy of *Bludgeon* which he had borrowed to read on the journey. They got seats on the lunchtime flight.

As the plane curved over the Baie des Anges Oliver said: 'I've never been so eager to get away from a place. Not even the *Daily Post* on a Friday evening.'

Rain did not doubt that by the time he reached his favourite wine bar the horrors would have been reworked into a series of amusing anecdotes. She said: 'It was supposed to be a treat. Remember the Great Idea?'

'I promise I'll never have another one.' He leaned across her to look at the flushed roofs of Antibes.

The water was the deepest blue. The sails of small craft were scattered near the shoreline. Oliver said: 'I'm surprised Foucard didn't ask you to stay, in view of what you'd told him.'

'I'm sure he meant to, but then one of his colleagues found some drugs in the frame of a picture Joseph was going to take home, and I think Foucard just forgot.'

She watched the children's boats until they were replaced in her view by the massed pines of Cap d'Antibes and an innocent blue sky.